Naming the Spirits

ALSO BY LAWRENCE THORNTON

Imagining Argentina
Under the Gypsy Moon
Ghost Woman
Unbodied Hope: Narcissism in the Modern Novel

Naming

THE

Spirits

by

LAWRENCE THORNTON

Bantam Books

New York   Toronto   London   Sydney   Auckland

NAMING THE SPIRITS
A Bantam Book / published by arrangement with Doubleday
PUBLISHING HISTORY
Doubleday hardcover edition / September 1995
Bantam trade paperback edition / September 1996

For Toni

Full fathom five thy father lies,
Of his bones are coral made.
Those are pearls that were his eyes,
Nothing of him that doth fade
But doth suffer a sea-change
Into something rich and strange.

—Shakespeare, *The Tempest*

And he said unto me, Son of man, can these
bones live? And I answered, O Lord God, thou
knowest. Again he said unto me, Prophesy upon
these bones, and say unto them, O ye dry bones,
hear the word of the Lord. Thus saith the Lord God
unto these bones: Behold, I will cause breath
to enter into you, and ye shall live.

—Ezekiel 37

Naming the Spirits

Prologue

Until the shooting started none of us believed we were fated to sing this long cantata of midnight's bones. Of course we were frightened. Some of us were petrified. But despite their guns and the lantern glowing like the eye of some huge animal in the dark, it was impossible to think of ourselves as candidates for extinction. After all, except for the teenage girl we were just twelve ordinary men and women in our twenties and thirties, indistinguishable from thousands of others. Try as you might, you couldn't have picked us out on a crowded sidewalk. Nor would you have had better luck stopping at an outdoor café on the Riachuelo hoping to glimpse one of us sitting over a coffee or a beer. There simply weren't any telltale signs that would let you say of a dark-haired woman in a green dress, or a man smoking a pipe: "There's a likely candidate." To see what set us apart would have required X-ray vision, not the kind that cradles bones and organs in eerie light, but something more technically advanced, capable of penetrating minds and revealing the ideas that brought down the wrath of the generals, ideas they believed were as dangerous as matches struck in a hayloft and which became synonymous with our names.

Absurd? Of course it was absurd. There were plenty of wild-eyed radicals in Buenos Aires grown overly fond of plastique, young men and women who had learned to love the persuasiveness of fire, but we didn't believe in violence. Even the two of us naive enough to have spoken out in public never raised a finger against the regime. Not that it made a difference. In those days, ideas alone were enough to make you disappear. That doesn't mean they were always careful about whom they took, which only goes to prove the truism that fine discriminations are among the first casualties of war, dirty or not. One of us came to their attention purely by accident, another by way of a personal vendetta that sprang from an ache in the loins. We never had time to find out what the girl had done.

In any case, once our names were inscribed in notebooks, on the backs of envelopes, receipts, and in one instance a candy wrapper—the man doing the writing having nothing else handy—they were impaled on a spike that stood on the desk of a general who had a nice view of the Plaza de Mayo from his office in the Casa Rosada. When a dozen pieces of paper had accumulated, he slid them off the spike as gently as if he were removing a flower from a shallow vase and told his secretary to make a list. Thanks to a new ribbon, the characters she typed were nicely black, and she thoughtfully doubled-spaced between each name and address for easy reading. By the time she rolled the sheet out of the platen and handed it to the men whose job it was to find us, it was no longer merely a column of names, a collection of easily pronounced syllables; the list had become a story of treason highlighted by accusations that would have been laughable had they not been so deadly.

Within the week the story began to unfold across the city in broad daylight and the middle of the night. It gathered momentum on street corners, in university quads and bars, becoming more complex as we were driven through suburbs and alleys, along Sarmiento Street and Cangallo Street and a dozen others, always with the familiar sounds of the city in our ears while our eyes registered details of routes none of us ever thought we'd take. We passed cafés and movie theaters, skirted parks where elegant women walked pure-bred dogs, drove by school yards filled with laughing children, stores where people browsed, steadily moving further away from where we had been forced into cars that bore no license plates. They kept us in different places until we were sent to a warehouse reeking of oil and there we stayed, often in darkness, before a panel truck finally took us away.

We arrived here many hours later. The dry scent of wheat in the air. Flashlight beams played across the darkness. One of the men said it was midnight. When we asked where we were, a gruff voice demanded silence. We complied because we had no recourse, because we still believed obedience mattered as they led us through a field wet with dew. Our procession, for it was that, solemn as anything you would see in a cathedral, was accompanied by the sounds of wing tips, sandals, high heels and tennis shoes rustling in the grass. When they told us to stop, one of them put a lantern on the ground and removed the chimney. A match flared, the wick caught and a yellow pool of light bloomed as it rose the length of our bodies. Huddled in a circle, we saw each other clearly for the first time. We were trying to match faces with voices heard in the dark as the lamplighter backed away, wisecracking to his companions.

At that moment a low-ranking policeman named Alberto Marqovitch was overcome by unexpected guilt. He would never understand whether it had been the girl's white dress, the tears glistening in her eyes, or the way she leaned against the woman beside her that had touched his conscience. All he knew was that he could not leave her with the rest of us and live with himself afterward. And so, fearful as he was for his own safety, Alberto stepped forward, pulled her away from Kikki and said boastfully that he was damned if he was going to waste something so fine and that he intended to have a little pleasure.

The girl screamed when Alberto closed his fist on the back of her dress, bunching the cloth so tightly in his fingers that the neckline pressed against her throat. As she struggled to get free, twisting left and right, Alberto laughed for the benefit of his friends and pushed her into a nearby grove of ombu trees where his flashlight made dizzying arcs across the branches as he answered her pleas to leave her alone with obscene descriptions of what he was going to do and how much she would like it. He kept it up until they reached the center of the grove and he looked back, relieved that the trees blocked most of the lantern light.

"All right," he whispered, releasing his grip. "Listen to me."

With a cry the girl raked her nails across his face. She tried to run, but Alberto grabbed her shoulders, shaking her so hard that her head snapped back and her moaning broke into rhythmic phrases. He begged her to listen. It was a ruse. A diversion. He wasn't going to hurt her. He'd taken her away because he wanted to save her. If she wanted to live, she had to imagine something terrible, had to scream as if she were being raped.

Alberto's words made no sense. She looked around wildly, gasping for air like a child who has cried too long. He was holding the flashlight at his waist, pointed up, so that the beam illuminating the scratches on his face made him look like something in a nightmare. His fingers dug into her shoulders. He said again that he was only acting. His words were clipped, bitten off, hissed between his teeth, but despite her fear, she recognized the urgency in his voice, the desperate tone. When she realized he was telling the truth, the unexpected relief made her cry again. She covered her face with her hands. Alberto pulled them away.

"There's no time to waste."

He switched off the flashlight and they were plunged into darkness broken only by the lantern's distant glow.

"Scream," he said. "Now."

And she did, forcing herself to imagine the unthinkable. It was so close to the truth that she felt her gorge rise. Time collapsed. There was nothing before, nothing after. She was trapped inside her high-pitched wail until she heard gunfire coming from the muted light.

The sounds we made in response to those cones of blue-white fire—a drawn-out screech, a curse, the name of someone's wife—cut off her voice as suddenly as if a tone arm had been lifted from a record. Those of us not killed outright, whose brains had not exploded, whose hearts had not been pierced, filled that yellow light with more noise than you can imagine. We screamed louder than a choir reaching a high note, louder than the whistle of an old-fashioned steam locomotive. It was the prelude to our story, source of every chorus, solo and recitatif of the bones' cantata, though we didn't know it yet. At the time we were only aware of the pain and the sound of our living voices raised in screams and howls until the breath went out of us.

While our voices faded Alberto and the girl embraced, felt the thud of each other's hearts. Alberto knew he had to fire his pistol to convince the others she was dead. She would have to stay there, he said, absolutely quiet, until they left.

"You'll see our headlights. Wait an hour, just in case. Then go for help."

Alberto rubbed his hands over his face and smeared blood on her dress in case someone came to look. Then he removed a Beretta from his waistband and fired into the ground three times. For a millisecond he saw her in the blue glare of muzzle flash.

He was just snapping on the safety when he heard the rustling leaves.

"Lie down!" he whispered. "Don't move."

He quickly pulled his shirt out of his pants and was unbuckling his belt when Ernesto Siciliano appeared.

"You bastard!" Ernesto said jovially. "You could have waited and given me a chance." He shone his flashlight on Alberto's face. "Looks like she put up a fight."

Alberto casually rebuckled his belt. In a sardonic voice whose authenticity amazed him, he said: "She was scared shitless. Anyway, there'll be others."

Ernesto played his flashlight over the girl. The beam traveled from her legs to her waist and her bloodstained chest. When it reached her face she flinched.

"Goddamn it!"

"What?" Alberto said, terrified. He too had seen the movement.

"She's still alive."

Before Alberto could say anything more Ernesto fired. The girl quivered, then lay still.

Miserable, his ears ringing, Alberto turned away with what he hoped would pass for indifference.

"Come on. I don't want to stay here the whole fucking night."

"A pity," Ernesto said reflectively. Then he draped his arm around Alberto's shoulders. "She really fucked you up. You'll have scars."

"It was worth it," Alberto answered. "She was a virgin."

Their companions had already removed picks and shovels from one of the cars. Alberto and Ernesto joined in the work. The earth was spongy because of a recent storm, but it still took two hours to make a pit large enough for all of us.

They were exhausted afterward. Ernesto sat on the truck's fender, catching his breath, while they debated burying the girl, deciding against it because they were tired and a single body was not important, especially in a place no one would ever visit. Someone produced a bottle which they passed around, congratulating themselves on how well things had gone. When they finished it, they knocked the fresh earth from their tools and returned them to the car. They drove off a few minutes later, the precise cones of their headlights concentrated on the dirt road leading to the paved one. But Alberto Marqovitch was not looking ahead. He was staring out the window, trying to stifle his sorrow and silently cursing Ernesto Siciliano.

Our story was supposed to end with the *matanza,* the massacre whose last traces were obliterated as the death squad carefully smoothed the earth with the backs of their shovels. The final breath that passed through the lips of the last who died was supposed to finish the narrative created by the column of our names. As far as the general and his cronies were concerned, it was over. That night they celebrated in restaurants on Calle Florida, or listened to *milongas* in a tango bar. They drank French wines and made love to wives or mistresses. That night, and all the ones that followed until the *Proceso* collapsed like a rotten building, eaten away from within, they believed our story had run out of words.

But they overlooked one thing, those soldiers and policemen and politicians who had invented a new verb for our language. As they calmly went about the business of defining the usage of "to disappear," they overlooked the fact that grief abhors a vacuum. It never occurred to them that even though we were gone we remained alive in the memories of our families. Nor did they know that the mundane details of our everyday lives, the ones that constituted the narratives of communal lunches, dinners, playing with children and going to movies, hadn't disappeared with us but were transformed into prologues to the untold stories of our last days and nights, white stories, unwritten but clamoring to be told, waiting for a pen to impress them on the page, a voice to give them form. No, as far as they were concerned, there was only silence, shattered inkwells, broken voices.

So you can imagine their surprise, their amazement and

chagrin, when clues to what they'd done began emerging toward the end of their dirty war. Names of people tortured in clandestine detention centers spoke from carelessly discarded cassette tapes and notebooks. After the travesty of the Malvinas, stories were discovered in the sepia tones of dried blood on prison walls, rose from the memories of reluctant witnesses. By the mid-eighties, stories were pouring forth as if from a broken dam, filling up the whiteness they'd created. But ours was not among them. Much as it needed telling, much as our families and friends deserved to know our fate, our story remained hidden in the mind of a girl who sought her name in the flights of painted birds.

Book

One

Awakenings

Immobile as a stone, the girl lay under the ombu tree all that night and the next day and the second night, her arms and legs rigid, her mind dark as the vaulting sky. Dew seeped through her dress, embracing her with an icy second skin. Had she been capable of dreaming, it would have been of floating underwater, borne along by a current far below the surface. But dreams do not thrive in the place where she had gone. That much, if no more, we can attest to.

The second morning dawned with a red slash on the horizon. Thin clouds threatening rain parted at noon, allowing the sun to fall slantingly on her body, drying the blood that had welled from her wound, baking it black. Drawn to the shape that lay like a discarded rag doll, birds settled in the branches and cocked their heads to observe this strangeness. A squirrel rose on its hind legs, regarding her curiously as it nibbled seeds. Colonies of ants marched over her ankles, circling her flesh like thin black chains that appeared to pinion her to the earth. A sensitive microphone placed beside her legs would have picked up the ticking sound of the insects' progress. But no matter how fine the instrument, regardless of its complex circuitry, it could not have detected the infinitely faint, bell-like sound echoing along the bullet's pathway, nor record the sudden sensation of pain that announced her return to the world. That privilege was reserved to us for whom the tiny sound was as loud as a cathedral's carillon. We listened throughout the night, urging it to continue with all the hope that comes to those afraid of being lost forever.

Finally, late in the morning of the fifth day, at the call of a blackbird flapping its wings so hard it would have taken flight had it not clutched a tree limb tightly with its claws, the girl's eyes opened. The movement of wings against the sky patterned by limbs and branches made her so dizzy she had to look away, her eyes slowly traveling to her legs, which seemed strangely long and thin as stilts. When she stood up she teetered awkwardly as a child in a woman's high-heeled shoes. The field spun, tilted, whirled, slowly came into focus. Once she regained her balance she stepped out from beneath the trees, looking left to right and back again as she searched for a landmark that might tell her where she was. She had no memory of the muzzle flash or anything that came before. The world was new, un-named, its details unfettered by a past. As she walked half-dazed to the dark patch of freshly turned earth still memori-ous of the sounds made by our killers' spades and shovels, our voices rose in unison, surrounding her with the names we so desperately hoped she would remember as she scanned the fields. But all she heard was that bell-like sound. A moment later she departed like a bird instinctively migrating along invisible pathways in the air. She went east through the fields, skirting windbreaks, shying away from buildings that did not have the look of the place where she belonged, stopping only when it was so dark she could no longer see her way. That night and many more she lay down in the grass like a small furred animal and fell into dreamless sleep.

In the morning she came upon a stand of bushes flour-ishing beside a pool and ate a handful of its bright red ber-ries. When she bent to drink she saw a girl staring back at her. She studied her face, the star-shaped wound, watched the girl's fingers touch it and spring away the instant her own brought stinging pain to life. Blue light flashed before her eyes. Her mind quickened toward two words. "I am," she said, and the other's lips parted, asserting that she was.

The day yellowed in blistering heat. With sweat bead-ing on her forehead and trickling into her eyes she wan-dered in the haze until she reached a road, and discovering the bounty of a half-eaten apple, sat down on the shoulder, savoring each bite, even the bitterness near the core.

She was hugging her legs and examining the apple seeds in her left hand when a truck pulled over. An old man got out and asked what she was doing there. She gave no sign she understood, staring blankly as he repeated the question. Because he was worried about her being alone in the heat of the day, he offered to take her into town. He pointed to the truck, nodded, encouraging her to follow. As they drove off he reached into the glove compartment and removed a piece of chocolate he had been saving for himself. She ate it greedily, licking the brown stains from her fingers and the wrapper. Half an hour later he parked in front of a store, saying that he needed supplies and that afterward he would take her home where his wife would care for her. She watched him enter, then got out and crossed the square to a narrow alley that led back to the road.

The sun was going down by the time Eduardo Ponce saw her on his way home from the granary where he had been working the last six months. Her figure rose up by the side of the road like a shadow, but closer than he thought. He still misjudged distances on the pampas, especially in the early evening when the soft light blurred the edges of things.

The condition of Eduardo Ponce's life over the last few years had forced him to retreat from all but the most necessary contact with people other than his family. At work he seldom spoke. In town, he conducted his business brusquely, ignoring the friendly overtures of shopkeepers who finally left him alone, assuming that his heart was misanthropic and mistaking a nagging fear for indifference. They would have assumed he would never stop and offer a ride to anyone walking in the country at the end of a long hot day. But Eduardo had not lost his compassion. When he saw the girl he pulled over, just as the old man had done hours earlier. Rolling down his window, he said he would be happy to take her to the nearest town a few miles away.

Without acknowledging him or breaking stride the girl detoured around the truck. There was time for Eduardo to notice her filthy dress, the chocolate smudge on her cheek and her wildly raveled hair before she glanced at him over the hood. Though their eyes met for only a moment, the contact was enough to make him shudder. He told himself it was nothing, that he had only imagined recognition. But it was too late. Something in the frankness of her gaze, the penetrating look, had liberated an old fear that made him subject to premonitions. As he watched her going along the road, Eduardo's hands felt greasy on the steering wheel. He knew that he should repeat his offer, ignore the sensation that was already settling in his gut even as he reached for the ignition switch. He gunned the engine and sped off, intent on putting distance between them as fast as possible.

Eduardo's boys were kicking a scuffed soccer ball back and forth when he reached the gravel drive. Tomás returned Manfredo's kick with a header and then turned, eager for his father's admiration. Eduardo smiled wanly, his gut churning with old distress. The boys ran to him with the expectation that he would play awhile as he usually did before dinner. Eduardo gave the ball a halfhearted kick and brushed by them. Over his shoulder he said he had to talk to their mother.

Beatriz Ponce, in her forties and a little stout in her print dress, looked up from the onions she was dicing for stew as Eduardo came into the kitchen.

"Come," he said anxiously. "We have to talk."

"I'm in the middle of dinner. Talk to me here."

"No," he said, indicating their bedroom with a nod.

"Why?"

"So the boys can't hear. Damn it, Beatriz, do as I say."

He went to their bedroom and turned, gesturing impatiently. Beatriz kept her eyes on him as she dropped the onions in the pot and wiped her hands on a towel. She did not appreciate being talked to like that. She went to him without forgetting the insult.

Eduardo closed the door and sat down on the only chair in the room, a wooden one without arms. He put his hands on his thighs and faced her, hoping she would guess what was coming, but Beatriz could not read his mind. All she detected was confusion, unhappiness.

"Are you sick? Did something happen at work?"

"There was someone on the road," he said shakily.

"So?"

Eduardo glanced at his hands. His left thumbnail was blackened from a recent accident with a heavy wood pallet. The backs of both hands were covered with scratches from work he never thought that he would have to do. Sighing, he looked up and told Beatriz what had happened when he saw the girl, how the old feeling had settled in the pit of his stomach. "It was a sign."

Beatriz's face slackened. The color drained away. They had lived with presentiments for years, and enough had proven true to make Eduardo believe he had a sixth sense that warned him of danger. Each time the feeling had come upon him in the past there had always been something concrete to hang his fear on—a stranger who looked at him suspiciously, a car he did not recognize, a phone that went dead as soon as it was answered. As far as she was concerned, this event lacked substance, and that only made it worse.

"You're just skittish," she said dismissively.

"Maybe. But I'm not willing to take a chance."

Beatriz sat down heavily on the bed. The springs squeaked. She heard the boys laughing. Her eyes filled with tears as she looked out the window and saw Tomás kicking the ball. She was sick of running, but she had seen the road in Eduardo's eyes; one lingering glance told her that he had made up his mind.

"We've only been here six months," she said miserably.

Manfredo ran to the window, waved.

"Better safe than sorry. We agreed a long time ago."

"How could she know anything about the boys? If she did, what makes you think she could find us?"

"Someone will. I can feel it."

Eduardo drank heavily at dinner and afterward in the sparsely furnished living room Beatriz had brightened with a few pictures and vases of flowers. He did not feel like talking to her and sent the boys to bed early over their loud objections. When Beatriz left he sat at the table a long time, feeling trapped in a condition to which he saw no end.

Well before dawn Eduardo went into the boys' room. Still half asleep and rubbing their eyes with their knuckles, Tomás and Manfredo listened as he offered the familiar explanation. Something unexpected had happened. It was essential to leave as soon as possible. When Eduardo left after getting them on their feet and telling them to pack their things, the brothers tried as they always did to make the best of the situation even though they knew something was terribly wrong.

The Ponces set out after a cold breakfast, Eduardo driving slowly because the sun made it hard to see through the dirty windshield. He was grateful to be on the road. Because of the way his thoughts were tumbling into each other, idea giving way to idea, image to image, he was too distracted to look out the window on his side when they passed a drainage ditch where the girl was sitting, having wakened minutes earlier. She stared at the truck with no memory of having seen it the day before, watching it grow smaller as she climbed out of the ditch, hesitated, then began walking in the opposite direction.

They reached the Souza brothers' granary at six o'clock, just when the men were arriving for work. Eduardo saw the tower, the lights in the office where the owners would be greeting their employees. Much as he respected the Souzas, Eduardo had no intention of telling them he was quitting, or of collecting the pay envelope waiting in the office, though he desperately needed the money. When he was in the grip of this particular fear, which had hounded him for years, he was indifferent to courtesy and practical considerations. So he drove by the granary without hesitating, and he did not stop later when he reached a town where he could have easily used a shopkeeper's phone to call the Souzas. All that mattered was disappearing without a trace, following the pattern that had become part of his life the night the boys were given to him and Beatriz. It was the fourth time they had moved out of fear that someone would discover Tomás and Manfredo were not their children.

The Villa
Deamicis

fter the Ponces fled we lost track of the girl for a while.
Maybe it had to do with our being distracted by these
thieves of children, but it seems more likely that we had not
yet learned how to follow our only hope through the vastness of the country, that we still lacked the necessary skill.

In any case, weeks of frantic searching passed before we caught sight of her again just as she was emerging from an alley in one of Buenos Aires' more fashionable neighborhoods. She meandered along the sidewalk, looking intently but without recognition at street signs and addresses. With the same vacant gaze she examined window boxes, trellises, potted plants, all the little touches that set one building apart from its neighbors. Once she peered into a window where a startled woman glared angrily before closing her curtains. Unperturbed, the girl proceeded down the block, her attention drifting from the sycamore and tipa trees to the sky framed by rooftops which looked like some blue mystery. When two couples approached, she ran her fingers through her hair and slowly dropped her hands to her sides, watching them impassively as they gave her a wide berth, instinctively shying away from this disheveled trouble in the filthy dress. They hurried by, glancing at her smudged face and scratched legs out of the corners of their eyes, shaking their heads in sympathy.

At the intersection she crossed to the south side of the street, ignoring the traffic, deaf to horns, screeching tires and a cursing cabdriver who stuck his head out of the window and demanded to know what the hell was wrong with her. She was heading back in the direction she had come from when she reached a brick apartment building with an ornate stained-glass door that showed a white seagull sailing over the port. Intrigued, she climbed the stairs bordered by an iron railing and traced the gull's outline with her fingertips. The tightness at the corners of her mouth eased; her eyes seemed less haunted as she glanced at the brass plaque embedded in the wall, running her fingers over the engraved letters announcing the Villa Deamicis. She tried the door. When it stayed closed, she pulled on the knob, pushed, retreated a step and looked down the street, eyes half-closed against the afternoon brightness while she interrogated the buildings, trees, traffic lights. After a moment she turned back and stared at the seagull. Anyone watching would have agreed that it seemed less a decision than an unconscious reaction when she raised her hand and knocked.

In his ground floor apartment next to the entrance, Guillermo Calvino was fortifying himself with another glass of Chilean burgundy while he watched soccer on a television equipped with a screen-sized magnifying glass recently installed to help his miserable vision. He was thinking of bringing the bottle in from the kitchen when he heard the knock through his door which he had left open for circulation. He reached for his cane just as the opposition's star stole the ball and fled downfield like a miserable thief. Guillermo struggled out of his chair, muttering that it was to be expected; whenever he tried to enjoy himself someone always interrupted, usually for no good reason. He was halfway across the foyer when he heard another knock.

"Yes, yes," he called impatiently. "I hear you!"

The crowd roared and he turned to look at the television, cursing the bastard who scored. Though all he could see at that distance was pulsing blue light ("cataracts," the doctor had said), he knew Fallaci was egging on the crowd, circling the field with his hands raised in self-adulation. Guillermo wished he could see the home team's hangdog expressions. Maybe they would be shamed into doing something, though he doubted it. The collection of misfits and castoffs changed over the years, but the team he perversely supported was a perennial loser.

Pivoting on his cane, he hobbled to the door. There was another knock while he fumbled with the lock.

"All right!" he said angrily.

The sun was directly behind the girl, reflecting off the shoulders of her dress so that she appeared to be surrounded by an aura. The odd play of light embracing her made him uneasy. Beggars never appeared on the street, much less in his doorway, waiting for a handout. He was disgusted by her matted hair. He was getting ready to slam the door in her face when something made him relent. Maybe it was the way she stood, with her arms at her sides, or the fact that she seemed so vulnerable.

"Yes?" he said irritably. "What is it?"

The dreamy expression remained, as if she had not heard a word he said. It was unnerving. He was beginning to feel irritated again when it occurred to him that she might be deaf, so he repeated the question, louder this time. In response, she raised her hand and smoothed a wisp of hair from her eyes.

"Well?" he said more evenly, "at least tell me what you want."

She frowned, then half-turned and gestured vaguely toward the street before facing him again. In a voice barely louder than a whisper, she said, "I . . . am."

Guillermo leaned forward on his cane, uncertain whether the words that had been spoken so tentatively, the space between subject and verb stretched out as if the connection were problematic, were simply an assertion of her existence or the preface to a name. While he waited for her to finish she glanced over his shoulder and without another word walked slowly to the middle of the foyer.

"Now wait a minute," Guillermo said. "What the hell's going on?"

In the reflected light from the shoulders of her dress the skin of her face looked transparent, like a pane of ivory shaved thin enough to glow from backlight. It was a beautiful but disturbing color, akin to the pallor of the dead. Guillermo's eyes were so bad that he suspected the glow was an illusion flickering on his retinas, but the translucence remained. He stood there, utterly confused, while her eyes drifted from the iron gate of the elevator to a vase of gardenias on the table beside the mailboxes. The girl examined the flowers before confronting the gilded pier glass on the wall opposite the door. She stared at her reflection, then stepped closer. Her fingers moved across her mouth and nose, coming to rest on the scar above her left temple which she examined as if she were seeing it for the first time.

Guillermo's unhappiness doubled when he heard the opposition's fight song. They had scored again. He wondered if Menéndez could do something spectacular as he went over to her.

"Now listen. You can't just barge in here. Do you know somebody in the building? Are you a relative?"

He tried to think of who might be most likely among the residents, but no one in particular came to mind.

"Please," he said, pointing at the door. "You aren't wanted here."

The girl did not move. Guillermo saw her in the mirror as well as a couple passing by on the sidewalk. Behind them a green Ford Falcon, bristling with aerials, passed quickly. The girl was a mystery. He tried to think of what he should do as the din of the crowd and the announcer's voice echoed in the foyer. He had a sudden, distinct impression that she possessed no past or weight of experience, and might as well have dropped from the sky. As far as he was concerned, the two words she had uttered were the Alpha and Omega of a story without antecedents.

None of his neighbors would have argued that Guillermo Calvino was a paragon of intelligence or decency. He could be faulted for his short temper, his failure to be courteous and for being excessively self-absorbed. For years he had refused to let anything interfere with the comforts he had earned from a long career with the railroads, which included royalties from a patent for a throttle that continued to make life easier for Argentine engineers.

But Guillermo could not be faulted for his perplexity as he stared at the girl. Lacking prescience, he could not have been expected to know she had arrived after a long journey, that her dress was filthy because she had slept in the open for many nights, that her legs were scratched from falls taken on the way, or that she was there because she had to be. All he thought about was whether he dared leave the front door open in the hope she would disappear. He glanced at the umbrellas in the stand, the full mailboxes, the vase of gardenias. There would be hell to pay if anything were stolen. Frustrated, he raised his hand close to his face to check his watch.

"All right," he said wearily, pointing his cane toward his apartment. "You can wait in there, but only until the others come back."

Guillermo went into the kitchen and poured himself a glass of wine. The girl was sitting on the sofa when he returned. He immediately started cursing his team who were committing more mistakes than schoolboys in a pickup game on a Sunday afternoon in the park.

A short time later, Gabriela Santini came home ladened with a satchelful of essays. She was tall and thin, and her dark eyes emphasized wavy black hair which her lover said reminded him of the ocean. She tried to ignore the blaring television as she put her bag down on the table beside the mailboxes and picked up the vase. The flowers were still sweet. After straightening them, she collected her mail and crossed the foyer to Guillermo's apartment. Since his heart attack, she always looked in on him as soon as she returned from the university. He seemed more out of sorts than usual, giving her a withering look and rolling his eyes. She thought he was probably drunk again, and was about to say that he had better start taking care of himself when she saw the girl.

"Take a good look. She came in an hour ago. Barged right through the door."

The girl had been staring at the television, but she stood up when she saw Gabriela and searched her eyes with a baffled expression. Gabriela sensed right away that something was wrong. It was not so much her appearance as her luminous blue eyes; they were bright and vacant, inquiring and unfocused all at once. She smiled at the girl, then addressed Guillermo.

"Who is she?"

The old man snorted.

"Your guess is as good as mine. The only thing she's said is, 'I am.' I tried to get rid of her, but she wouldn't leave."

" 'I am?' "

"That's right. Maybe she's crazy."

The girl's face remained expressionless. Either she had not heard the insult, or it had made no impression. Her filthy dress and odd expression fit no categories, defied context. Gabriela had intended to go up to her apartment and have a drink before grading the essays, but Guillermo was obviously at his wit's end.

"Why don't I give her something to eat?"

"I don't care what you do so long as you're quiet."

The kitchen was a disaster. Guillermo's sink overflowed with dishes and the countertops were littered with

opened cans, cutlery, empty milk cartons. A slice of dried
pizza lay on a chipped plate. Gabriela rummaged through
the cupboards until she found a box of tea. While the water
was boiling, she took some rolls out of the bread box, heated
them in the oven and spread them with apricot jam. When
the tea had steeped she laced it with honey, put everything
on a reasonably clean plate, and took the food in to the girl
who ate quickly without looking at either of them.

"Do you feel better now?" Gabriela asked.

The girl blinked.

"Won't you tell us who you are? We can get in touch
with your family."

"For Christ's sake!" Guillermo complained. "Can't I
watch television in my own apartment?"

"There's something the matter with her."

"Is that my fault?"

"A little kindness won't hurt."

"I let her in, didn't I?"

"That's not what I mean."

Thoroughly disgusted with the old man, Gabriela
picked up the girl's cup and took it into the kitchen for more
tea. Holding the strainer over it, she poured out the hot
maté, catching the soggy leaves and knocking the strainer
clean against the sink. It made no difference that Guillermo's rudeness was traceable to his heart attack. Sick as
he was, he should be ashamed of himself for the way he
treated the girl. She would tell him, if not now, then later,
when things calmed down. Old men, she thought. And old
women, too. She hoped she would not lose her sense of
courtesy when she became one of them.

She was coming in from the kitchen when she saw
Chloe Fuentes, the resident astrologer, holding the front
door open for Eva Gille who had her arms full of groceries.
Chloe's husband, Jorge, followed them. Gabriela disliked

him. Besides being vain about his looks, which led him to wear his hair slicked back in imitation of Juan Manuel Fangio, his conservative ideas made him impossible to be around. Still, she was glad to see them because Chloe's presence always cowed Guillermo. He seemed to think her charts were a form of voodoo.

Eva took the elevator while the Fuentes sorted their mail, which was voluminous because of Chloe's newsletter and magazine subscriptions. Gabriela was going out to tell them about the girl when the Cristianis arrived with Orestes Escardó who was carrying rolled-up canvases and a bundle of framing wood.

Jorge took one look and grimaced.

"I suppose this means the building's going to stink of paint again."

"Why don't you fuck yourself, Jorge?"

"Stop it," Chloe said. "I'm in no mood for the two of you."

Orestes winked at Jorge, then said hello to Gabriela. Chloe glanced up from her mail, pursed her lips. She had done Gabriela's horoscope earlier in the week and warned her to be careful.

"I told you that you shouldn't even be out on the streets until Monday."

Roberto Cristiani smiled discreetly as he opened his mailbox.

"I'm fine," Gabriela said. "There's a girl in Guillermo's apartment."

"What?" Mercedes said.

"I'll be damned," Orestes laughed. "I thought he was too old for that."

Chloe groaned.

"Can't you think of anything besides sex?"

"Only when I try, sweetheart."

"I'd appreciate it if you were more polite to my wife," Jorge said. "I don't give a damn how you talk to your whores."

"She might be ill," Gabriela said to Roberto. "Would you mind taking a look at her?"

Roberto and Mercedes exchanged a quick glance. Their whole demeanor had changed within a few seconds, especially Mercedes' who acted like she'd seen a ghost. She made an odd fluttering gesture with her hand as she and Roberto hurried toward Guillermo's door.

"She's been here for hours," the old man complained as they stared at the girl.

"One," Gabriela said. "And she hasn't put you out."

Roberto had spent the afternoon in surgery. Before his daughter disappeared the discipline of the operating room always stimulated him. Now the work left him feeling wrung out. But it wasn't fatigue that made him seem to sink into himself; within a minute's span he had witnessed a prophecy fulfilled.

"I'm Dr. Cristiani," he told her in a shaky voice. "Gabriela said you aren't feeling well."

The girl regarded him blankly, then turned back to the television. Roberto had noticed the scar from across the room. Now he touched it, feeling a slight depression beneath the smoothness. He dismissed the possibility that had immediately occurred to him, that it had been made by a bullet. At the same time, he could think of no other explanation for such an injury.

"Can you tell me what happened?" he asked.

The girl continued looking at the screen.

"This is ridiculous," Jorge said. "I think we should throw her out."

Mercedes had been quietly watching the girl, doing all she could to deal with the sudden change of mood that had begun with Gabriela's announcement. Only a few hours ago she had been seeing pediatric patients in her office. She had finally diagnosed the problem of a three-month-old baby and was immensely relieved for the child and his mother. Now her eyes were bright, on the verge of tears. Recoiling slightly at Jorge's words, she shook her head and said, very softly, "It's dark outside. She isn't hurting anyone."

"She's in trouble," Orestes told him. "Anyone can see that."

"So now we're taking in bums off the street?" Jorge asked.

Guillermo groaned and turned off the television.

"I give up," he said to no one in particular. "Maybe I'll move to the pampas, go live with my cousin and have a little peace and quiet."

No one paid attention. Moving to the pampas was one of his favorite themes when he was drinking, along with how lousy things were in the city.

"She can stay with me tonight," Gabriela said.

"Now wait a minute," Jorge protested. "What about tomorrow?"

"What difference does it make?" Mercedes snapped.

Gabriela was surprised that Mercedes seemed so edgy. As Jorge went out to the foyer and slid the deadbolt home Gabriela held out her hand and told the girl they were going upstairs.

Jorge came back and looked pointedly at Orestes.

"If you're expecting visitors, that's too bad. For all we know she might've escaped from a detention center. What happens if one of your girlfriends blabs about seeing her? The police might get wind of it and think we were involved. They're already suspicious because of Ana María. You can fill in the blanks."

Orestes glanced at Mercedes, then faced Jorge.

"Your mouth's big as a toilet," he said.

"Bigger," added Chloe. "Do you always have to be such a fool?"

"It's all right," Mercedes said quietly.

"Come," Gabriela told the girl.

Jorge and Chloe stayed with Guillermo while the others took the elevator to the second floor. When they got out, Roberto said he would check on the girl in the morning.

Gabriela showed her around the apartment. When she asked her if she wanted something to drink she stared at the bookcases. Leaving her in the living room, Gabriela ran water in the tub. Once it was full, she unwrapped a new bar of soap, then went to her bedroom and retrieved a nightgown, underwear, slippers, then rummaged through the closet for a dress and sandals. The last two items she left in the spare room with a fold-down bed and took the others into the bath, laying them out on the counter beside the sink. Then she brought the girl in and pointed to the tub.

"Take as long as you like. The clothes are for you, understand?"

She looked even younger in the prim nightgown buttoned up to her neck. After showing her where she was going to sleep, Gabriela went back to the bathroom and picked up the clothes that lay heaped on the floor. She took them into the kitchen, ran water in the sink, added detergent and dropped them into the foam. The underwear and socks came out fine, but scrub as she did she could not get the stains out of the dress.

By the time she finished the girl was lying down. When Gabriela sat on the edge of the bed she pushed herself up. Leaning against her, the girl ran the fingers of her left hand across the bodice of her nightgown, tracing the embroidered flowers while Gabriela considered half a dozen possibilities that might explain her arrival.

Down the hall the Cristianis were sitting at their dining room table, arms extended, hands clasped, the drinks Roberto had poured untouched. Old grief shone like polished silver in Mercedes' eyes, a look brought up against her will and all the more pronounced in her drained, washed-out face. The overhead light emphasized the lines around Roberto's eyes and mouth as he asked the question neither ever seriously thought they would have to consider.

"What are we going to do?"

"Do we have a choice?" Mercedes said.

While they stared at each other we tracked their thoughts backward in time, rewinding them like film in a projector, ratcheting back and forth until we located what we wanted—a quiet neighborhood on a balmy night long before the girl went up the steps to the seagull door.

Calle Córdoba was lined with cars for half a block in both directions. The Cristianis cruised along in their diesel Mercedes and parked where the street intersected Avenida Arboles, in front of Pedro Augustín's house. They followed three other couples along the sidewalk to number twenty-nine, where they went through a wrought-iron gate into Carlos Rueda's garden. Twenty-five or thirty people were already there. The sheen of tables painted cobalt blue rippled like water when the shadows of the branches moved. Lantern light cast a yellow glow on the potted plants, trees and flagstones.

The Cristianis looked around, uncomfortable as children the first day in a new school. A sad-faced man motioned toward two empty chairs. Roberto thanked him with a nod and took Mercedes' arm, nervously guiding her between the rows. They settled back, grateful to no longer be on view, waiting as anxiously as everyone else for the man they had come to hear. Carlos was visible through the glass doors. He was bent over a guitar whose music suddenly broke off and left them stranded with its fading notes that seemed to blend uncannily with the scents of cyclamen and roses.

They had learned about him from Chloe Fuentes. One of her friends whose grandsons had disappeared regularly attended the sessions in Carlos' garden. While Carlos had never been able to see what happened to the boys, Dolores Masson's faith that he might was sustained week after week by stories that led to miraculous returns. When Dolores told Chloe about Carlos' gift, she immediately thought of the Cristianis. If she were in their place, she would grasp at any possibility. She knew they were skeptical about such things, though they were too polite to make fun of her as Guillermo and some of the others did whenever she talked about horoscopes or what she had learned at the metaphysicians club she belonged to. Besides having an indefatigable faith in horoscopes, Chloe advocated parapsychological fads and was a fervent devotee of Gurdjieff and Ouspensky.

One Saturday afternoon she met Roberto and Mercedes just as they came into the foyer looking worse than they had since Ana María disappeared. It didn't matter if they dismissed what she had to say; she would hate herself if she kept quiet.

"You aren't going to believe this," she blurted out, "but there's a man who sometimes knows what happened to the Disappeared. He's even brought some back. I have a friend who swears it's true."

If Chloe had spoken to them a day earlier, the Cristianis might have quickly slipped away with a polite excuse that they were too busy to talk, rolling their eyes at each other as they entered the elevator and joking on the way up about the latest example of Chloe's capacity for nonsense. While their faith in rationality was still intact that day, their resistance to the inexplicable had been weakened as surely as if they had been attacked by a virus.

During the previous week they had compiled a list of police stations and civil offices and set out one morning in search of information about Ana María, entering precisely ordered rooms smelling of polish and disinfectant, rooms where sparkling counters and chairs set neatly against the walls spoke of authority and knowledge. After they politely explained their purpose, the responses varied only in degrees of contempt shown by policemen and functionaries who either dismissed them outright or went through the charade of thumbing through folders before saying there was no record of their daughter. They visited five police stations, stopped for a drink in a run-down café, went to seven more, growing more desperate with each stop.

They were exhausted by mid-afternoon, but Mercedes insisted on going to the Casa Rosada. A sergeant waved them away. It was not possible to speak to anyone. Roberto pounded his fist on the desk. Another soldier appeared, told them to get out. Roberto wanted to grab him by the collar, tell him this was their daughter they were talking about, refraining only because it was clear the soldier was spoiling for trouble. When they left, the hollow echo of their footsteps seemed to stain the air trapped in that polished granite hall.

So they were tired and distraught by the time they met Chloe Fuentes. With the day's pain and frustration still fresh, neither had the energy to invent an excuse. Roberto stood by the mailboxes with his arms folded. Mercedes took off her scarf and shook out her hair. Their passivity surprised Chloe; it was the last thing she expected.

"I'll tell you what I know," she said hurriedly.

They listened while Guillermo's television droned in

the background, juxtaposing her description of Carlos' powers to the voice of a woman giving the weather report. Chloe's words were slipping by the defenses that had always kept the mysterious at a distance. A fissure had developed in their skepticism, flooding their minds with unexpected light. At exactly the same moment they thought: What if it's true?

Then, faster than the idea had occurred, the chink closed. As the moment passed they exchanged a quick glance, embarrassed by the desire to believe they still saw glimmering in each other's eyes. The excitement that had begun to animate Mercedes' face gave way to slackness. Roberto unfolded his arms, managed a half-smile.

"That's very interesting," he said flatly.

"Thank you," Mercedes told her.

Chloe noticed the change but could think of nothing to add as they headed for the elevator, obviously intent on getting away from her as fast as possible.

By all rights that should have been the end of their understandable lapse in judgment occasioned by grief and helplessness but most of all by the desire for things to be other than they were. Everyone experiences such moments. Everyone has done what the Cristianis did in the days that followed as they upbraided themselves, felt disgusted. It was all very conscious and rational, what you would expect of two physicians embarrassed by the detour they had made into the inexplicable. After entertaining the possibility that what Chloe said might be true, they went in the opposite direction and stopped talking about Ana María altogether, which they mistakenly thought might be a way to avoid the glaring whiteness a disappearance makes.

But grief has its own way of dealing with things. Just as they were making progress, Roberto decided to take a different route on his morning jog. Usually he ran into the heart of the city, stopping halfway for bread at a bakery he had patronized for years. For some reason he turned left instead of right at the bottom steps in front of the Villa Deamicis and was soon running through the park where they took Ana María when she was a child. The sight of the swings left him close to tears. He got hold of himself by the time he returned, but the old misery had threaded through his mind, linking memories and shards of thoughts.

Mercedes knew what had happened as soon as he came inside. She watched him drink a glass of water, then head into the living room to do his push-ups.

"Roberto? There's something I want to say."

He looked at her quizzically.

"Can you wait till I finish?"

"It's important."

He unzipped his jacket, draped it over the back of a chair. He was, he realized, feeling worse by the moment. She acted as though she were embarrassed.

"What's wrong?"

She sighed, then looked straight at him.

"I've been thinking about him."

He scanned her face, judged her comment an observation and not necessarily a subject for discussion. Sometimes she just liked to get things off her chest. He wanted that to be the case now because he did not feel like talking until he had a chance to get hold of himself. He nodded and then dropped to the floor, straining hard against his weight as if the extra effort, the resistance, might clear his mind.

"Are you going to say anything?" she asked.

He did ten more push-ups before he got up.

"What's the point? I thought we agreed."

He felt hypocritical, but it was better than telling her about the images streaming through his mind.

"What have we got to lose?" she asked.

Roberto saw the swings, Mercedes pushing Ana María, her beaming smile. In an instant his resolve to look toward the future fell apart.

They dressed without speaking, aware that their decision was so tenuous the wrong word or intonation would kill it, crush the possibility. After breakfast they went upstairs.

Chloe greeted them at the door with her red hair done up in awful pink curlers that clashed with her red flower-print robe. Feeling stupid, Roberto said, "This man you told us about. How do we get in touch?"

Chloe could see what the question cost him. Excited as she was, she said nothing and invited them in with a curt nod. They stood awkwardly in the middle of the living room as she put on the oversized glasses hanging from a cord around her neck and rummaged through stacks of papers on the desk where she prepared her charts. Finally she found a scrap of pink notepaper no larger than a playing card.

"Calle Córdoba," she read. "Number twenty-nine."

"Is there a phone number?" Mercedes asked. "Do we make an appointment?"

Chloe shook her head.

"I understand that people just go. There's a gate at the side of the house that leads to his garden."

At the end of a long day at the hospital, during which they had to force themselves to pay attention to things any intern could have done without thinking, they went to dinner at a grill whose dark wood paneling and wrought-iron chandeliers wrapped the place in the aura of tradition. They could usually relax in the ambiance, easing the strains of the day with martinis as they watched *asadores* dressed like gauchos cut slices from huge sides of meat stretched tightly on spits over open fires. But the considerable charms of La Cabaña did not touch them that night. The martinis seemed too dry, the grilled kid indifferent. Mercedes cut hers into tiny pieces she left uneaten. Roberto managed to consume half of his with effort. After a day of thinking about Carlos they were feeling uncertain, and stretched out their stay with aperitifs and coffee while they tested their resolve, debating whether it would be better just to go home. They might have if two of their colleagues had not come in and headed for their table with the determined expressions that the Cristianis had come to recognize as masked pity for their loss of Ana María. They got up quickly, told their friends they were late for an appointment and hurried out the door, knowing before they reached the car that they were going through with it.

They had envisioned a flamboyant, theatrical-looking man, but their imaginings were at odds with the one walking toward the rattan chair set up at the edge of the flagstones. Of middling height, thin, with close-cropped hair that fitted him like a skullcap, Carlos' chiseled features were as ascetic as a monk's. Having assumed someone larger than life, they were naturally disappointed. Roberto had a sinking feeling, as if he had wandered into a fundamentalist's tent filled with true believers. The image left him helpless and he thought bitterly: It has come to this.

Carlos searched their faces, moving deliberately from person to person until he had made contact with everyone. The serene way he sat with his hands on the arms of the chair contrasted vividly with the intensity of his gaze. Roberto had never seen eyes like those before, and he was grateful when Carlos looked at someone else.

"I promise nothing," Carlos said suddenly. "I describe only what I see. Now, tell me your stories."

A woman sitting in front of Mercedes stood up.

"My name is Imelda García. My son Francisco called one afternoon a month ago to say he didn't feel well and was coming home early. His friends saw him leave the building, and that was the last anyone saw him. I came to find out what happened."

"What does he look like?"

"Like me," she groaned. "Everyone says so."

She was shaking, her body mimicking the tremor in her voice. It was absurd, Roberto thought. Repulsive. The whole thing seemed outrageous. It was stupid to have gotten mixed up in this. A fool would have known better. Yet he found himself looking expectantly at Carlos, the way a kid stares at a magician, amazed to be thinking that he might actually be capable of pulling a rabbit out of a hat. Memories of Ana María floated into his mind and his skepticism broke on them, shattering like waves against a shoreline's rocks. The vague hope that had come to him throughout the day took hold again as Carlos leaned back and stared at the lanterns, his brow furrowed in concentration, his eyes distant yet oddly focused. The only sound was of the wind in the trees, the odd note struck on a wind chime.

Finally he said, "I'm sorry. I see nothing."

Imelda bunched the fringe of her *rebozo* in her hands. She tottered. Roberto rose just as the man sitting next to her reached out and helped her down.

"This happens sometimes. Don't be discouraged. Tell me your stories."

Roberto reached for Mercedes' hand, squeezed it, cleared his throat, aware that he was taking Carlos at his word because there was nothing else left to do. But he stood there resisting as Carlos turned to face him, holding back a little longer. Finally he spoke in a voice barely above a whisper.

"I'm Roberto Cristiani. My daughter was involved with some students who passed out leaflets and held some demonstrations. We told her to be careful, but she's headstrong. She said, 'If I don't do it, who will?' When she left for the university that morning I expected to see her at dinner. We'd planned on going to a play. But she didn't come home. Some students saw her being pushed into a car on her way to school."

His silence made him feel hollow. He was appalled that there were so few words to tell her story.

"Her name?" Carlos asked.

"Ana María," Mercedes said. "Her name is Ana María."

The garden walls were not nearly high enough to send back echoes, but it seemed to Roberto that his daughter's name was sailing through the air, its five syllables Mercedes had pronounced in a pinched, desperate tone sounding again and again.

Carlos nodded and stared at the flagstones. When he finally looked up a change had come upon his eyes, a kind of glimmer that had been missing when he spoke to Imelda García. As he began to speak, the timbre of his voice shifted from a soft, almost apologetic register to a deeper one that was more resonant and assured.

"Somewhere in the city there is an old building reeking of oil. It was used as an assembly point, a place where people were taken and made to wait until plans were laid. The lights were rarely turned on so no one ever saw the others clearly, though they heard voices, and from time to time saw a sliver of light through the door when someone new was pushed inside. One night the door opened. A truck backed up to it. They were forced inside and then they rode in darkness for many hours."

Suddenly Carlos broke off. The lantern light washed over his face. He appeared exhausted as he closed his eyes. When the truck's doors opened everything began spinning. His mind was filled with glowing lights, moving lights, then one still light at the center.

"There was a grove of trees. Fields of wheat. A new moon came up the next night and there was a disturbance in the air, the sound of wings as an owl flew from its cover across the sliver of moonglow. After five days a girl left that place and walked until it was too dark to see. She ate whatever came to hand, slept in the open. I don't know if she is Ana María, but she has been traveling for a long time, coming to you because she has nowhere else to go. Take care of her, whoever she is." Carlos slumped in his chair, still seeing a girl walking in an open space.

Roberto sat down awkwardly, afraid to look at Mercedes. They joined hands and watched Carlos bestir himself, regain his strength, listening while others rose to speak a name, offer fragments of stories without endings. Carlos revealed a death, a miraculous escape. His voice went flat when he failed to see the grandsons of Dolores Masson. But even though they heard each word and learned the rhythms of Carlos' speech which rose and fell, speeded up and lagged according to the intensity of what he was vouchsafed to see, the remaining stories were like distant music, or figures seen from far away, all secondary to the image he had given them of a girl walking through endless fields of wheat.

For days afterward they heard Carlos' words echoing in the hospital's corridors, sounding behind the din of traffic. After a while it all began to seem dreamlike. As the effects wore off they found themselves thinking of that evening as a kind of theater to which they had naively succumbed, and soon felt embarrassed that they had ever believed in it, as if they had cheapened both their memory of Ana María and the grief which held her like a setting does a gemstone.

By the time they had dinner with Orestes Escardó months later, they had come to terms with the need that had driven them to Carlos, accepting it as a desperate aberration which had only renewed their sense of loss. They had planned to see an old Fellini film later, after Orestes dropped off his supplies. He had talked about it in the car, and their minds were full of clowns and rainbow colors as they came through the seagull door. When Gabriela told them there was a girl in Guillermo's apartment, her words rocked them back on their heels.

Perched like gargoyles on the pier glass, we saw wild expectation flaring in their eyes. Who could blame them? Though Gabriela had not pronounced their daughter's name, hope filled up the absence, giving them a thousand explanations for her silence. Heartsick and appalled, we watched them cross the foyer, preparing ourselves for what was coming as they reached the door of Guillermo's apartment, the blaring of his television sounding like the music of deliverance, its melody pitched to the remembered sound of their daughter's voice which vanished the moment they saw the disheveled girl. And just as we felt the disappointment bearing down on their hearts while Roberto examined her, so we felt their confusion after they bade good night to Gabriela and returned to their apartment, confounded by the truth of Carlos' prophecy and the weight of his injunction. None of us remained unmoved when Mercedes asked if they had a choice. There they were, caught between the fresh sorrow of their loss and the inexplicable presence of the girl who had stepped out of Carlos' imagination. The thought of caring for someone who reminded them of Ana

María was like an iron bar across their chests, bearing down on the cores of their beings where Carlos' words had taken root. One look at Mercedes told Roberto that she was thinking the same thing.

"You're sure?" he asked.

"The only thing I'm sure of is that something's going on we don't understand."

The following evening, after she had been left alone in Ana María's bedroom, the girl went over to the dressing table and stared at a photograph. Circled by an ornate silver frame, her long blond hair falling gracefully across her shoulders, Ana María stood with her arms around her parents, smiling. The girl's eyes shifted back and forth between the three faces but always returned to Ana María's, interrogating it for some clue to the emotion that had come upon her. It was as though she were swimming at night, kept away from the shore by an unseen current. The closest she came to recognition was the time she had been walking and discovered the pool where another girl looked back at her and she had recognized the face as her own. That was not the case with the girl in the picture. This one was not her. This one was separate.

Her attention soon drifted away to the details of the room. When Mercedes and Roberto had left her there it had seemed strange, alien. Now she felt that she belonged, as if she were sharing it. She was aware of Ana María's presence when she opened the closet and trailed her fingers across the linen blouses, the skirts and creamy silken dresses. She slid out the bureau drawers filled with scarves and underwear, a rainbow of soft pastels.

At first she was satisfied just to look at the things, touching them for the pleasure of their softness. But soon they recalled the emotion that had come to her as she stared at the photograph. She returned to the bureau and picked up the picture. There was something wrong with the stillness she gazed at. The frozen smile and unmoving body were as unendurably sad as the neatly folded clothes in the drawers, the dresses hanging lifelessly on padded nylon hangers in the closet. She faced the open closet with its paralyzed shapes and colors. Going to it, she removed a green dress from its hanger and held it out, her eyes traveling from the bodice to the hem and along the narrow sleeves that descended from puffed shoulders. She imagined how the girl's long blond hair would look against its emerald green as she began to move, swaying slightly back and forth. Then she took a step, another, and began to dance. She danced the dress around the bed and to the window and in a circle before the dressing table, her steps as graceful as any ballerina's, the skirt of the empty dress billowing out to match the swirling of her own. She was dancing to a feeling, a toneless rhythm deep within her mind, and was too preoccupied to notice Mercedes opening the door, drawn to her daughter's room by an unfamiliar sound. Mercedes stood there watching, fascinated and appalled as the girl continued her dance, unaware that she was compelled to make the green dress move, or that she was doing what she could to force imagined life into its slackness as she twirled and twirled.

So it was that the girl came to stay with the Cristianis, upsetting the careful patterns of communal living developed over the years and throwing the Villa Deamicis into confusion that only increased when its residents theorized about her arrival and her past. Except for Jorge, they thought she was too young to be an enemy of the regime, too lost in herself to have ever been normal. They agreed that her pallor was the sign of an unnamable affliction, that silence was her element as the air is a bird's. Though she never spoke, her presence renewed the fear that had come upon them after Ana María had disappeared. Jorge Fuentes regularly demanded that the Cristianis send her away, complaining that she had forced them into a dangerous conspiracy, but the others accepted her as a communal burden and devised a schedule so she would never be left alone.

By the time the regime collapsed, the residents of the Villa Deamicis had settled into their new routine. Falcons no longer prowled the streets. The generals were imprisoned, their death squads a thing of the past. But people who have endured terror do not suddenly fling open their windows to let in the sun. For a long time they observed its warmth without quite believing that it once again belonged to them. Their minds were marked with suspicion, with the still fresh sorrow they felt for Ana María, and with the mystery of the girl which nagged at their minds like a fretful child. There was nothing we could do to help them, no way to share our knowledge that she had ascended the stairs to their seagull door in a desperate effort to get back inside the story of her life.

Testimony of
Jaime Goyisoto

I'd heard of Carlos Rueda. Even in a city as large as Buenos Aires someone that remarkable can break through the static and claim a place for himself, especially with people who've gotten so desperate they'll try anything. And I understand what drove the Cristianis to him. It was no different from what happens when you've exhausted all the resources medicine has to offer and make a pilgrimage to a place like Lourdes, hoping for a miracle to stop the disease eating you up from the inside, or wanting to hear again, or walk. Though it must be easier for true believers than it was for Roberto and Mercedes. Imagine the conflict in their minds —physicians visiting a seer! Now that was a leap of faith.

As they sat there trying to come to grips with Carlos' prophecy, their hearts were aching with disappointment that he had failed to conjure Ana María. The wound of her disappearance was renewed, as raw as it had been the day it happened. Knowing what they felt put me in mind of my family. The same longing ran in their veins, and I couldn't stop thinking about my wife and son wondering what had become of me.

It started with a soldier's impromptu theatrical performance one day while my son, Aldo, was coming home from school. He was late and had taken a shortcut past a military garrison. He was minding his own business, but there was a cannon on the lawn out in front and you know how boys are about guns. A knee-high chain fenced the lawn off from the sidewalk. He stepped over it and went to take a look. I believed him later when he said he hadn't touched the cannon. He was just checking it out when a guard appeared and asked what he thought he was doing. Aldo told him he was just looking. The guard said it was a restricted area and he had no right to be there. Then he decided to teach him a lesson. He put his pistol to Aldo's head, pulled the trigger. The chamber was empty, but the sound of the hammer on the firing pin must have been loud as a bomb in my poor son's ears. He was so terrified he ran all the way home, almost two miles. Thank God my wife was there. She said he cried all afternoon, and he kept it up after I got home from work. Irene and I spent the evening trying to calm him down. I'll never forget the look of terror in his eyes. It was still there when we put him to bed, though he'd finally stopped crying.

The next morning I woke up to the sound of my wife screaming. It came from Aldo's room and I ran in to find Irene standing at the foot of the bed, sobbing uncontrollably. You want to know why? I'll tell you. Because Aldo's hair had turned white. That's right, white hair. On a ten-year-old.

I stood there doing what I could to get hold of myself, so outraged I could hardly breathe. Aldo knew something was wrong with his hair from the way we looked at him. Irene went over and put her arm around him but he got up and looked at himself in the mirror over his dresser. His face became white as his hair. He touched his temple and without saying a thing started to cry.

I'd never done anything violent in my life, but as I watched Aldo revenge was all I could think about. Without a word I left the house, drove like a maniac, slammed on the brakes in front of the garrison. Two guards were out in front and I ran at them, screaming and tackled the one closest to me. His rifle went flying. I was on top of him, my hands at his throat, when the other swung the butt of his rifle against my head. I remember the sound, like a melon being dropped on a kitchen floor.

As I came to I heard them laughing. Why they didn't arrest me is a mystery, but they let me stagger back to the car and go home with what turned out to be a concussion.

When I was well I started going to meetings. What happened to Aldo had forced me to see the light, and the more I saw the angrier I became. Everyone had plenty of grievances, but none had to see what I did when I went home. Aldo refused to go to school or play with his friends. Out of desperation Irene bought some hair dye. The color was shiny black and made him look like an old man trying to be young again. He hated it and I helped him wash it out.

It was about that time I got involved in some things, nothing violent, you understand, but enough to call attention to myself. Enough, it turned out, for my name to make its way onto the list.

They came for me at work, drove me away, taught me things about pain I'd rather not go into. Let's just say that all the rumors about what they were capable of were true.

A month or two passed before I was taken to the warehouse. It was so dark I could hardly see the people already there. The rest were brought in over the next few days, and then a funny thing happened. The guards didn't say anything, but we knew that no more people were coming, that the twelve of us were it. That's when we started telling our stories, saying who we were, what we'd done with our lives, how we'd ended up in the warehouse. One story a day, always after the evening meal of some vile-tasting soup. I suppose we talked about our pasts rather than howling at the injustice of what they'd done to us because it let everyone cling to who they'd been. For the last few nights a guy named Jacob sang revolutionary songs in his ruined voice until he couldn't do it any longer. We had time to get through everyone's story except the girl's before they took us away.

And then, well, you already know what happened. When the bullets hit I thought of Aldo's hair and the sadness of his face wreathed by unnatural age. His hair seemed to burst into flame, one strand at a time. As it became a pall of the whitest smoke I'd ever seen, drifting over everything,

I realized that I'd seen the announcement of my death the morning I went into his room.

After the goodness that claimed Alberto's heart had been defeated by Ernesto's bullet and the killers drove away, it was so quiet we could hear the moon gliding through the sky, the mangled roots above us trying to find purchase in the soil. Our despair was the despair of the lost, the forgotten. Hope had been sucked out of us like air from a bell jar. Then, a few days later, we saw the girl move and you can imagine our elation when we realized that she was returning to the world. Though she didn't respond to our names rising up around her, circling her like a swarm of butterflies, we stayed close and still do, desperately hoping against hope that she'll remember us as I remember the whiteness of Aldo's hair.

Book

Two

King of
the Hill

Since the Villa Deamicis is crucial to our story, and since we've reached a place where the action slows down, a kind of adagio before the tempo moves ahead more vigorously, we want to take advantage of the moment and describe the place in more detail than we've had a chance to do.

The old Italian who built it, Giancarlo Deamicis, took great pride in the foyer, remodeling it until a year before his death, when he finally pronounced himself satisfied that it matched his memory of a villa in Palermo whose interior he once glimpsed while delivering milk, years before he immigrated to Argentina and made his fortune on the pampas. The floor was covered with black and white tiles imported from Italy, smooth and creamy as Carrara marble. To offset their starkness, he had the wall paneled with mahogany veneer. There were light fixtures shaped like half-moons, their edges rimmed with metal filigree. The light was mute but good; a soft yellow, like sun on a hazy day.

The stained-glass door was inspired by Deamicis' arrival in the city after a long journey on a freighter. He had been sick most of the time, but as soon as he stepped onto the dock he felt wonderful. He had looked around the city and seen a pearl-white seagull circling overhead and looking down, as if to welcome him. The image stayed in his mind during the long years he was accumulating his wealth, and the first thing he did when he bought the building was to hire an artist to design a door with this remembrance of that long ago day.

Important as the door was, the centerpiece of the foyer was a large pier glass Deamicis had come across on a visit to Rome. Six feet high, and nearly as wide, it occupied the wall opposite the door. The first thing residents saw when they came home was an image of themselves backlit by the tree-filtered light from the street. Deamicis had put it there because he thought it only fitting that people see themselves entering their sanctuary, leaving the cares of the world behind. But there was more to the placement of the mirror than that. Deamicis had loved irony the way other men did food or drink, and the shadowy shape people saw when they came in fitted his tastes perfectly. Whenever someone moved in, Deamicis took them to the door and told them to look at their image. "It's like Plato's cave," he said. "What's real? The shadow before you, or the person standing there in the nice yellow light after you close the door?"

Over the years, sometimes with the advice of the residents, sometimes on a whim of his own, Deamicis changed the pictures in the foyer. Eventually, he settled on three scenes of the pampas and a painting by Orestes Escardó, a large blue and white abstract called *Impression 36* in honor of his birthday.

The explosion of colors aptly represented the force of Orestes' presence in the building. Except for the Cristianis and Gabriela Santini, who accorded him a certain latitude, he offended everyone else with his nocturnal behavior which Jorge Fuentes likened to that of a cat in heat.

Orestes worked tirelessly in his studio during the day and spent his evenings on the prowl for women. The requisites for his attention varied according to his mood, but he was always on the lookout for a certain *brío* in the eyes, a creative twitching of a skirt, an *hauteur* in reaction to his outrageous jibes. In response to Eva Gille's accusation that he made *roués* look like saints, he said that his pleasures were not those of a collector but of an aesthetician who loved everything about women and craved their love in return, even if sometimes only for a night.

Orestes was unfailingly polite as he reconnoitered his favorite bars. If he found no one suitable, he strolled the midnight streets, moving among long-legged beauties whose leather miniskirts streamed with reflected neon lights. He searched their eyes, noted shades of lipstick, the swing of hair, made his pitch which was so outrageously frank that even the ones who dismissed him out of hand wandered away laughing, cheered by what he said. And if his luck was such that he reached the end of the last street without finding someone to follow him into a bar, he drove to La Boca where he was well known among the artists, touring the brightly lit alleyway of Caminito Street whose buildings were painted in screaming primary reds and blues and greens. Failing there, his last recourse was the waterfront where he tipped his fedora low over his eyes and danced a tango so lascivious that even the whores were offended.

When he succeeded, he brought his companion back to the Villa Deamicis whose insulated walls were not thick enough to mask the sounds from his apartment. These included a game of chase requiring him to roar like a lion as well as shouting endearments that ended with him laughing at the sheer joy over what was coming. People did their best to ignore the commotion, piling pillows on their heads, getting up for a midnight drink or talking sleepy trivia to pass the time. If they happened to be up late visiting in an apartment next to his, someone invariably repeated the building's nighttime refrain—"I hope he catches her soon!"—with a mixture of indignation and secret envy, listening until he did, usually with a whoop. Then they returned to their cards or conversation that always seemed a little flat and desultory in the wake of his success.

On weekends Orestes usually had breakfast with the Cristianis who had taken pity on him years ago because he refused to cook anything decent for himself. He ate most of his meals in local cafés. When he dined at home, it was inevitably on pastry or cakes from the same bakery where Roberto bought bread on his morning run. Orestes judiciously perused everything in the display cases, gravitating toward those items with brightly colored icing and interrogating the baker about the number of layers and the flavor of the fillings before he settled on the richest of the lot which he took home in a large white box, dipping his finger into the frosting from time to time. Because his body burned up food as fast as he ate it, he never put on weight and was therefore the envy of Mercedes and Gabriela who only had to look at something made with cream and butter to gain a pound or two.

On the first Saturday after the girl moved in with the Cristianis she was startled by a loud knock on the door. Mercedes had noticed that unexpected sounds made her uneasy and quickly told her not to be afraid; it was only Orestes. The girl looked at her blankly. His name floated into her consciousness like a balloon, sailed away without giving her a face. Only when Roberto opened the door and she saw Orestes did she have a vague recollection of encountering him before.

Clutching several canvases and a drawing portfolio, Orestes stepped inside, faked a stumble, gaped at her like a clown.

"Good morning one and all," he said.

His bright pink shirt and green pants reminded her of parrots, his stick-thin body of a clown. She tried to remember where she had seen such things as he made a funny face and laughter welled up inside her, bursting on her lips like bubbles.

"Look," Orestes said. "My little white bird from nowhere knows how to laugh."

He approved of the Cristianis taking her in. Something about her touched him. It went beyond her dazed eyes, was a kind of vulnerability he had never encountered. She seemed without boundaries, undifferentiated.

"Flown the coop," he added softly, "and forgotten her way home."

"It's the first time she's laughed," Mercedes told him. "Good for you."

After breakfast Orestes leaned the three paintings against the wall. They resembled nothing the girl knew, but the bright patches of colors and geometric designs made her head swim.

"What do you think?" Orestes asked. "I'm taking them to the gallery today."

"I like them," Mercedes said.

"And these?" Roberto asked, nodding at the portfolio.

Orestes laughed as he put it on the table.

"Recollections of the war."

He made a strangling sound, raised his eyebrows, stuck out his tongue. The girl shrank back, wide-eyed.

"Don't," Mercedes said sharply. "You're scaring her."

She watched him out of the corner of her eyes, afraid the awful expression would come back.

When the girl neither moved nor changed expression, Orestes turned to Roberto.

"Do you think she understands?"

"I'm not sure," Roberto answered.

"Sometimes she does," Mercedes said defensively. "I'm positive."

"It could be amnesia," said Roberto. "I suppose you've noticed the scar. I think it might be from a bullet wound."

Orestes had seen it that first night, but it had never occurred to him that she could have been shot. He did not know what to say.

"Let's change the subject," Mercedes said pointedly as she led the girl to the sofa.

She sat next to Mercedes, trying to unravel the tenor of their conversation. Sometimes pairs of words, even three or four broke out of the jumble, arrayed themselves in familiar

configurations. The rest were mere sounds that matched the
movement of their lips. She wanted Orestes to make her
laugh again. Instead he opened the portfolio and removed a
pencil drawing. They saw the familiar face of a middle-aged
man shaded by a visored hat. His narrow eyes glowed above
a smug mouth that showed the beginning of a smile.

"Generalísimo Galtieri," Roberto said.

"His true self, the way I imagined him in that pink shit
house they call Casa Rosada, dreaming of what else he
could do." He passed the drawing to Mercedes. "It's part of
a new series I call *The Eighth Sin* in honor of the seven
deadlies."

"Which you know by heart," Mercedes laughed.

"Or by something else," Roberto said dryly.

"I'm serious. What's left out of the list? Sloth, gluttony,
envy, they're all sins of the body or desire. Whoever invented them overlooked another. Power. Since power in our
country is located in the military, I decided to draw it in all
its manifestations. There's one for every rank, from the
dumbest private to our beloved generals."

He handed them half a dozen sheets of thick creamy
paper. The drawings were parodic, hilarious.

"Were you thinking of Daumier?" Roberto asked.

"Goya." Orestes watched their reactions, obviously
pleased. "Now," he added, "the *pièce de résistance.*" He removed a sheet from the back of the portfolio. "It's called,
King of the Hill."

Roberto took the drawing and held it up to the light.
Two potbellied men stood on top of a hill facing each other,
naked except for jackboots and enormous hats bearing general's insignias. They grasped enormous penises in both
hands, brandishing them like broadswords. A chest lay at
their feet, its top open, exposing a map of Argentina.

"The winner gets the prize," Orestes said.

Roberto smiled and handed it to Mercedes who made a face. Yesterday she had seen a child in the emergency room, the victim of a neighbor. The drawing vividly brought it back. "It's disgusting," she said. "Put it away before she sees it."

But she had. The swollen penises seemed to expand the moment she glimpsed them, devouring the space on the paper, then the space in the room, pushing her off-balance so that she was tumbling backward into memory. Out of its spinning a man emerged, looming up in a dark place, shutting out the light, his body like a wall. Her voice echoed off it when he put his hands on her. His fingers felt thick as sausages. His beard scratched her face. She was falling, falling, crushed, the sudden pain unbelievable, filling her whole being. The words she tried to shout were silenced by the flatness of a hand pressing on her mouth as she descended into a darkness of her own making, shutting out the pain, alone in a place she retreated to, one she never knew existed.

The pity of it. That's what we thought. At the moment we forgot our need, our reliance on her to remember us, remember where we were. We knew what had happened, why she escaped into the darkness, what she'd feel if the protective metaphor suddenly collapsed. And so we tried to place ourselves between her and the scene that had come to life in her mind, stretch ourselves so tall we'd block it out. But our effort failed, and for the next few nights she dreamed of falling into herself, into some deep blue place. During the day she sat with her arms crossed, knees pressed together, staring out the window. Mercedes was furious with Orestes for showing them the drawings of the naked generals, assuming that the enormous penises had shocked the girl but having no idea that she had traveled into the past on those images and was struggling to return. For three days she barely moved. On the fourth morning she woke with only a hazy memory of her feelings, her mind purged but sensitive, as if it had been bruised by grasping fingers.

The Wall

Cecilia Rueda woke at dawn, thinking about a sentence. The night before she had given in to her editor's suggestion handwritten on a yellow slip stuck to the page. Now she realized she should have followed her instincts.

Carlos turned over as she slipped out of bed, mur-

mured something, went back to sleep. She put on a robe and went out to the kitchen, switched on the light. After the coffee was made she went into the living room where the manuscript lay on the coffee table, surrounded by empty cups, pencils, erasers, notebooks and a plate with the remains of a meal. Its ten chapters overlapped like dominoes, all thinner than she wanted. Her reading glasses were folded on top of the last one. Slipping them on, she picked up the manuscript cross-hatched with arrows connecting circled and bracketed passages to places higher or lower on the pages. Words were scratched out, replaced with successive revisions, as many as half a dozen forming little ladders over the typed lines, mementos of her search for better ones to convey a meaning or the texture of an emotion. Lengthier additions in her bold hand ran like filigrees along the margins, their positions in the text indicated by arrows and asterisks.

The sentence was on the next to last page, gnarled as she had feared, its meaning obscured by the wrong verb. She lined out her editor's suggestion and inserted the original above it. Then she read over the page, fairly pleased but aware that she could recast every line in more burnished language. Her dissatisfaction with the page spread to the rest of the book which seemed sketchy, inadequate. Images raced through her mind. For every sentence she had written there was another that should amplify it, extend its meaning, add color, weight. There were details she had not spent enough time on, the slant of light when the guard came into her room, voices echoing in unseen corridors. All the words she had written and worried over and changed time and again were only symbols for what should have been said, like a ship's signal flags. The book seemed like a skeleton with missing bones. She wanted to find them, but it was too late. She had already planned to spend the day reading it aloud with Carlos and Martín Benn before handing it over to her editor.

Cecilia felt sick thinking about it as she pulled her legs up and circled them with her arms. She stared out the window at the brightening city where *The Wall* would soon take on a life of its own. She had written with desperate energy, aware that with each passing day the war was receding further into the past. Her words were needed to keep it fresh, offer more proof of the obscenity the generals had visited on the country. Though it would never be the book she wanted, it was good enough, it told the truth. The counterforce at work, the desire to hold on to the manuscript and rewrite all its sentences, had less to do with a need for perfection than it did with her feelings for Teresa. *The Wall* was her daughter's story as well as her own, filled with pages describing their captivity together and her emptiness after Teresa was taken away. Watching the sun flood the city, she suddenly understood why she wanted to gather the manuscript in her arms and endlessly remake it; letting it go would be like abandoning Teresa whose fate would solidify in the descriptions, the images. As she turned her eyes away from the sun, she imaged the words of her book carved into a huge slab of stone memorializing her daughter, a crypt of words, massive and unchangeable.

Martín arrived as they were having breakfast.

"Do you want something?" Cecilia asked after she let him in.

"I had an omelet at the Rafael, but I read better with a little alcohol."

"Bloody Mary?" Carlos asked.

"You know her name."

Carlos made Martín's drink, poured plain tomato juice for himself and Cecilia.

"It's in there," Cecilia said, pointing to the living room.

Carlos pulled the overstuffed chairs close to the coffee table while Cecilia divided the manuscript into three sections, putting hers on the arm of her chair and handing the others to Carlos and Martín.

"Who wants to start?"

"It would help to hear you read," Martín said. "I'll have a better idea about the cadences."

Carlos looked at her.

"I don't mind," she said, nodding to him, though it was obvious that she would rather not.

It took the whole morning to get through the first section. Carlos and Martín listened for breaks in rhythm, violations of her voice, stopping her occasionally to make suggestions. Once she came to a part that made her voice quaver and she handed the pages to Carlos, asking him to read them and looking out the window while he did, trying not to hear the words about Teresa that were like a knife cutting to the bone.

They broke for lunch, then Martín read through dinner and Carlos finished the last section at five minutes to ten, his voice shaky as he read the final sentence. He carefully put the pages down on the table and glanced at Cecilia.

"It will make a difference," he said.

"It's the best thing anyone has written about what happened," Martín added, stopping his praise only because he saw that she was not interested in hearing any more. "I'd ask for a nightcap, but I'm bleary-eyed as it is."

He got up and put on his jacket. They followed him to the door and Cecilia kissed him on the cheek.

"Thank you," she said.

"Call me when you feel like celebrating."

"It will be a while."

"I know that, but you need to."

Cecilia locked the door and joined Carlos on the sofa where she put the ninth chapter on top of the tenth, the eighth on the ninth, working backward until she had assembled all of them. She stared at the title page a moment before putting the manuscript into the typewriter paper box. As she slipped on the cover she remembered the image of the stone.

"It's finished," Carlos said.

She looked at him, eyes brimming. "It will never be finished." She rubbed her forehead. "God, I'm tired."

Carlos got into bed while she applied cleansing lotion to her face, then methodically wiped it off with cotton balls, removing the accents until her skin glowed in the lights framing the mirror. Traffic sounds came up from the street, music from the building next door. She always looked younger without makeup, scarcely any different than when they had met and were so greedy for each other. But that had changed. The past still had its hands on her body, bruising it with memories. He was afraid neither of them could ever forget enough to recover the old spontaneity. He did not realize that she was crying until she turned away from the dressing table and held out her arms. Throwing back the covers, he went to her, slid his hands around her waist.

"I miss her so much," she whispered.

He stroked her hair, said he did, too. Then he felt her arms coming up his back, her hand soft on his neck. She came closer, pressing against him, concentrating.

Two months later she drove home from the doctor's office beating the heels of her hands on the steering wheel, crying, unable to believe she had been so stupid. One moment she had been looking at herself in the mirror, the next she was falling into emptiness, the echo of her voice rattling in the *estancia's* corridors. As she had turned to Carlos she remembered the little plastic case in the medicine cabinet, but her mind skipped past it, plunging ahead to what she needed *then* to stop the falling. But not taking a minute in the bathroom had been more than impatience. That was the least of it. Tracking the idea, she quickly shifted and pulled around an old truck belching smoke. Because at that moment, in an obscure, muddled way, like some love-stunned girl half her age consumed with the idea and ignoring everything it meant, she had wanted it to happen.

Carlos was working in his study, the new play's manuscript a pool of white beneath the lamp. He turned when she came in, his smile fading as soon as he saw her.

"What's wrong?"

"Everything."

She looked out the window, back at him.

"I'm pregnant. I was pretty sure a week ago, but I didn't want you to worry." Her eyes were dull, confused. "I don't think it's all right," she added. "Do you?"

Trying to gauge her feelings, he hesitated before answering. "I need to think," was all he could say.

After a dinner neither felt like eating they stayed at the table, purposely leaving a space between them for their thoughts. Carlos kept picking up and putting down his wineglass, his mind circling the same questions Cecilia had asked herself.

"We don't have to decide right away."

"Soon," she said, looking at him sharply.

"I realize that. All I'm saying is that there's plenty of time."

"I was thinking about Teresa on the way home, what

would happen to her if we went through with it. There would be pleasure in a baby, but at her expense, our memory of her. Does that make sense?"

Carlos looked at her quizzically, not sure that he was tracking her thought.

"That a baby would diminish her?"

"I'm afraid it would dim my memories. When I look at the pictures of us now it's already like she's been cut out, air-brushed into oblivion. It would be worse with another baby, wouldn't it? I mean that's all we have left."

Carlos glanced at the photograph of the three of them on the end table. He heard the glass breaking again, Teresa crying for help. He saw the men coming at him, looming out of the darkness. He tried to get back to the present, but it was too late. The words he had spoken the night he told her story in the garden of the old house on Calle Córdoba were already returning. He saw her walking into the whiteness, disappearing.

The next day, with Carlos by her side, Cecilia phoned a doctor she knew about and set a date. The night before their appointment in his office in Palermo she tried cooking, but could not concentrate. The list of ingredients danced in front of her eyes. Carlos stared for half an hour at a page of his manuscript, unable to think of anything for his characters to do. Finally he picked up his guitar and began playing a few short exercises to warm up, then a Villa-Lobos prelude, losing himself in the melody. It had been Teresa's favorite, and as he imagined her standing in the living room an idea crept in from the corners of his mind, taking shape as his fingers spread in memorized patterns along the guitar's gleaming neck. He played one more chord, felt the overtones, the dying notes vibrating through his body. Grief had obscured the truth. Teresa's memory could never be diminished by another child. He looked up to find Cecilia standing in the doorway between the kitchen and living room, her eyes focused on the guitar, then rising slowly to meet his.

"We can't," he said. "I realized when I was playing."

She nodded, came to him. "So did I."

A month later Cecilia was in her publisher's office, insisting on control over the cover design. Federico Tortoni was reciting all the reasons for denying authors that privilege.

"It has to be eye-catching," he said dryly. "This isn't a nonprofit organization. We exist to sell books."

"It also has to tell the truth."

She took a drawing out of her purse and slid it across the desk.

"This is what I want."

Federico looked at it, frowning at the overlapping half-circles. *The Wall* was inscribed a third of the way down the page, and her name was at the bottom.

"I want it pale yellow. The color I had to look at."

"Nobody will notice it. And your name should be at the top. We want to capitalize on your fame."

"It's the story that's important, Federico, not me."

He stared at the drawing with evident distaste.

"Couldn't we have a window, maybe with bars?"

"There was no window."

"Covers don't have to be literal."

"This one does. Otherwise, I'll find another publisher."

"You mean it?"

"I do."

Federico examined the drawing again. "Can we at least enhance the lines, bring out the swirls?"

"So long as you don't alter the pattern."

"I've never let anyone do this."

Cecilia stared at him.

"All right," he said with a sigh. "I'll send it to the art department."

"You'll let me see it before it's printed?"

"I'll call. Is there anything else?"

"I want it to come out on a Thursday."

"Why?"

"Because that's when the mothers march in the Plaza de Mayo."

The publication party was in Federico's apartment on the tenth floor of a building on Calle Florida. The tables in the entry were piled high with copies of the book whose cover was only a little brighter than Cecilia had wanted, though not enough to complain about. When she arrived with Carlos and Martín she was immediately surrounded by people from the publishing business, as well as journalists she had worked with over the years.

"Give her a chance to catch her breath," Federico said.

He guided them to the bar and kept his guests away until the three of them had drinks.

"I didn't expect so many," Cecilia said.

"This is an event," Federico told her. "People are curious."

Manuel Butler, a reporter for one of the daily papers, stuffed a sausage in his mouth and squeezed between Cecilia and Federico.

"Are you done being protective?" he said to Federico.

"Ask her."

"Whatever you want to know," she said.

"Within reason," Martín said.

"Reason and journalism is an oxymoron," Manuel said. He took another sausage from the tray a young woman carried through the room. "I read the galleys the day they arrived. It's wonderful. I don't mind telling you it made me cry. But there's something I'm curious about. You said in the Preface that you wrote the whole thing in your head, assigned each paragraph to a swirl of plaster on the wall."

"Yes."

"I write everyday. If I don't get down what I'm thinking about, I forget it in five minutes. I know about mnemonic devices, but this is a whole book. How did you do it?"

"The eternal skeptic," Martín said. "You think she's exaggerating?"

Cecilia smiled at Martín.

"He's only doing his job."

"And I'm only feeling avuncular."

"Have you ever had to remember something?" Cecilia asked Manuel.

"All the time."

"I don't mean for your stories. What I'm talking about is something you need to survive. It isn't easy to explain."

"I'm patient."

"I had to remember. Not the way we do most things, like where we were at a particular time of day, who said what to whom. I knew I could do that. But I was afraid of forgetting the tiny details. I had to record everything the way it happened, every sensation. It was my story, our story, but it didn't start with us and it didn't end with us. I'm trying to say that it was too important to forget, to re-create later, like you do from notes. It had to be entire, the way it was. You find resources for such things."

Claudia Ortiz, the book reviewer, looked at her skeptically.

"It was an amazing feat then, like someone who claims to have memorized an encyclopedia. You're saying you made up nothing? That it's like a photograph?"

"As I said to Manuel, necessity does strange things."

Claudia sipped her champagne.

"That's why you killed the guard? To tell the story?"

"Wait a minute," Martín said.

"I was just following the idea."

Carlos had been listening quietly, but he put his drink down and turned to Claudia.

"She has a right to ask," Cecilia told him.

He thought she was holding up under the questions better than he could have done. With a glance at Martín, he nodded toward the balcony and took his old friend by the arm. Outside he said, "I told her somebody would ask about it. You know what she said?"

Martín shook his head.

"That she was obligated to talk about everything."

"Including Teresa?"

"Including Teresa."

"Federico's planning a big promotion. How do you think people are going to react?"

"Only a few people heard my stories. The newspapers are telling what happened now, but there's a difference with a book. You keep books, pass them from hand to hand. It will help everyone remember."

Carlos walked to the edge of the balcony. For a long time he had not wanted to see the city whole. Now he looked at the lights, a scatter of diamonds, his mind working back and forth across the array. "What do you see?"

"Lights. Darkness. Is this a quiz?"

"I see stories. At least places where they should be, ones I haven't told, couldn't. Ones I began and lost."

"There are plenty you saw to the end."

"They aren't important anymore, Martín. There's all that light, space I couldn't fill."

"You did what you could. Amazing things."

"Not enough."

Martín put his arm around him. It was all he could think to do. They stood there awhile before Carlos went on.

"I'd like to think that one is Teresa's. That the lamp in a window, a streetlight, the sign over a bar's door is the light I saw her walking into. Sometimes it all comes flooding back, waves of images breaking through time, erasing the line between past and present. Sometimes I feel her presence, as if she weren't far away. I concentrate, try to find the path that led me to the other stories, half afraid I'll see something terrible. One night I dreamed there was a knock on the door of our house on Calle Córdoba. I knew it was Teresa trying to get back inside. I ran downstairs, ran all the way across the city. No one was there. I peered inside. It was empty. Then I went around to the garden and nothing was there. Flagstones, trees, plants, even the iron chairs and tables were gone. It was just a barren plot of ground, dusty in moonlight. I knew she'd been there, that she thought she'd come to the wrong place and walked off into the darkness. I stood there shouting her name, saw its letters flying away in a cloud of dust."

The next afternoon Carlos and Cecilia stood on the margin of the Plaza de Mayo, watching people gather near the center of the square beneath a lambent sun. The pastel facade of the Casa Rosada mocked the power that once resided there. Only the guards remained in their cerulean blue uniforms, gold-fringed epaulets, visored hats, President Alfonsín having been too leery of the army to order a toning down of its splendor. As the women began to march, Cecilia withdrew a white scarf from her purse and carefully tied it over her hair. Then she and Carlos crossed the street and joined the procession, falling into line behind Dolores Masson who carried a sign with photographs of her grand-

sons pasted above the inscription: WHERE ARE ROGER AND
JOAQUÍN?

Except for the noise of passing traffic, the only sound announcing the advent of *The Wall* was of footsteps. The
scrape of their shoe leather against pavement, the click of
heels were perfectly audible here, where our bones nour-
ished the soil which brought forth grass green as emeralds.
By that time *The Wall* was already in dozens of bookstores,
stacked on counters, on floors beside cash registers, in long
rows atop display cases, its yellow cover attracting attention
even though many people were supersaturated with memories of our dirty little war. It should come as no surprise that
there were those who put it down after thumbing the pages
and spent their money on something else, believing that too
much outrage and shame had already accumulated in their
minds. As far as they were concerned, there had been too
many words issued in decrees, orders, typed on lists and
whispered in darkened rooms. What they wanted was time
to heal, forget, space to go on with their lives.

Now that the war was over, none of us blamed them
for wanting a little peace and quiet. We bore them no ill-will
because their desire was perfectly natural. Fortunately, for
every person longing for forgetfulness another was avid for
words, in need of explanations like a thirsty man craves
water, a hungry one food. Rather than putting their hands
over their eyes to shield them from things they had no desire
to see, these people descended on the stores and stood in
long lines waiting to pay for their copies of *The Wall*.

Over the next few days Cecilia's publisher realized that
he had made a serious miscalculation. Much as he admired
her work, Federico Tortoni had ordered a small first printing, uncertain whether in a time of emotional exhaustion

people would willingly read of terrors lightened only by Cecilia's claim that Carlos had kept her alive by an unfathomable act of imagination. Federico survived in a difficult business because he possessed a talent for gauging the public mood, which he translated into numbers of books in a complex arithmetic that kept the house afloat and put food on his table. Pleased as he was by the glowing early reviews, he had resisted publishing a larger run, despite his assistant Fabienne Deluze's prediction that *The Wall* would sell out quickly and they would suffer an unnecessary loss while going back to press.

And she was right. By the end of the first week Federico had to order a second printing. Even as those books were being boxed for shipment, more orders were pouring in. "I told you so," said Fabienne, cupping her hand over the phone. Nodding in agreement while he waited to speak to the printer, Federico decided to give her a raise and seriously considered buying himself a new car to replace his aging Fiat.

Federico had no idea that Cecilia's words were loosening the tongues of readers who not long ago had hidden behind closed doors. People who had spent the war like wary cats poked their noses into the open air, crying out with late-blooming rage and indignation. Country folks as well as *porteños* in fine linen suits acknowledged that in her frenzy to purge herself of the likes of us, Argentina had eaten her own kind like an enraged sow consumes her young. Cecilia's book released them from fear, untied the knots whose invisible strictures had bound their lips.

The Wall scattered the fear of an old woman who had seen her neighbors leave their house with two babies in the middle of the night, strengthening her backbone so that she could visit a nearby police station and give them a name, a date and the number of a license plate. It encouraged a baker to come forth, a man whose sugar-coated hands had trembled for years whenever he thought of what happened on the street one day as a young man left his shop with a bag full of pastries. A prostitute who worked the alleyways near the docks, snaring sailors with her lilting voice, and reading voraciously whenever she was alone, called to the police who always harassed her and offered information about a clandestine cemetery. That same week a chef at a fashionable restaurant revealed what he heard one night in the parking lot when six officers had talked too much. Cries from a warehouse returned to the watchman of a nearby building who had been so terrified he had willed himself into forgetfulness. A professor bent over Aquinas raised her eyes and stared at the table lamp, suddenly aware that she could remain silent no longer about a certain colleague.

Cecilia's story spread across city and countryside, entered apartments, villas, farmhouses. Rumors of what she described disturbed the sleep of Guillermo Calvino who dreamed that he was young again and driving a train through a vast wasteland where a young girl without a face stood by the tracks, waving him down. He stopped the train, and while it hissed and groaned the girl climbed aboard and began singing in a high-pitched voice as he set off again, the engine chanting a deep bass accompaniment. Orestes Escardó painted a general ripping up the bronze plaque marking Kilómetro Cero, which he used to shield himself from knives and bullets. At Esperanza, Amos Sternberg read it aloud to Sasha, reminding this tongueless woman that Cecilia was the wife of the man who had appeared at their *estancia,* heralded by flights of birds.

Doctors and lawyers read it, along with housewives who put aside their ironing, students who ignored their homework, soldiers, policemen and informers in whom it created a little thrill of fear. A copy reached the monastery where Alberto Marqovitch had gone in the hope of saving his soul, begging for work as a custodian, and daily humbling himself even more egregiously than the monks. The book made its way into his hands one sultry afternoon when he abandoned his mop and started reading in the shade of an ombu tree, Cecilia's words plunging him into deep despair as he remembered the motionless form of the girl he had tried to save.

Bookstores in Buenos Aires were not the only ones that found it impossible to keep her work in stock. Shops in regional capitals, seaside resorts, little hamlets on the windswept plains of Patagonia, where reading had always been a special grace for people who would otherwise find themselves staring at the horizon all day long, sold out as soon as the cartons were opened. Harried owners made calls to Tortoni's and wholesale distributors frantically trying to keep up with the demand.

Because we had a stake in its success, we urged the drivers of delivery trucks to bypass favorite roadside hangouts and press on, encouraging them to drink and eat on the move because we knew how time worked, that it was like a wound in the flesh inexorably knitting itself together, forming scar tissue over the trauma until the flesh forgets its violation. And since the place where we were was lost in the mind of the girl who had walked away, we took our hope where we could find it, believing that Cecilia's story might touch the memory of someone who could guide our families to where we were.

A van carrying half a dozen copies blew a head gasket on a remote stretch of road, forcing the driver to lay over at a truck stop until a replacement arrived from the city. He drove faster than usual to make up time, and late the next day reached the dusty farming town of Santa Rosalita, where the books were quickly unboxed and placed in the window of a shop two blocks away from the general store where Eduardo Ponce was employed.

When he had run away months ago, Eduardo had been sufficiently frightened to drive until long after dark. He had no particular destination in mind, only the names of half a dozen little towns culled from the map tearing at the folds he kept in the glove box. His sole requisite in choosing them had been that they had to be small and a considerable distance from any of the large regional cities. He knew from his experiences of the last few years that he would recognize a suitable place when he found it. He drove straight through the next two towns east of the one where he could have called the Souzas, refusing to stop even when his back began to ache and his eyes burned from the heat, enduring the hypnotic glare in the hope that he would recognize something in the next place they reached that meant he had found his new home.

Neither Eduardo nor Beatriz spoke more than a dozen words all day. His attention was concentrated on the prospects of safety each town presented, the chance for anonymity. Though Beatriz shared his fear of being discovered, having become used to looking over her shoulder years ago, she did not invest every object with symbolic meaning as Eduardo was prone to do. Miserable but resigned, she contented herself by watching his face as they drove through a town, knowing from the way he frowned that he was rejecting it for reasons she had no interest in hearing about. Otherwise, he drove stone-faced, except for once late in the afternoon when he saw a distant figure on the road and was so shaken that his knuckles turned white from gripping the steering wheel so tightly until the figure resolved itself into a man on horseback. Beatriz knew what had happened. She reminded him that the girl was many miles behind them. He glared as if to say that maybe things were not always the way they seemed, then glanced at the boys in the rearview mirror, promising to stop soon so they could have something cold to drink.

Cramped in the tiny backseat, Tomás and Manfredo quarreled whenever their space was invaded by a foot or hand. Except for that, they were quiet. Adept in sudden upheavals, they knew something very serious was going on and hid their confusion in silence as they tried to believe that everything would soon be fine. But something was always wrong with the towns they reached after dark, either the way streetlights reflected off the fronts of buildings, or the width of a square, or the way a sign blinked on and off.

It was close to midnight when Eduardo pulled up in front of a small inn, using one of several aliases to register. He gave the bed to Beatriz and the boys, sleeping on the sour-smelling rug where he was plagued by nightmares. He rose at dawn and allowed them a hasty breakfast before they got back on the road, and drove until late afternoon when they reached Santa Rosalita. Though nothing in particular recommended it, he knew immediately that this was the place. He nodded to Beatriz, then told the boys that they would have fine adventures.

By the following afternoon they had rented a small house on the outskirts of town. Beatriz cried over the dilapidated kitchen and thought of the infinitely better one she had left behind. When the boys complained that their room was too small, Eduardo spent an hour showing them how to fix it up. As far as he was concerned, the house was perfect. He could see the pampas from every window. Cars coming along the road were visible a kilometer away. All in all, things were as good as they could be under the circumstances, and they improved on the following Friday when he found a job clerking in a hardware store that supplied farmers and ranchers. Before going home to tell Beatriz the good news, he telephoned his benefactor, the general who had given them the boys, saying that he had been forced to move again, but assuring him that everything was fine. He had a job and would not have to ask for a loan to supplement expenses as he had done in the past.

General Guzmán was in his study, his feet propped up on a mahogany desk. He was still shaken from his time in prison. He felt the humiliation that lay like a scar across his heart every time he breathed. Before the government had granted amnesty he had been prepared to cooperate, something he had vowed never to do during the trial. Like the others, he had been questioned about what he knew of stolen children. Like them, he denied knowledge of such things. But in the confines of his cell Guzmán had soon begun putting together a list of things he would offer the authorities, and Eduardo Ponce's name was on it. He was glad it had not come to that because Eduardo had been a loyal and faithful servant, deserving of the boys.

While Eduardo talked the general watched the songbirds he kept in lacquer cages, making little gestures with his mouth to encourage them to sing. He was appalled when Eduardo explained why he had run away again, but since he felt sorry for him, and saw Eduardo's freedom as a little victory over those who had brought him down, Guzmán answered that it had been prudent and encouraged him to hold on. The old women who were still making a fuss over their missing grandchildren would soon give up, he said. It was only a matter of time. Once they did, Eduardo could resume a normal life.

After hanging up, Eduardo surveyed the quiet street, filled with pleasure by the general's words. On the way home he allowed himself the luxury of thinking about returning to the city, reentering its bustling life, which he had come to love even more in exile. In the meantime, he would make the best of Santa Rosalita, accommodate himself to its shapes and sounds and vistas. He craved the ordinary as an antidote to flight, was greedy for commonness. The banalities of life were treasures which bought a tentative peace of mind.

Beatriz sang as she scoured the filthy kitchen, was filled with pleasure when she lined the cabinets with butcher paper. Her greatest triumph was managing to make the oven work. Eduardo bought several gallons of paint at a discount from his employer and reveled in transforming the dirty white walls of the boys' room and the kitchen to soft cool blue. He felt as if he were repairing his own life as he nailed down four sprung boards on the porch and shored up a sagging supporting beam. When he finished the work he bought two wooden chairs from a secondhand furniture dealer so that he and Beatriz could sit outside in the evening and enjoy the long dying of the light.

At first the renovations were enough to distract the boys, but after things were settled they complained that there was nothing for them to do. Eduardo told them they had to learn to love the pampas, savor the freedom of the fields which were more vast than the ones where they used to live. He took them on long walks where they discovered herds of sheep and cattle, saw gauchos on horseback, strange and lovely birds. Gradually, the pampas began to exert its hold on their imaginations.

On weekends Eduardo drove them into Santa Rosalita for soccer games played on a dirt field on the far side of town. He bought an old ball from the coach of the local

team which Tomás and Manfredo practiced with every afternoon. Eduardo resumed his habit of playing with them
before dinner, showing them tricks he learned when he had
been a striker on his college team.

His job was dull but undemanding. As soon as he arrived in the morning, Eduardo put on a blue denim apron,
tied the strings in front, and went into the storage room.
The first task of the day was unpacking new merchandise
and stocking the shelves. After that, he laid out new tools
smelling of fresh oil, filled plastic containers with nuts and
bolts, stacked rolls of bailing wire on the sidewalk where it
was easier for the ranchers to load onto trucks, finishing all
of his tasks before the first customers arrived. It was easier
work than his job at the Souzas' granary where his back
began to ache early in the day from carrying hundred-
pound loads, and developed into bone-deep pain well before
the end of his shift. He congratulated himself on no longer
being exhausted, and that his boss, a taciturn man in his
sixties, largely left him alone. Of course there was no semblance of the power he had once enjoyed as a government
functionary, no rubbing elbows with influential men or con-
tributing modestly to their decisions, but Eduardo was satisfied with his work and certain that Santa Rosalita was a
perfect place to wait out the hysteria of those so eager to
undo the past.

Maybe it will surprise you that the Ponces never questioned what they'd done, never considered what it meant to
have transferred the boys from one car to another in the
middle of the night and driven away without a thought
about their mother, who they knew was dead, or their father, who they knew was hiding. But they hadn't at the
time, and they didn't later, either. Eduardo and Beatriz
managed to draw a curtain between themselves and the

family, shut out any feeling whatsoever. It sounds far-fetched only if you ignore how they and everyone else who was cozy with the regime thought about those of us who were disappearing. We were enemies of the state, you understand, guilty of the worst treason. Remember how the Nazis demonized the Jews? The propaganda films showing rats running for cover? It was easy for the Ponces, the generals, the soldiers and police to think of us as vermin. Consequently, taking children was of no more significance than adopting a stray cat's kittens. At the same time, it was another way to prosecute the war. Those who handed over the children to those who took them discovered that kidnapping was a bloodless way to increase the dissidents' pain, a way to twist the knife without making a mess.

In all the time since they'd spirited the boys away neither Eduardo nor Beatriz felt anything other than elation and growing love for Roger and Joaquín Masson. Guilt was something the boys' grandmother had to imagine coming alive in a word or gesture or the sight of something strange. That's why every time we saw the Ponces our outrage was renewed, intensified. We wanted revenge for the way they'd taken the boys, changed their names, obtained forged birth certificates. We devised terrible reversals of fortune, imagined their discovery, arrest, imprisonment. But it never got farther than a dream. The vengeance we wanted, imperfect as it was, came about in a totally unexpected way, developing as slowly as one season fades into another.

This is how it started. It was Eduardo's habit to have lunch at a café that was always packed at midday because it served generous slabs of meat and good cheap wine. On his way there one Wednesday, thinking about whether he should order beef or pork, he glanced at the window of the general store. Ever since his boss entrusted him with the hardware displays, Eduardo had been interested in how other merchants presented their wares. The general store's windows were always a mess. Sundries, patent medicines, girdles, ready-made clothes were stuck in with no effort to balance the items or make them attractive. Scanning the window always gave him a sense of superiority. But that day the feeling was stripped away the moment he saw the books. Five copies of *The Wall,* their pages splayed out like accordion bellows, rested between two pyramids of bottles. The red subtitle, *The Story of a Disappeared,* glowed against the lemon-yellow jacket. Eduardo watched the clerk handing a copy to a rancher he had a passing acquaintance with, a man who had seemed levelheaded whenever he came into the hardware store. Now Eduardo knew the truth and hurried across the street so he would not have to speak to him.

Tasty as the pork was, he did not enjoy it as much as he would have had he not seen the books. The content was predictable, no different than what was appearing more and more frequently in the papers he read contemptuously, one-sided distortions of the *Proceso* by someone who would not understand the truth if it hit her in the face. The more he thought about the lies, the angrier he became. He left half his lunch on the plate and ordered a second glass of wine, then a third, declining the invitation of some men at the corner table to join them at dominoes. He wanted to indulge himself in pleasant outrage about the slanders that were undoubtedly strewn across the pages of the book like so many piles of cow shit.

Eduardo was a little drunk by the time he returned to work. On the way, he glared at the clerk of the general store who was standing in the doorway, ignoring her comment that the day had turned out to be nice after all. He went into the storage room and tried to concentrate on inventorying the paint when the owner came back and asked him to fill an order for nails. Feeling fuzzy from the wine, and preoccupied with the ideas that had ruined his lunch, Eduardo followed him out and picked up the scoop lying in one of the bins. As he filled a large sack the sound of cascading nails increased his anger. He thought about what the leftists had cost him, remembering the office where he once worked, his elegant wood desk, enumerating the enormous sacrifices he and Beatriz had to make. The injustice of it all took hold of him as he poured one more scoopful into the sack and took it over to the counter where he dropped it angrily on the scales.

"I said galvanized," the customer told him. "Not steel."

His boss gave him a disapproving look. "Pay attention," he said.

Eduardo wanted to tell them to stick the nails up their asses. Instead, he grabbed the sack and went back to the bins, dumped the steel nails and began scooping up galvanized ones. Being insulted by a common shopkeeper was an affront to his dignity. He dug savagely into the bin, took the sack back to the counter and left it for the owner to weigh, returning to the storage room with a faint sense of victory that was not enough to salvage his pride. The day was ruined. He looked around at the boxes waiting to be unpacked and slashed one open with a linoleum knife, wondering how he could stand doing this for four more hours.

By quitting time he had a raging headache. The condition of his life loomed up as he drove home, surrounding him with a choking embrace. For the first time since settling into Santa Rosalita the old feeling returned, the sense that an invisible net hung over him simply because he and Beatriz had desired children they could not have themselves.

He reached the house in a terrible mood and barely

spoke during dinner. The boys fixed their eyes on their plates. Beatriz had learned long ago that the only thing to do when he was in one of his moods was to ignore him and wait for it to pass.

Eduardo drank steadily throughout the meal, a slow soaking of cheap wine. Afterward he went into the kitchen and uncorked another bottle, reminding himself bitterly that plonk was all he could afford these days. He tipped the bottle up; the wine had a sour vinegary taste, worse than what he'd had with dinner. He passed through the living room without looking at anyone and slammed the door behind him.

Tomás glanced at Manfredo, then Beatriz.

"I know," she said. "But he'll be fine. He's been working very hard lately."

As Eduardo watched the sun pool on the fields, then slip below the horizon, he sipped the wine, muttering as he always did when he was drunk, inventing universal truths with himself as the beleaguered victim of the idiots who had been too timid to run the war as they should have done. He always enjoyed the maudlin thoughts that came to him when he was alone and could indulge himself, floating through the evening on a pleasant tide of self-pity.

As the pampas disappeared into the darkness, Eduardo's anger over the ideas that had sprung to life when he saw Cecilia's book slowly faded, leaving him with the delicate aftermath of anger. He finished the wine, thought about going inside for another bottle, but it was too comfortable sitting there. He slumped in the chair, resting his head against the cushion, content to feel the wind and watch the stars, give himself up to fragments of thoughts, memories linked like charms on a bracelet.

The stars were moving around. He blinked, tried to

make them stand still. Instead they kept coming down, and in their rush the girl appeared, staring at him, her face growing larger as it hung in the star-studded sky where her eyes glowed like two blue moons. She was saying his name, her voice sharp, staccato, as if her lips were pressed to the mouthpiece of a loudspeaker. She said it again and again, every second or third repetition of the word in her high-pitched voice intensified by the piercing squawk of electronic overtones. His name seemed to echo in the sky, announcing to the universe who he was.

Eduardo fumbled for the bottle, remembered it was empty. Rising unsteadily from the chair, he gripped the bottle by its neck and threw it toward the blossoming acacia tree, stumbling as he did so into the yard where the flowers fell in a shower illuminated by the weak light coming from the house. Brushing himself off, he got up and went inside. Beatriz was reading in the bedroom. He was pale, his eyes liquid and glassy.

"What's the matter?" she asked.

Eduardo said nothing as he lurched across the room and fell onto the bed, rubbing his hands over his face to get rid of the image of the girl. Then he passed out, sleeping dreamlessly through the night while the tiny yellow blossoms continued to fall, patterning the grass which the next morning was bright as gold.

The Double
World

Gabriela Santini stood in front of the class with her hands on her hips, eyes sweeping over the room like a lighthouse beam. Her students knew what she was doing. They waited until her brightness came their way, then stared at their books or doodled in the margins.

The problem was that Gabriela hated to lecture. That was what all her professors had done. She still remembered some spectacular talks when the final points were made just as the hour was up, falling into place like the tumblers in a lock. But most of the lectures had been excruciating and she might as well have been listening to a tape recording at home, curled up in bed. In her own classes she insisted on asking questions that forced her students to dig into the texts and think, rather than mindlessly accepting whatever she said. It never bothered her to stand in front of a silent room as she was now, letting the minutes tick away while the tension built until someone couldn't stand it any longer and blurted out a response. Then she leaped on the observation, divided it into more questions so they realized what she wanted them to see and their truculence blossomed into dialogue.

Today no one was taking the bait. She looked around the room one more time before deciding that she had to fall back to her second line of defense, playing devil's advocate. She went over to the south wall, leaned against it, glared contemptuously.

"So it's a mistake to read Sophocles. Why waste time on a Greek who's been dead two thousand years? I agree. For the life of me I can't understand why he remains in the curriculum. Everything we need to know can be found in contemporary authors, right?"

Stone silence. Everyone looked at her now that it was safe. A few were angry that she had insulted them, but they remembered she had used the same ploy earlier in the term and refused to defend themselves.

"All right," she sighed. "You want a lecture, I'll lecture. For half an hour. Then we start all over again."

She unraveled the plot of *Oedipus*, explaining how its

themes foreshadowed the mystic resolution at Colonus, then spent ten minutes summarizing critical positions.

As far as Gabriela was concerned, the day was a total loss. They were soaking up facts like sponges, refusing to engage the text. She glanced at her watch, saw she had five minutes. Stepping away from the lectern, she walked around the desk and stopped in front of Olivia Arnoldi, one of her brightest students.

"Help me," she said. "What's wrong? Why is this so difficult?"

"I don't know," Olivia said. "Maybe because he just seems like a victim. He's a hero. He saved the city. He didn't know Jocasta was his mother, or the old man was his dad. It seems like overkill to me."

"That's right," said Umberto Crasci. "He made an honest mistake, two honest mistakes."

The girls on either side of Umberto nodded and glanced at Gabriela, interested in how she was going to get out of this. A moment later the bells chimed, but Gabriela was not ready to let them go.

"That's how you all feel?"

Everyone nodded. They were ready to leave. Outside, the quad was filling up with students and faculty members. It was too late to counter Olivia and Umberto.

"I understand. You're myopic. You can't see the forest for the trees. I want you to think about something for next time."

She went to the blackboard and drew two lines, labeling the bottom one, "action of the play," the top, "influence of the gods." Then she drew a line between them and wrote "synchronicity" in capital letters.

"This is where the two forces come together. I want you to think about the relationship. The play is both temporal and spiritual, of the earth and the heavens. The action moves on two planes at once. Remember Jocasta's skepticism about oracles? See where it takes you. That's where we start next time, with a quiz."

They all looked perplexed, which was exactly what she wanted. She stuffed her notes into her bag and quickly headed out the door before anyone could ask for help.

In her office she exchanged her high heels for the walking shoes she always wore to and from the university, then gathered up some papers and a review of *The Wall* she wanted to reread on the way to Manzoni's, where she intended to buy a copy before going home. She could have gone to the bookstore adjacent to the campus, but decided to take a bus across town because the author was scheduled to be there, signing copies. Gabriela treasured signatures the way other people did china or postage stamps. A shelf in her apartment was reserved for autographed books. It was not a matter of celebrity. She had yet to meet a writer who looked any different from the people she saw every day on the streets, even the famous ones. It was just that there was something intimate in their names which personalized the book and made each sentence seem written exclusively for her. Sometimes the autographs even affected her critical judgment, leaving her disposed to overlook things which in an unsigned book she would have pounced on, underlining an offensive sentence and chiding the author in a marginal note.

She bought a newspaper at a kiosk near the bus stop and paged through it while she waited. She was pleased with herself for inventing the Oedipus diagram and thought about ways to exploit it in class as she skimmed the news, her attention only half-focused until she came to a story about the Disappeared. Forensic experts had developed a

method to identify remains by matching DNA extracted
from bones with that of relatives. She wondered if the Cristianis knew anything about it. Remembering Ana María depressed her, and it worsened when she saw two young men
flirting with Olivia across the street. The girls were, had
been, the same age. It was still hard to believe Ana María
was gone, even after all this time.

Gabriela was glad when the bus appeared down the
block. Just as she stood up, a derelict came by and began
rummaging through the trash bin next to the bench, withdrawing a discolored sack he quickly eyed before stuffing it
in the pocket of his filthy coat. She got on as soon as the bus
stopped, grateful for the hissing hydraulic doors that closed
between her and the man. She hated his red-rimmed eyes
and glanced away, inadvertently looking up at Hirsch's office window before forcing her eyes toward the buildings
running off in the distance, baroque soot-stained edifices
fronting each other like sphinxes.

Our hearts went out to Gabriela because we knew
what no one else did on the bus; that that accidental glance
had opened the door to a painful memory. While the others
watched indifferently as the traffic passed down the canyon
of buildings into the heart of the city, Gabriela saw the pain
of the dead war staining the air like exhaust. It had been a
terrible mistake to look at Hirsch's window. Stupid. Idiotic.
Because now remorse was coming back, seeping into the
cavern of her heart, rising like water that will not be contained. We could only watch and sympathize as she fought
to keep it down until she reached her stop and quickly
backtracked half a block to the store.

Manzoni's had been in business for sixty years. The
building housing it was even older, dating from the turn of
the century when it had opened as a haberdashery for the

young blades who displayed themselves on the boulevards. Gabriela frequented half a dozen bookstores in different parts of the city, but Manzoni's was her favorite port of call, the place she felt at home. Most of the others were new, sporting plastic shelves and counters that gave off a slightly medicinal odor, astringent and vaguely offensive. Here you smelled the mustiness of the old books that occupied half the shelf space—something akin to mushrooms or truffles—whose earthiness countered the crispness of the new volumes and seemed to promise that they too, if they were good enough, would be around to smell like that some day.

She also went there because of the owners, Oswaldo and Marta, a couple in their seventies who were in the business because they loved books. Whenever she came in, one or the other gave her a look, welcoming her as part of the fraternity who would rather read than do anything else. They always seemed a little fly-specked, like the windows and counters. Oswaldo's face inevitably sprouted a few days' beard. It had occurred to Gabriela more than once that she was probably destined to end up more or less like Marta in her shapeless dresses and cardigans that almost reached her knees. They employed two women close to their age, and rounded out the staff with a cat named Plato which usually stretched out on top of the counter next to the cash register, opening a slitted eye now and again to observe the world. When he was bored, Plato jumped down from the counter and padded over to the aquarium near the door where he sat gazing dreamily at the tropical fish floating in the aerated water like bits of colored glass. On the days authors appeared there was a coffee urn in the back along with a samovar of tea surrounded by cakes and pastries. As Gabriela entered she nodded at Oswaldo who was talking to some women in front of the wall covered with framed pho-

tographs of Borges, Bioy Casares, Cortázar, García Már-
quez. There were sepia-tone prints of a young Thomas
Mann and Hemingway with his foot on a dead antelope.
Next to him Gertrude Stein looked resolutely grim.

The new books were piled in no apparent order on a
long table in the entryway. She recognized half a dozen
titles from reviews. She was always book poor, spending
more than she thought, and finding herself eating frugally
for the last few days of the month. A quick calculation told
her that nothing had changed as she picked up four volumes
and asked the woman at the register to hang on to them.

Six tall shelves ran the length of the store, ending at an
alcove where a wooden staircase snaked up the wall to what
looked like a choir loft but served as the office. Customers
queued up halfway down the center aisle. Gabriela took her
place behind a young couple thumbing through a collection
of photographs. As the line inched forward she examined
the shelves. She was in the art and geography section, surrounded by oversized books devoted to Rembrandt, Degas,
Miró, their glossy covers imprinted with famous paintings.
She saw a book emblazoned with the interior of the Teatro
Colón, another with a picture of the pampas showing a
wheat field and a lone ombu tree. Shuffling into the classics,
which were divided into sections of books in their original
languages, as well as Spanish and Portuguese translations,
she removed a copy of *Oedipus* and let her eyes stray over
the flaring letters of the opening lines. She paged through to
Jocasta's dismissal of oracles and decided to read it to her
class, give them a sense of the rhythm of the Greek.

The couple in front of Gabriela shuffled forward and
she followed, skirting a frayed oriental carpet held down by
worn leather chairs where two old men were reading peri-
odicals, oblivious to the crowd. She was a little surprised
when she saw Cecilia sitting at a table piled high with copies

of *The Wall*. She had expected more signs of stress. Her hair
was pulled back, emphasizing the structure of her face. Except for her blue-green eyes framed by sadness she looked
fine, better than that, elegant in a simple black dress and
gold earrings. Gabriela guessed that she was in her late thirties, though the long-sleeved dress could add or subtract a
few years. As Gabriela waited for the line to move she
thought there was something vaguely familiar about Cecilia,
as if she had seen her before.

Cecilia smiled at a young man as the woman sitting
next to her smoothed down the title page before sliding a
copy of *The Wall* across the table for her signature.

"Your name?" she asked.

"Arturo."

"That's all?" she laughed.

He nodded nervously.

"Thank you for coming," she said when Gabriela
reached the head of the line. "What would you like me to
say?"

Gabriela shook her head. She had always thought it
was presumptuous to ask writers for a personalized inscription.

"Just your name is fine."

"You're sure?"

"Yes. You must be exhausted."

"Grateful. So many people."

"It's a tribute," Gabriela said.

"I think a recognition of what we've all been through."

Gabriela waited until Cecilia had signed her name and
handed the book to her. This was always a special moment,
as if something intimate passed between her and the author.
This time it was more intense. The unread words already
touched her life through the Cristianis.

"Do you mind if I ask a question?"

"Of course not."

"A couple in my building lost their daughter. I was wondering if I should give them the book."

Cecilia's smile faded. She hesitated a moment before saying, "That's up to you. What happened to me, to my daughter, was part of a pattern. They might find some comfort in that. Beyond that I don't know."

Mercedes needed something, Gabriela thought. She wore her work like armor during the day, but every night she came back to a building redolent with bitter memories and was vulnerable again, unable to lose herself in the troubles of children.

Gabriela opened the book as she waited in line to pay. Cecilia's name was written neatly just below the title. Leafing through, she found there were no chapters, only sections separated by an ornament that repeated the cover design. She paid for the books and walked back to the stop where she had time to read the Preface before the bus arrived. Cecilia's words had an elegiac grace that was deeply moving. As she took her seat she decided to pass it on to the Cristianis when she finished.

She stayed holed up in her apartment over the weekend. It was the way she liked to read, carving out large chunks of time so she could immerse herself in a text, enter its world, see it whole. For years she had been in the habit of reading with a pencil, underlining sentences, cross-hatching pages with arrows, asterisks, marginal comments, to impress the contents on her mind, but it had not occurred to her to reach for one when she curled up with *The Wall* on the sofa. She read as she used to before books became her profession, letting the words enter her mind without the critical stance she had assumed so long ago.

On Sunday morning she reluctantly put it aside in order to make notes for her class, elaborating her strategy for explaining the double action of *Oedipus*, but images from *The Wall* kept playing through her mind. She saw Cecilia preparing crudités for dinner, her abduction, her escape one night when she lost a shoe, which Carlos later found. She could not get the moment out of her mind when Cecilia had to make the awful bargain only to see Teresa disappear again. Nor could she forget the murder of the guard.

When she returned to the book the two stories ran together in her mind. Suddenly she realized that the power Cecilia attributed to her husband paralleled that of Sophocles' panoply of gods. Two thousand years apart and the texts were making similar assertions about a double world. She wondered if her students had read *The Wall*. She would tell them about it, then use it to illustrate her diagram. Maybe then they would see what she had wanted them to.

She read the last chapter while eating a dinner of pasta and canned marinara sauce. The discovery of the parallel had kept her from confronting another idea that had been building in the back of her mind, but the final sentence of *The Wall* brought it into focus: "No one remembered ever dies."

Usually she finished a book with a sense of triumph, aware of a victory over the images, themes, argument, but she closed *The Wall* with a sense of shame. She heard the elevator groan as it descended the oil-scented shaft and paused before it started back up. Glancing at the clock, she saw it was 1 A.M. Orestes was on the prowl. She thought of his friendship with the girl, wondering if he saw something the rest of them had missed. She forced herself to dwell on it less for the girl's sake than her own, needing relief from the feelings that had surfaced. But it did no good. Regardless of how she looked at it, she could not discount the truth. She had been complicit. It was true that inaction was a kind of action, omission no less tainted than commission. She went over to the window and gazed at the city's lights. At night, Buenos Aires always seemed decked out for a celebration. She heard laughter. A couple passed beneath a streetlight and back into darkness. Everything goes on, she thought, as if what had happened had never occurred, was lost as some ancient city beneath centuries of drifting sand.

In bed she spun the dial of the radio on the nightstand until she picked up Vivaldi. She pulled the quilt up to her chin, suddenly in need of warmth and wishing her lover, Franco, were spending the night, or that she had gone to his apartment. She wanted out of herself, wanted the refuge of touch, sensation, to ease the ache of memory. The years of the *Proceso* replayed themselves in her mind. She remembered the day Ana María had been taken, and then, because she could not avoid it any longer, the afternoon that Hirsch had disappeared.

She had been reading essays in her office, the door open, when someone from the history department ran down the hall. She heard him stop, then his footsteps on the linoleum floor as he dashed back and stuck his head in the door.

"They've taken Hirsch."

It was not the kind of thing you have a ready answer for. She heard him repeating the words down the hall, a senseless refrain that only belatedly took hold of her. She went out and saw Estela and Gómez standing in the hall, disbelief smeared across their faces. She hadn't said anything. She simply started toward the stairs, breaking into a run. As she reached the stairs, she heard Gómez cursing, saying he didn't believe it. At the second floor landing she pushed the door open and headed down the corridor. Half a dozen ashen-faced colleagues were gathered in front of his office. Estela and Gómez caught up, and the three of them went in. Gabriela stared at the coffee-stained manuscript spread across his desk, the smashed glasses on the floor. The images registered as pure phenomena, things beyond her frame of reference. Estela made a sound halfway between a groan and a cry as she pushed by them, stopping in front of the desk where she raised her hands to her ears and held them there as if she were trying to keep out sound. A moment later she rushed over to the bookcase, grabbed a box of tissues and dabbed at the manuscript. The pages were all soaked, stained with dark brown blotches.

"He's finished," Gómez said quietly.

Gabriela had been on the verge of asking what Hirsch could have done, but she knew perfectly well that she didn't have to. In those days, there were plenty of pretexts and assumptions that had nothing to do with reality. She had always believed she would be strong enough to speak out if the time ever came. She had thousands of fine sentiments in her head culled from years of reading, scenarios from plays and poems and novels with heroic figures fighting off the barbarians at the gates. But the bent metal frame of Hirsch's spectacles surrounded by tiny pieces of glass were stronger than any image in her mind. They screamed at her, announcing that the sanctum had been invaded, that not even the privileged world of the university was safe. She should have turned on her heel and gone downstairs to the quad, climbed onto a table and given an impassioned speech to students and faculty, demanding that they take a stand. Instead she retreated without saying anything to Estela or Gómez or the others, returning to her office where she sat for an hour staring out the window at the quad.

Later, in the classroom, she had placed her notes on the lectern and talked about Neruda, saying nothing about what had happened. As she looked at the class and heard her voice going on and on, the broken glasses rose up in her mind, slanted against a black background, for all the world like a playbill outside a theater. The bent frame seemed crushed by an enormous weight, the shattered lenses evil and threatening. The gleaming shards had kept her from testifying. They seemed pointed at her heart. Ana María had not yet been taken, and it was the first time the meaning of the war had come home to her. Until then, those who had disappeared had been ciphers. But no longer. They were all Hirsch; she could be Hirsch if she were foolish enough to protest.

She lectured on "The Heights of Macchu Picchu" for an hour without asking a single question, hiding behind the poet's words, hiding behind the lectern when she should have been outside, urging insurrection. She would never forget that day, regardless of how long she lived. It was like a scar across her conscience, as ineluctably there as the one on the girl's forehead. It had been her crossroads, she knew, the moment that had changed her life.

It would not have mattered if we had possessed the power to enter her mind, speak in soothing tones and say that we, the Disappeared, understood, had known the same fear and forgave her frailty. It would not have mattered because Gabriela could not forgive herself. Now that the war was over there was no way to heal the wound, no opportunity to climb the barricades. We could only watch her drift off to sleep hearing sentences from *The Wall* rise like wind, seeing Hirsch's glasses and the pale, uncomprehending eyes of the girl who could not speak.

Before the White

On the following Friday Mercedes enlisted Gabriela to stay with the girl while she and Roberto took in a play Orestes had been urging them to see. Written by an old friend of Carlos Rueda's, it damned the Church's complicity with the government and had sold out every night during its first

week. Its popularity was not surprising; anything that criti-
cized the still warm corpse of the regime drew audiences
thirsty for truth after the long drought of the generals.

The Cristianis and Orestes successfully avoided stepping on feet as they squeezed between the knees of people
in their row and the curved backs of wooden seats in front
of them. No sooner had they settled down than someone in
the back shouted "Bravo!" clear and distinct over the mur-
mur of the crowd. They turned at the same time, craning
their necks to see what the commotion was about. Applause
and more shouts came from the back where the doors
opened from the lobby. The sound quickly traveled the
length of the house, crescendoing as more people recognized
Cecilia standing with her hand on Carlos' arm. She wore a
long-sleeved burgundy dress with a strand of pearls that
stopped just where her belly began to swell. Clearly surprised, Cecilia looked around as people rose singly and then
in whole rows to give her a standing ovation. A few had
seen her in the garden of the house on Calle Córdoba, preparing the lanterns for Carlos. Those who had neither read
her book nor visited the garden asked who she was and then
they applauded, too.

Carmen Valenzuela, an old friend of the Ruedas who
was playing one of the Mothers of the Plaza de Mayo, appeared in a yellow silk dress that gleamed in the houselights.
She walked, smiling, to the center of the stage, clapping as
she went. Soon the rest of the company pushed through the
opening in the brocaded curtain and joined in the applause
as Luisa went to the edge of the stage.

"Bravo, Cecilia," she cried. *"¡Viva!"*

Her acclaim drove the audience into another frenzy.
Carlos stepped back a few paces, and with a simple gesture
offered Cecilia to the crowd. She kept her eyes on him a

moment, then nodded to Luisa and slowly turned her body in a half arc, raising her hand in an awkward salute.

Once the applause faded, Cecilia and Carlos went to their seats only to be forced to stand for another round that began with the people in their row and quickly spread.

Satisfied at last, the audience settled down. Luisa Valenzuela let her eyes linger a moment longer on Cecilia before leaving the stage, followed by the rest of the company. Minutes later the houselights dimmed, the pulleys creaked and the curtain rose on a set representing an office. The cardinal, resplendent in a purple soutane and skullcap, sat behind a desk reading a report and frowning as he turned a page. Looking up, he regarded the audience, then started taking notes. There was a knock on the door on the right side of the stage.

"Come," the cardinal said.

A priest entered and carefully closed the door, waiting deferentially until the cardinal finished.

"You see the problem?" the priest asked in a tentative voice.

"Of course, and I don't like it."

The priest sat down.

"I have some suggestions," he said. "Perhaps if we—"

"Sacrilege!" thundered a voice from the back of the theater.

Had the cardinal and the priest not suddenly looked toward the audience, dropping all pretense of acting, people would have thought the shout was part of the play. But it obviously wasn't. A tall man with a shaved head and a fierce expression stood in the aisle with his hands on his hips. Behind him were a dozen men wearing fatigue jackets with black armbands on the sleeves.

"Stop in the name of God!" he shouted.

Someone in the audience booed. A woman yelled, "Get out!" The manager appeared, objecting vigorously. The one with the shaved head pushed him away.

"Opus Dei," he declared. "The Falange of the Faithful!"

With a sudden, histrionic wave of his hand, as if he were commanding troops, the leader started forward, followed by the others who tooted little brass horns and swung noisemakers over their heads. They spread out like sentinels along the aisle while the leader strode to the stage.

"This is heresy!" he yelled at the actors. "Take off those clothes!"

The cardinal approached, looked down.

"What the hell are you doing?"

"Stopping these insults to God and country. Take off that soutane!"

"You want it," said the cardinal angrily. "Come and get it."

"You," Orestes said to the man standing at the end of their row. "Get out of here!"

The Falangist blew another note.

"Fucking Bolshie!" he said viciously. Then he looked around at the audience. "This is filth. Respect the priesthood!"

"Fanatic!" Orestes shouted.

"Idiots!" howled someone else.

The Falangists tooted their horns louder. They swung their noisemakers as if they were decapitating chickens. The one Orestes had singled out made an obscene gesture at him before going on and joining the leader and three others who had climbed onto the stage. Chanting, "Down with Communists!" they started knocking over the props. When the cardinal tried to intervene, the leader ripped open the front of his soutane and the priest ran for the wings.

After flipping over the desk, the leader went to the edge of the stage, motioning for the others to follow. When they were lined up beside him he looked down at Cecilia.

"I know who you are," he spat out. "It's a pity you returned." Raising his eyes to the audience, he shouted, "May the Disappeared stay disappeared forever!"

As his colleagues took up the chant, a man in the audience quickly edged out of his row and took a swing at one of the Falangists. The blow landed on the Falangist's shoulder, and before the man could set himself to throw another punch he was beaten to the floor. Pandemonium broke out. A woman screamed. The houselights came on and people started running up the aisles. Mercedes stood with her hands over her ears, trying to drown out the chant. She saw the Ruedas standing in front of the stage, arguing with the leader. Taking her arm, Roberto guided her down the vacant row and up the aisle where people massed in front of the exit, moving slowly into the lobby. As they stepped outside two police cars pulled up to the curb, sirens blaring.

"Are you all right?" Roberto asked.

"I need fresh air," Mercedes said weakly.

"What about a drink?" Orestes asked.

Mercedes nodded, hearing his words as if she were half-sedated. The chant was still in her head. She could not believe the way they had relished the words.

In the first café they came to Orestes ordered brandies. When the bartender delivered them, Orestes handed a glass to Mercedes.

"Drink. The whole thing."

He ordered another round, paid.

"That's how it got started," he said contemptuously when they sat down. "Soldiers and priests in bed together. Gladiators and capons."

Mercedes fumbled for a tissue.

"They believe it."

"What they believe doesn't matter."

"That's easy to say."

"It's true. There are pockets of them everywhere, will be for a long time. You know that. They can't let themselves believe it's over. The *Proceso* is all mixed up in their heads with God. True believers are always the last to give up."

Images of Ana María raced through her mind. She was doing her best to deal with the fragmented narrative of memory that obeyed no sequence, casting up moments in her daughter's life from childhood to maturity and back again.

For the next two hours they talked about the assault, but they still felt wretched by the time they left. On the way to the car, each syllable of the chant sounded in Mercedes' head, clear as the notes of a distorted bell. A derelict in a filthy jacket and pants appeared at the mouth of an alley, staring at them with bloodshot eyes. Mercedes noticed that he was holding something with both hands, eating. When he saw her looking he held the thing out, offered it to her. She turned away quickly. Arrays of lights dotted the night. She let her gaze roam across the little patches of yellow glowing in the windows of office buildings, apartments, rising in a random pattern to the darkened sky. She started counting, numbering the lights, saying the words to herself so as to drown out the others.

Carlos and Cecilia had gone directly home, the obscene chant etched into their minds as if by acid. We, too, still heard the voices shouting, threatening to drown out the softer sound of our cantata. Cecilia's eyes filled with tears. Carlos' glistened in the apartment's lights. Looking at them, we saw everything they'd suffered come to life again. If we'd had eyes of flesh and blood, we would have wept with rage, raised our voices in howls of protest. But we could only watch silently, mournfully, as Cecilia went to bed feeling ill and left Carlos in the living room.

Lying in the dark, Cecilia replayed the evening in her mind, saw what had promised to be a pleasant, satisfying night shed its skin and become the evil thing into which she and then her daughter had disappeared. She'd seen the hate before, had memorized its shapes and colors, memorialized it in her book. She remembered thinking of *The Wall* as a granite slab chiseled with her words. But the hatred wasn't dead. It remained alive in the Falangists' robust voices. She thought of the child growing within her. Instinctively, she put her hands on her swollen stomach, lay them there like bands of steel to ward off the words and the filthy meaning they conveyed.

Carlos drank a glass of wine, then another. He, too, could not get the words out of his mind. And so he did the only thing he could to stop the pain. He sought the solace of his guitar. He played a piece composed long ago in memory of his daughter, singing in a soft whispery voice words that had come to him on Calle Córdoba, the last ones of the story he had told about the pampas when his vision failed. We knew that between each word he heard the chant mocking his desire, applauding all he'd lost. And then we heard the timbre of his voice grow stronger. He sang the final words again and again the way a writer repeats half a sentence in his head, hoping to find a way to make the whole cohere. He lingered over the word "white," repeating the sound of the color that was no color, singing it hard and singing it soft, accompanying himself with brittle chords and single bell-like notes as he tried to coax an image from the bursting

light, urging himself onward, determined in spite of everything to make the whiteness speak.

When the Cristianis and Orestes came in, Gabriela and the
girl were sitting on the rug in front of the television, watching a documentary about the pampas. The coffee table was
littered with dishes containing the remains of omelets. The
girl sipped hot chocolate, licking a thin brown line off her
upper lip as Roberto tossed his jacket on a chair.

"How was it?" Gabriela asked.

"Horrible!" Orestes said. "Some religious fanatics
broke it up."

"They said terrible things," Mercedes added.

Roberto was still shaken, but out of deference to Mercedes he tried to appear calm. He looked at the screen as he
went over to the bar. Half a dozen gauchos in baggy pants
and high boots were standing around a campfire at dawn.
They always rose early, the narrator said, facing a day of
hard work with relish.

"Does everyone want brandy?" Roberto asked.

"Absolutely," said Orestes.

"A small one," Mercedes said.

"The same," Gabriela said as she got up and motioned
for Mercedes to follow her into the kitchen.

"Something strange happened a little while ago."

Roberto removed a platter of antipasto from the refrig-
erator. Orestes took a piece of rolled-up salami and popped
it in his mouth.

"How strange?" Orestes asked.

"Maybe surprising is a better word, or unexpected. Everything was fine during dinner. Afterward, she paged
through some magazines. You know how she likes to look at
the pictures. I felt like listening to some music and put on

Villa-Lobos. As soon as it started she leaned her head back, stared at the ceiling. Then she got up and wandered around, as if she were searching for something, tracking an idea. Her expression wasn't like any I've seen before. When I asked if anything was wrong she didn't even acknowledge me. Instead, she went over to the window and looked outside. Her behavior was so odd I tried to think of what had caused it and decided it had to be the music. I mean that was the only thing that was different. By the time I'd taken the record off she'd gone out to the balcony. I followed and told her it was too cold, but she wouldn't listen. She pulled away and just stood there looking at the lights. I got a shawl from Mercedes' closet. I don't think she even noticed when I put it around her shoulders. She stayed out fifteen or twenty minutes, and when she finally came in her expression had changed. She seemed confused. Then, and this is what I was thinking about when I said it was strange, she pulled up one side of her dress and ran her fingers along the hem. I turned on the TV and made some hot chocolate. That seemed to calm her down. You can see she's fascinated."

Roberto finished pouring brandy into four snifters and glanced at the girl.

"You're positive it was the music?"

"What else?"

"I wouldn't make too much of it," Orestes said as he took another piece of salami. "Music always reminds me of things."

Roberto stood with the decanter in his hand, marshaling his thoughts. So far as he knew, the girl's reaction to the music, and now the television, was the first time she had responded to stimuli. He thought of what he knew about amnesia, remembered the eerie glow of the X ray clipped to a light panel. He had looked at it a long time, unable to believe what it showed, unwilling to accept the evidence. The fact of the matter was that the girl should be dead, at least in a coma. Instead, she was sitting there, fascinated by the documentary. He hated not being able to account for his feelings. Whenever it happened, he had an out-of-body experience, as if his emotions belonged to someone else. It went against the grain of his being. He was still not willing to concede the mystery, telling himself that some explanation was available. He had put off talking to Raúl Espinoza. Now, as he put the decanter on the tray, he decided to speak to him. Maybe he could make something of it.

Mercedes took the antipasto into the living room. The girl did not look away from the screen where four gauchos were seated around a fire, roasting meat. The narrator explained how the cult of the gaucho persisted, from the habit of drinking maté tea through silver straws to the use of Creole colloquialisms among the educated. "Even their eating habits are influential," said the narrator as the images switched to a restaurant where *asadores* were grilling sides of beef. "All Argentines dream of the pampas."

"Cecilia Rueda and her husband were there," Roberto told Gabriela.

Mercedes looked at him, trying to keep her spirits up. The problem was that something had happened when she saw Cecilia's swollen belly, a sense of jealousy and loss all mixed up together. She felt herself withdrawing into the old depression.

"There was a standing ovation," Mercedes said. "It seemed as though everyone knew who she was. Seeing her made me remember whole passages she had written."

Gabriela had given her *The Wall* with the instincts of a professor which always overcame her diplomatic side. The pain evident in Mercedes' eyes made her wonder if she had done the right thing.

"Maybe I shouldn't have given it to you."

"No, I'm glad you did," Mercedes said reflectively. "It's just that seeing her was a shock, especially with all that happened afterward. I admire her. And I believe what she said about Carlos keeping her alive in his imagination."

"I don't," Roberto said, looking at the girl and remembering how Ana María used to sit in exactly the same way.

Orestes made a face.

"Why don't you let go once in a while? You might learn something. There are more things in heaven and earth. You know how it goes."

Irritated, Roberto said, "Sometimes you get on my nerves."

"You're not the only one who's told me that."

"I can imagine," Roberto said, smiling slightly.

"Part of my charm. It's my duty to be a thorn in somebody's side at least once a week."

A commercial came on and the girl leaned back against Mercedes' knees. Roberto was sorry he had snapped at Orestes, putting his rudeness down to the incident at the theater, which had upset him more than he thought. He felt raw inside, abraded. Now he needed to defend himself.

"Listen. You can't help being blunt, I can't help being skeptical. After Ana María disappeared, I felt so alone that I wondered if I'd ever be connected again. Then I read about someone who'd gone through the same thing and suddenly there was a recognition that I inhabited the same pattern of experience. I don't have to believe in the supernatural to be moved by what she said."

Roberto was a little surprised by his confession, but he felt better than he had in a long time. He had bottled up too much, he thought, let himself become isolated.

"She's a remarkable woman," he added.

"But scarred," Gabriela said. "I remember the way she

looked at Manzoni's. She was very gracious, but you could see the loss in her eyes."

"And in her book," Mercedes said. "On every page."

Two gauchos were herding a flock of sheep, followed by their dogs. The land was brown and flat. Argentina's pampas was immense, the narrator said, stretching hundreds of miles west and north of Buenos Aires. "The only indigenous tree in the region was the ombu, until Spanish landowners planted European varieties as windbreaks. Though it is still barren, it is beautiful to the gauchos. It was them Mallea had in mind when he wrote, 'it is a flat countryside under an unequal sky. Human destinies disturbed no more, with their conversations and surprises, only the earnest dialogue with the clouds, the fate of the invisible wheat which grows from the fallen and reborn grain.'"

The camera panned across a wheat field, then the scene shifted to a branding party. Two gauchos threw a calf to the ground; it bawled as smoke rose from seared hair and flesh.

"I keep thinking about what I'd have done if I'd been in her place," Mercedes said, "if I could have written about it. When she saw her daughter only to lose her . . ."

She shivered involuntarily and crossed her arms.

"Don't," Roberto said.

Mercedes swallowed hard, blinked back tears. She was coming undone inside, felt hollow as a gourd. She had embarrassed herself but there was nothing to do about it, nothing she wanted to do about it. Without a word, she got up, piled the dishes from the coffee table on the tray and took them into the kitchen where she ran water into the sink and tried to find some comfort in the familiar work of washing, the feel of the hot plates, the lemony scent of the soap. Too many things were going on at once, intersecting planes crossing and recrossing, bringing the past into the present.

She dropped a plate and started crying as she stared at the pieces scattered across the floor.

When the plate broke the girl jerked her head away from the television.

"You scared her," Gabriela said. "She practically jumped out of her skin."

Mercedes came out of the kitchen, drying her hands on a white towel and apologizing.

"I need to talk," she said.

The scene on the television shifted to a farm. All the buildings had red roofs. Hills rose in the background, their arroyos purple against sunburned grass. The girl scooted closer to the television.

Roberto reached for Mercedes' glass, asked if she wanted another drink. She shook her head.

"Maybe we should go," Gabriela said.

"No," Mercedes answered.

"You're sure?"

"As I can be of anything." Nodding toward the girl, she added, "I can't look at her without thinking about her mother. Then I think how strange it is that she's here and Ana María isn't. I'm going to tell you something. Months before she came we went to see Carlos Rueda. And you know what happened? He predicted she'd come here. He told a story about her being in the pampas, that she was on her way here, to the villa. He told us to take care of her, and we have. But I'm not her mother."

The girl was standing in front of the television, its glow visible behind her, lighting the sides of her dress. As the credits rolled she looked at them slowly, one by one, her eyes intense, their brightness seeming to rise up from deep within her. She clasped her hands, joining her fingers. The muscles in her jaw tightened. She was remembering all the times Roberto and Mercedes had said their names and that of the street where the Villa Deamicis was and the names of the people who lived there. Until she had heard the strong, clean notes of the guitar earlier in the evening, names had only hovered in the air like swarming insects, part of the strangeness that enveloped her. But everything began to change when she listened to the chords and glissandos, the player's fingers squeaking on the strings when his hand slid up and down the neck of the guitar. She had recognized the melody, recalled how notes looked, little black circles with tails moving up and down across the lines. The confusion had started to lift then, and the names had stopped flying around. The word Mercedes uttered had gone inside her, deep down, as if it were part of the music. She took a step toward Mercedes and the tension in her face eased, replaced by an amazing smile.

"Before the white there was a mother."

The next morning she went into the dining room and said Roberto's and Mercedes' names while they were eating breakfast. Mercedes cried and Roberto did not look quite so sad.

On Monday she said Chloe's name and Chloe laughed and said she had to learn more words.

The next day Gabriela was so happy when she spoke her name that she sang a song.

That Wednesday she stayed with Orestes, whose name made her laugh when she said it, its syllables tickling her lips. He said his name in a funny way, "OOOREESSS-TEEES!" repeating it loudly until she laughed again. Then he led her around the apartment, telling her the names of his paintings and the names of turpentine and spirits of ammonia, which sounded just like they smelled.

The names of other things were also coming back. She said "chair," "table," "pictures," "music," "bread," repeating the words again and again for the pleasure of their sounds and the greater pleasure of feeling less lost now that she knew what it was she sat on, touched, saw, ate and drank.

In the days that followed it seemed as if hoards of words were floating in the apartments in the Villa Deamicis as well as in its halls and foyer and even the courtyard filled with plants. You can imagine our elation. If the words for things were now at hand, names of people could not be far away. We followed her from room to room, down halls, outside into the midday sun, listening for just one name, however hastily uttered, that would open her memory, remind her of where we were. We stayed as close to her as tango dancers on a polished floor, looked into her eyes with more passion than you'd ever see in a dancer's heavy-lidded gaze. You'd have thought she'd hear our phantom breathing. If we could have turned ourselves into pure sweet air we'd have filled her lungs and made a name explode from her startled lips.

Yes, we did all those things, thought of dozens more, but nothing worked. It was as if she'd never heard us say who we were in the quiet of the warehouse. And so, defeated and morose, we had to content ourselves with watching her catch other words and names as if she were hunting butterflies, then listen as she fashioned stories which never came out the way she wanted. She made things gold that should have been gray, soft when they should have been hard, sad when they should have been happy.

At first it hardly mattered to the residents of the Villa Deamicis. They were so relieved that speech, however garbled, had replaced her silence that they feasted on mere sounds. Only after weeks had passed and her stories continued to confound sense did they begin to worry. She knew they were straining to understand and tried harder, but what she said never meant the same to them as it did to her. They nodded, smiled, told her to go on, say whatever she wanted to. And always, when she finished, they asked who she was and that word never came.

Testimony of
Alessandra Ricci

A voice, high-pitched, full of longing. The broken silence like a crash of thunder. Stunned as they were, mouths agape, Roberto and Mercedes welcomed it as a sign that madness had not claimed her mind. Standing in front of the television, the girl seemed to come into focus for the first time.

Pallid, dream-scarred, she was no longer a distant figure on a far bank, barely visible through a screen of leaves. She had stepped onto the shore. Who could blame them for believing that she was of their world, after all? Roberto's mind, Mercedes', spun round and round, their thoughts whirling away from Carlos' prophecy as they sought to place her within the explicably mundane. Orestes had no such need. For him, her voice was pure pleasure, like color laid down in glistening thickness upon a pristine canvas. What Gabriela heard was sweet as unexpected music wafting across a barren field.

Over the next few weeks, recovered from their surprise, they approached her carefully so as not to disturb whatever source brought speech to lips that had parted only once before to say, "I am." Avid now for certainties, they did what you'd expect, asked who she was, looking for the key that would unlock the strangeness of her life.

To me, her voice was resonant with hope, her words gleaming with the brightness of Ariadne's Thread that might lead my bones to the place where they belonged. Even more impatiently than they, I waited hungrily for the words that would unfurl her past. And then my heart—I have one still, only of an order different than your own—gave way to sadness as she returned their questions with a vacant stare. More than ever before, I understood the relationship between words and things, how love lives in the words that convey it, entering the mind of the beloved like the scent of jasmine on a summer's night. And how words kill love and bodies, too, for they had started the motors of the cars that came for us, took us to the warehouse and, finally, here. Words had been my undoing, had put my name on the list.

I knew exactly which ones they were, the time and place where they were uttered. It was a Tuesday night in a café students favored near the university. We were in shock over the abduction of a professor we all admired. There, in the blue haze of cigarettes, the brightness of neon flashing from behind the bar, we felt safe to vent our rage. It was our lair, sacrosanct, immune. As we drank I felt a rage building within me greater than any I had ever known. Sometime later I made a fiery speech, damning the government. I remember everything I said, remember the feeling of power flowing like blood through my veins while I stood there beseeching the crowd. Everyone was moved, even the strangers. Moments after I began, the place fell silent. Attentive faces, approving nods, gestures of support. Afterward loud applause, shouts of "Bravo!" piercing an atmosphere thickened by my conviction and naiveté.

A week later, as I was leaving my apartment, two men dragged me off the sidewalk and pushed me into the backseat of a car. This is incredible, I thought. My mind filled with pictures of abductions I had heard of, but I could not imagine that it was happening to me. What did I do? I yelled, and the next instant I understood. I saw again the crowd in the café and among them were two or three I'd never seen before. I remembered catching their eyes, seeing approval shine, remembered them applauding. I looked at the man in the backseat next to me. He had the soft features of a priest. A faint smile lifted the corners of his mouth. He was one of those I'd seen.

In the detention center they wanted the names of my friends. Subversives they called them. Evil slime. They wanted to know why I'd become a traitor. I told them I wasn't. That I had only spoken what thousands of others thought. What was the crime in that? It was, they said. You're just too stupid to understand. Then they wanted my body, which they took and took, and after that they wanted pain. Only when they had everything did they return me to my cell.

I sought refuge from what they'd done in sound. Whenever I moved my bracelets jangled. I always wore them with the earrings that my lover, Marco, gave me. He could never stand it when I was out of his sight, I couldn't stand being away from him. We had planned to go away that weekend. Be together where we didn't need to worry about prying eyes. I told the girl I'd spent the morning before they took me thinking of nothing else.

So you can understand why I wanted her to find her name and ours. If she did, surely information about what happened would eventually reach Marco, offer him the consolation of knowing where I was, end the questions that followed him like animals throughout the long hours of the night.

But there were no names, only broken stories, misshapen as things in dreams. I was left with the memory of a gaucho's song, a lament for a lover, the music of the pampas stretching farther than the eye can see, perhaps farther than the sound of words can carry.

Book
Three

Collage

God knows we wanted to intercede on the girl's behalf, explain what she couldn't to the Cristianis, that she had traveled down the corridors of music to a cache of words whose usage was as new to her as those in a foreign language. We wanted to counsel patience, help them see how desperately she was trying to marshal what she'd found into sentences that could hold her thoughts and feelings. But doomed to the agony of silent watching, we could offer neither advice nor succor.

She loved saying their names and those of the other residents, loved to name everything she saw. After her long silence Roberto and Mercedes had greeted her first sentence as joyously as they would a newborn child, but soon enough they began to wonder if silence might not be preferable to the interminable repetition of names and sentences whose meanings were deformed, poor broken-backed arrays of words deprived of sense. Baffled, troubled, they debated going to see their old friend, the eminent psychiatrist, Dr. Raúl Espinoza, putting it off day after day like a woman who finds a lump in her breast procrastinates and hopes it will go away. But when no improvement came, they made an appointment, hoping that Raúl might possess the wisdom to decode her mangled speech.

Unlike some of his colleagues, Raúl Espinoza did not believe that an unadorned office was the most suitable environment for patients to unburden themselves. On the contrary, he contended that beautiful things put people at ease and helped them make discoveries that might otherwise take weeks or months. Everything in the office had been carefully chosen for its suggestive qualities. He brought objects from his home and tried them out to see how they looked on his desk and tables. He hung pictures, took them down, went to galleries looking for better ones. The photographs of the pampas he settled on had been made by a woman well known among the artists of Buenos Aires. He bought all six, convinced that they would catch the attention of patients whose eyes strayed from his, lead them down unremembered avenues of thought. The same day he had found an amusing wood carving of three monkeys resting their chins on their hands and thought he would put it on his desk before he happened to visit a pawnshop and discovered the glass horse. The moment he saw it he knew it was perfect, specific enough for patients to focus on, suggestive enough to lead them to other things. He liked to think of it as the horse of the unconscious, galloping through fields of repressed events and hidden thoughts.

As soon as Roberto introduced the girl she scanned the top of Dr. Espinoza's desk which held a tape recorder, a blue ceramic jar filled with pens, the glass horse. Head high and ears back, it was running, its body reflecting the light from the windows behind her. The planes of its muscles were bright and multicolored. She could see through it, though the part of the desk it magnified was hazy.

Dr. Espinoza looked at her patiently as he leaned forward and put his elbows on the polished surface of the desk.

"Can you tell me your name?"

She said she could not remember, that it was in the place on the other side of the horse.

Raúl glanced at Roberto before saying, "Where?"

"I don't know," the girl answered. "Not even there."

"Sometimes girls have three names. Or four. One is all I want. I'll say some, and you tell me if one is yours."

He began reciting in a soft, reassuring voice. She liked the sounds of the names he said. Some she had heard, she was sure of it. If he said hers, she hoped she would know it. She watched the words form on his lips and break like bubbles into sounds. He said the names like questions. Each time he spoke his voice rose at the end and his forehead furrowed and his eyebrows rose. She wanted to help him, wanted to be one of the names like the desk was the desk, the glass horse was the glass horse, but she was not any of them. Saying otherwise would be like calling the desk a horse, the horse a picture on the wall. There was a questioning expression in the doctor's eyes as he raised his hand and smoothed his mustache. She could feel the warmth coming from him, the interest and concern. It was the same with Roberto and Mercedes. They all wanted her to say her name as if they were thirsty and who she was would quench their thirst. She felt the dryness in them, the soft tissues of their throats yearning for moisture. She listened as he said more, and Roberto and Mercedes joined in, filling the room with new names and ones they had already used, but none were who she was. After a while she knew they would never say it.

"I am the girl who came to the house," she said finally. "The one who went away."

"Where were you?"

"I don't remember."

"Where did you go?"

She closed her eyes, concentrated.

"A dark place. Then a white one."

"Where were these places?"

"Somewhere."

Dr. Espinoza shifted in his chair, put his hands flat on the desk.

"Tell me about your mother and father. Do you remember their names?"

"There was a mother before the white."

Mercedes looked at her, her eyes welling tears. She wiped them away with the back of her hand as Raúl switched off the tape recorder and looked at the girl.

"Would you mind if we talked by ourselves for a minute? Would you feel lonely?"

Lonely meant what she remembered when she had looked at the television the night of the music. She did not feel that way now, only a little lost in the haziness of things. She shook her head and looked out the window. Cars and people passed along the tree-lined street. Outside, everything was free of the haze, clear and precise in its details. She tried to consider what that meant, but her mind veered away from an answer.

"We'll be right back," Mercedes told her. "It won't take long, will it, Raúl?"

In the outer office Raúl leaned against the wall and crossed his arms. He regarded them with a bleak expression.

"She just appeared on your doorstep?"

"In the middle of the day," Mercedes said.

"And you have no idea where she came from?"

Mercedes glanced at Roberto. His eyes told her he was thinking the same thing; that it was too complicated to explain and would only embarrass them.

"No," she said.

"You probably know what I'm going to say."

"Probably," Roberto told him.

Mercedes looked at her hands.

"I'm not certain, but the inability to use words properly or remember her name points to aphasia."

"We thought that was it," Mercedes said.

"There's no therapy. It's like coma. Psycholinguists have studied it to no effect. All we know is that the condition exists as a result of brain disease or injury. In her case, it's obviously the latter. The X ray you sent over shows a serious trauma. How she survived is a puzzle. I've never seen anything like it. Have you?"

"Never," said Mercedes.

Roberto shook his head in agreement. "So what's your prognosis?"

"Your guess is as good as mine. She could remain as

she is, sentient but without the ability to use language in any logical way. Or she could regress. Language could desert her altogether. From my experience, I think you should be prepared for that possibility. Of course it's always possible that mental function will return. Stranger things have happened. My opinion is that the first two are much more likely. I'm not telling you anything you don't know."

Raúl pushed himself away from the wall.

"Have you thought about what you're going to do? I know it must be difficult."

"Wait and see," said Roberto.

"I wouldn't get my hopes up. In cases like these you sometimes just have to throw up your hands. For all we know, she'll always be mystery's daughter."

As soon as Dr. Espinoza and the Cristianis left, the girl got up and wandered around the office, stopping in front of the south wall where three pictures showed the same region of the pampas in the morning, at noon and at dusk. They were black and white, printed on grainy paper to increase the contrast. The morning picture made her happy. She liked the newness, the light flooding down from the sky and spreading like water across the fields. The one shot at midday made her think of stillness, like a bird sitting motionless in a tree. The picture taken at dusk had the quality of a dream. As she studied it she saw a tiny flaw in the middle, a place no larger than a fingernail which was blank and whose whiteness disturbed the picture's mood. She stared at the space a moment, then abruptly turned away, feeling strangely disconcerted.

The doctor's black leather chair was pushed back against the wall behind his desk. She sat in it, swinging from side to side. The glass horse looked different on this side of the desk. Backlit by the windows, it was bright and even more appealing. She picked it up, surprised by its weight. She liked the way the light turned liquid on its surface, the way the transparent body magnified the pattern in her dress. Most of all, she liked the shape of the lean body and the grace of its running, one back leg and one front one barely touching the surface so that horse and earth gave the impression of a continuum, as if the horse were taking the earth with it in its running. There was a story in the horse. She searched for it just as she had searched for her name among the ones the doctor had spoken, turning the figure this way and that, as if motion might release the words. She saw only scattered light devoid of meaning and disappointedly returned it to its place.

She depressed the key labeled "Rewind" on the tape recorder. The machine made a high-pitched whirring sound. She pushed the "Play" key, heard the door open, muffled footsteps, then Roberto saying, "This is Dr. Raúl Espinoza." Their conversation was quieter than when they had actually spoken; otherwise, it was a perfect replica of all their words, the creak of the leather chairs, the sound of the pen when the doctor put it down beside a yellow notepad. Maybe words did not die like people and animals, like the bird she had seen in the courtyard of the Villa Deamicis dying on a flagstone. She heard herself say, "I am the girl who came to the house" when the door opened and Dr. Espinoza appeared, followed by Roberto and Mercedes who looked very sad. "The one who went away," her voice said.

Dr. Espinoza sat on the edge of the desk.

"So you know how to make it work. Have you used one before?"

She did not know. She had simply done what she had seen him do before he left the room. Besides, she was thinking about what she had just said.

"Like the horse," she told him.

"What is?"

His other voice was asking her where she had gone. She heard herself say a dark place, then a white one.

"The girl who went away with the other ones."

His voice on the machine asked if she knew the names of her mother and father.

"Do you mind if I turn it off?"

He pushed the "Stop" button and looked at her again.

"Does the horse have a name?"

"He has a story."

"Will you tell me?"

The glass horse gleamed. Its mouth was open, its mane flying out behind. She examined the brightness for a clue, letting her eyes wander over the tensed muscles, the bent legs that did not touch the glass earth and the straight ones that did. The story was there but it would not come out. No matter how hard she concentrated, the story remained silent, lay in the liquid light like a frozen dream.

When they passed through the revolving doors sunlight stabbed her eyes, made them sting. She raised a hand to shield them from the glare, wishing she were still in the cool office where she might have remembered something that would have pleased Dr. Espinoza and Roberto and Mercedes. She thought they were disappointed, but on the way to the car Roberto said she had done very well and so did Mercedes. Then her mood lightened. She was glad to be in the car, watching people on the sidewalks flowing along, bunching up at intersections, hurrying across the streets like startled pigeons when the lights changed. After the time in the pampas when she had walked so long before seeing anyone, when she had been grateful if an owl appeared in the sky, she was greedy for faces. Roberto had taken a different route to the doctor's office, one that passed through tree-lined neighborhoods. She liked this one better, liked the busyness of movement, the bright storefronts whose windows mirrored cars and people. She felt a deep longing for the old men and women, the young girls walking three abreast, arms intertwined, the men in suits and those in bright shirts with slicked-back hair. She had people once, before the pampas, and while she was there, too. She remembered them in a special light, dark with yellow in it, like the colors of the scarf worn over the shoulders by a woman entering a shop. Seeing her and all the others was like eating. The different gaits of pedestrians, the subtle variations of faces filled an emptiness like the one that had been in her stomach all the days she had walked. And sounds satisfied another hunger that had begun when the bursting stars had taken her into silence. She opened herself to the rush of traffic, the purring cars and rumbling buses spewing smoke. They were good sounds but the best ones were voices. Roberto's and Mercedes' for the way they soothed her, then Orestes' and Gabriela's, strong as bells. Chloe's was like silverware on a plate, Eva's like ice tinkling in a glass. She remembered the sound her voice made on the tape recorder, a small shy voice that was not like the one she heard when she spoke. Her head contained all the sounds she was hearing and the remembered ones, too. She remembered Dr. Espinoza reciting the names and heard them again as he repeated them on the tape, and how she could not find her own among those he offered, no matter how hard she tried. Maybe if she had pushed the right button the tape would have said it, remembered her and the names of the ones she had known before the bones. But maybe there wasn't a name. Maybe she was only a sound, like a bell, or like water in a fountain. Maybe she was only colors fluttering in the wind, like the blue and white flag waving over the pink building they were passing, or the white kerchiefs worn by the women carrying signs and walking in circles.

As they drove Mercedes watched the crowds, a blur that momentarily came into focus when a woman with a bright yellow scarf turned into a boutique. Her disappointment with Raúl's diagnosis was giving way to a deeper, more complicated emotion, an ugly thing she did not want to acknowledge. She had made a terrible mistake saying what she did about mothers and childless women the night the girl found her voice. The conditions the words invoked haunted her, enlivened her imagination as they approached the Plaza de Mayo. She imagined Ana María in her blue blazer and gray skirt coming out of her room that last morning. She remembered her, years earlier, skating on a broad sidewalk in the park, her arms suddenly thrown out for balance as she tottered, fell. Her memories gave way to marching women, the old soldiers of the plaza. She watched them circling the cenotaph, a procession of hooded faces beneath white scarves, drawn along by names inscribed on placards and photographs. She was not surprised when she recognized Cecilia Rueda walking arm in arm with two of the grandmothers. Mercedes let her eyes linger on her as they drove by. She wondered where her strength came from. Then she remembered the last line of *The Wall.* She had thought Cecilia meant her own daughter, but now she realized her mistake.

"Next week," she told Roberto, "I'm going to join them."

The lobby of the building housing the grandmothers' office was narrow and lit by low-wattage bulbs. Roberto scanned the registry, located the number at the bottom of the second column. There was no elevator, so they took the stairs and both were winded when they reached the landing on the fourth floor. Mercedes had convinced him to come on the strength of an invitation from Dolores Masson a few weeks earlier.

"I feel humble," Roberto said, remembering the dark core of the *abuela's* pupils aglow with old grief but edged with pity.

"That's how we're supposed to feel," Mercedes answered.

When they reached the door there was no sign, only the number, 402. Roberto knocked. A gray-haired woman in her sixties opened the door, regarded them suspiciously.

"Yes?"

Roberto told her who they were.

"Dolores invited us," Mercedes added.

"Of course, the doctors. I'm sorry, but we have to be careful. Come."

She waved them into a waiting room furnished with a Naugahyde sofa and an end table. A few magazines were neatly stacked on the table, along with a newspaper.

"Please," she said, nodding at the sofa. "It won't be a minute."

Neither felt like sitting down. They had come to learn more about what drove the *abuelas* and they were nervous. Their commitment to the Thursday marches had extended their personal sense of loss, attenuated it so that the boundaries they had so carefully marked for their own protection were giving way, opening to the outside world, which made them both vulnerable and excited.

Dolores Masson appeared in the door leading to the main office. Without her white kerchief she looked even more elderly than she did in the Plaza de Mayo, an ordinary old woman who had taken upon herself extraordinary tasks. The line between her brows remained even when she smiled.

"I want you to meet my colleagues. We always have tea this time of day."

The woman who had answered the door and three others about Dolores' age sat around a table piled high with neat stacks of manila folders and spiral notebooks. Each of the women rose and shook hands as Dolores introduced them. After he released Isabel Furzi's hand, Roberto let his eyes stray to the wall behind the table. He had noticed the snapshots of children as soon as he and Mercedes entered the room. There were several hundred, ranging in size from the little one by two-inch pictures taken by machines in amusement parks to glossy five-by-eights made with excellent cameras. Unlike the photographs carried in the plaza, some of which were blown up life-size, these remained as they had been printed before desperation required that they be removed from family albums and brought to the office where they were tacked to a large corkboard, overlapping each other like fish scales. There were adults in them, too, parents, grandparents, uncles and aunts. Roberto recognized two of the women at the table. But the subject of the collage was the children. Sleeping babies, playful three-year-olds, little girls on tricycles, a boy holding a ball so large it obscured everything but his eyes. He had expected nothing like this, had imagined bare walls, maybe a reproduction or two of some pleasant scene. He felt the children's eyes on him as Dolores told him that the pictures were their *raison d'être*, there to goad them when they were tired, energize them when they were disappointed.

"There are two hundred and seven pictures," Dolores said, "all the cases we have documented so far. We thought a long time before doing it. Then we realized we had to. Our own are in our memories, bright as day. We needed the others to remind us that we're not the only ones who suffer."

"You do all your work here?" Mercedes asked.

"Yes. It's better not to be at home." Dolores straightened up. "So now you see us in our lair."

"The old lions," Isabel Furzi added.

"But still with teeth." Hermione Golding laughed. "At least some of us."

After tea Dolores looked at them frankly.

"My friends wanted to know why you were interested in us so I told them about your daughter. When did it happen?"

"Years ago," Roberto said. "August 4, 1979."

"Did she have children?" Isabel asked Mercedes.

"No," Mercedes told her. "She was in her second year at the university."

"My daughter was eighteen," said María de León. "She wanted to be a nurse but she married her sweetheart out of high school. She was six months' pregnant when she disappeared. They kept her alive until she gave birth. The black market in newborns was very busy. There was a premium on them. Most were given away, a few sold to the highest bidder. Those they couldn't place they shipped off to orphanages or abandoned in city parks as far away as Valparaíso. It was the dirtiest thing they did."

"Spoils of war," Dolores said. "Little jewels. We will do what we have to to find them all."

"We've made progress," Isabel added. "Some have been returned. When they were stolen they simply vanished, but we have ways, and now there's help from the government. The National Bank of Genetic Data."

"I know about it," Mercedes said. "They store blood samples of relatives that can be matched against the children's."

"Three cases have gone to court," María said grimly. "We won all of them. The kidnappers were sent to jail. They thought they'd done nothing wrong."

"All the stories are in these files," Dolores said, indicating the folders. "The thieves thought no one could trace the babies. But they didn't know that blood tells its own story, that nature made signs in the blood they couldn't alter the way they did the children's names."

"It's difficult," Isabel said. "But new information comes in every day. We sift through every piece, exhaust the possibilities. We're lucky because no one suspects old women. It's easy to plant spies posing as housekeepers. We discovered a little girl that way only months ago, the granddaughter of Mariana Ortiz who couldn't be here today. A senior policeman offered Estela to a man named Ferenzi a few days after her mother and father disappeared. We know he told Ferenzi, 'This one will never see her parents again.' And we know what Ferenzi said. He boasted that he was the one who had killed Mariana's daughter and son-in-law, so it was only natural he should have their child.

"Mariana never gave up. She always believed she would find Estela. It happened because of a photograph. We placed an advertisement in a newspaper with Estela's picture and received a tip. Someone saw a resemblance to a little girl attending school in his neighborhood. Dolores waited outside one day, posing as a professional photographer. Though it had been years since she had seen her, Mariana knew the moment she looked at the pictures that it was her granddaughter. She went to court and the judge ordered genetic testing, but the Ferenzis moved to Uruguay.

Their mistake was coming back to Buenos Aires. The authorities tracked them down. The test was made. Estela's blood was a perfect match of Mariana's. They were reunited and Ferenzi and his wife went to jail."

"So it's detective work," María said. "The government does what it can, but it has more important things on its mind than stolen babies. We have friends in high places, but there are still people in the new government loyal to the old who tip them off when we get close. Some of the generals are involved, now they're out of prison. They take a personal interest in subverting us. It's a form of revenge on those who brought them down."

"What it amounts to," Dolores told Roberto, "is piecing together what we know of the children's stories. I've been looking for my grandsons a long time now. For two years there was nothing. Then a clue. They disappeared with my daughter-in-law, Marta. Now we know that after they killed Marta, Roger and Joaquín, they were two and three at the time, were given to a childless couple by General Guzmán. He was an old friend and benefactor of a man named Ponce. They have moved many times, always just before we find where they are. I keep looking for myself and also for my son, Rubén. He took my granddaughter Felicité out of the country because there were too many memories. I miss them terribly, but someday, I feel it in my bones, someday I will find the boys. When I do, Rubén and Felicité will come back and we will make a life together."

Dolores poured more tea, looked at Mercedes.

"There is a rhythm to these things, a balance. During the war, all the momentum was on their side, the killers and the kidnappers. But things have changed. It isn't a perfect government, but at least it's democratic. We have the authorities on our side, the blood tests, other allies. For a long time these thieves of children were able to live happily, but no more. They're afraid now. They can never stay in one place very long. That would be a fine punishment, never being able to put down roots, if it weren't for what it does to the children. So I don't wish flight upon them, only fear. I console myself thinking about how it eats into their hearts, makes them paranoid. This is my form of revenge and I am at peace with it. I have earned the right to this feeling. We all have. I expect the two of you have experienced similar emotions."

"At first," Mercedes said. "For a year there was great anger."

"The difference between us," Roberto said, "is that you have this couple to concentrate on. With us there was no single person. I suppose it would help if we knew who was responsible."

"People are finding out," Isabel said.

"The forensic team," Dolores added, "the ones who call themselves the Ezekiel squad, after the Scriptures. You know about them?"

"I know about Juan Reyes."

"They are doing a great service," Dolores went on. "One day we may learn where our children are buried and that will help. They are already finding bones. Clues they turn up lead to those responsible. I would like to be able to look these people in the eye, just once. It would be the end of the chapter, sad, but an ending. There are so many who need help, so many names to restore because they were stolen, too."

Roberto could see all the way to the ground floor through the space in the corkscrew stairwell. He looked even though it made him dizzy, as if the round open space were concentrating his thoughts. The faces of children seemed to rise up to meet him. Before Ana María disappeared he had often thought about what it would be like to be a grandfather. Now he was immensely grateful that she had not married. At least he only had her to mourn.

As he walked out into sunlight at the bottom of the stairs, an idea worked its way through his depression. We could sense it falling into place as he headed for their car, sense the way its increments found purchase in his mind and came together in a flash. Besides marching, there was something he could do for himself, Mercedes, the old women. He knew little about forensic pathology, but he could dig.

Egypt's Eyes

he east windows of Chloe Fuentes' corner apartment

opened on to the street, those on the west, where the bal-

cony was, to an enclosed courtyard filled with plants. There

were two cane chairs on the balcony, a table and a magazine

rack for Chloe's journals. It was a neatly ordered space

where she could read or just enjoy the plants Deamicis had been so proud of, and whose continued health had been assured by a provision in his will that the gardener he hired before his death would continue caring for them.

Chloe had never given a thought to the difference between the austerity of her balcony and the spectacular disarray inside. She had long ago grown deaf to her husband's complaints, and whenever a friend was indiscreet enough to suggest that the room seemed cluttered, she immediately dismissed the remark and forced their conversation in another direction. The fact remained that her apartment looked more like a storehouse than a living space. Its sofas, chairs, tables, settee and sideboards were of the highest quality, and they still retained a certain elegance, despite being so antiquated that more than one client thought he had wandered into a museum whose purpose was the preservation of vestiges of a long-defunct way of life. The walls were crowded with paintings in heavy gilt frames, modern aluminum ones, as well as photographs torn from magazines and tacked to the paisley wallpaper. The subject of the images was, in order of their importance, the stars visible in the heavens above Argentina; men and women posed in speculative attitudes; abstract representations of spiritual states; a plethora of cabalistic signs; and several photos of an Indian guru.

Two large trestle tables, their ends pushed together, stood against one wall and formed her primary work space. Three smaller ones stood on the opposite side of the room, in the dining area where the sideboard held photos of friends and family as well as some cutouts from magazines of spiritualists she admired. The surfaces of these tables, as well as the corners of the rug, were awash in a sea of paper. There was typewriter paper, carbon paper, crepe paper and colored wrapping paper of every imaginable shape and size. There were rolls of butcher paper on the worktable and more stacked against the walls which she used to make her famous oversized charts after doing preliminary sketches and summaries on smaller sheets. Four open boxes of blue and white stationery used for correspondence were stacked next to two-inch-square adhesive pads on which she wrote afterthoughts and then stuck on the charts so that they sometimes looked like fields of yellow butterflies.

Chloe resisted taking care of the girl for a long time, pleading that she was always behind in her work and could not afford the distraction. But everyone in the Villa Deamicis knew that her husband's truculence was behind the excuses and finally Eva Gille protested, shaming her with accusations that Jorge was running her life. Soon afterward she relented in order to salvage her pride.

The first time the Cristianis left the girl with her Chloe looked at her and said, "I'm glad you're here. I really am. But I'm a busy woman and I can't spend the day providing entertainment." As she led the girl through the apartment, thinking that she needed to be introduced to the clutter, Chloe was immediately gratified by her interest. Her eyes flashed, and she even smiled at the photo of the guru. Chloe patted her approvingly on the shoulder.

"Do what you like. Just don't interfere with my work. I get too much of that from my husband. I'll tell you when it's time for lunch. We can have it on the balcony."

Chloe believed that her words had made a general impression and left her on the settee while she went to her worktable, eager to finish a chart for a friend who regularly consulted her. Unrolling it, she checked her calculations. It was as she had feared: Blanca's houses lay in perilous conjunction.

While Chloe considered the consequences, the girl wandered around, revisiting the pictures and objects that had caught her attention. She was amazed by the amount of paper, charmed by the colors and sizes. There was a stack of yellow typewriter sheets on a table beside the settee. She picked one up. It was like rough silk. The feel was vaguely familiar, as was the color. Sitting down, she put the sheet on her lap and thought about it. There was another shape inside it, she realized, just as there had been a story in the glass horse. It was waiting to be released. She seemed to remember folding a similar piece of paper lengthwise and in other ways as well. She absently let her fingers follow the movements of her memory. After folding it once and halving its width, she pinched the fold between her fingernails, running them the length of the sheet and leaving a crisp sharp edge. Then she folded the end of one corner to make a sharp point, making more folds and creases, each modifying the shape further, streamlining it, transforming the yellow paper until a cranelike bird emerged with pointed wings and an elongated beak. It had a name she could not recall, something soft and sweet. She balanced it in her hands where it seemed poised for flight. Then she went over to Chloe and held it out for her to see.

"Very good," Chloe said in an irritated voice. "You know origami. Now leave me alone."

Bent over her chart, Chloe missed the pleasure in the girl's face when she heard the word that allowed her to remember the classroom where she had learned to make these paper creatures, nor did Chloe notice the girl returning to the settee where she methodically set to work again, inspired by an idea that made her fingers tremble. Once she had made a dozen more, she took a handful of colored pencils from one of the small tables and began drawing likenesses of herself on the upper surface of the wings, doing so in the hope that someone might recognize her face and tell her who she was. On one she drew herself wandering through the city, a tiny stick figure dwarfed by buildings whose windows looked like eyes. On another she put herself in the Cristianis' living room, surrounded by people but sitting alone, off to the side. She drew herself bending over the rainwater pool, drew the sun with ragged rays to convey its brightness.

Tears were streaming down Chloe's face as she plotted Blanca's fate. She was so caught up in her predictions that she did not hear the girl open the doors to the balcony, or the sound of her footsteps as she returned to gather the birds and carry them outside where she carefully placed them on the wicker table.

It was one of those perfect Argentinean days with an onshore breeze, just enough to ward off the heat and stir the leaves. We felt its warmth, smelled the faint perfume of flowers wafting up from the courtyard as she took one last look at the blue *porteño* sky and reached for the bird nearest her hand. Holding it between thumb and forefinger, she raised her arm and in a fluid motion launched it over the railing, following its flight with a hopeful expression as it caught a jasmine-scented updraft and rose in an arc before suddenly losing momentum and falling sideways to the courtyard. Looking down at the yellow shape, she wondered why it had not sustained the momentum imparted by her hand, deciding that it had not loved the air enough, at least not as much as it needed to. She launched the next and then another, each going a little farther than their predecessors before they lost their purchase in the air and tumbled to the flagstones, where they lay like wind-blown flowers. Perplexed, she stared at the fallen birds, her mouth tight with disappointment. Then she went inside.

Chloe looked up when the girl opened the door to the hall and asked what she thought she was doing. The girl ignored her and headed out while Chloe quickly followed, her slippers making a slapping sound on the carpet. With one hand on the railing, the girl went down the stairs while Chloe shouted "Stop!" She passed through the access door to the courtyard and collected the birds while Chloe watched, relieved that she hadn't run out into the street. Once they were back upstairs, Chloe went out on the balcony with her and watched her launch them all again. The birds made no effort to fly, having been bent and otherwise battered by their successive falls. The girl's face was red from the effort, her eyes despondent.

When Chloe told the Cristianis about the paper birds, neither of them gave the incident much thought. The girl fashioned another dozen from some drawing paper in Orestes' apartment the following day and tossed them from his balcony with the same results. She repeated her efforts when she stayed with Eva, and afterward with Gabriela who volunteered to care for her because she had no classes.

One Saturday night the girl lay awake long after she had gone to bed, her imagination teeming with flights of multicolored birds falling as if they had been shot from the sky. The problem was not their shapes. Each was perfect, their wings swept back to gather air, bodies narrow, every fold neat and crisp. Their inability to fly had another cause.

Unable to sleep, she went to the dressing table, turned on the lights rimming the mirror, studied herself a long time. She was the girl she had seen in the pool and in the pier glass, but she was afraid that what she was looking at was an illusion, that she might disappear if she turned off the lights. Then the darkness would claim her, take her back to the place where faces had leered in the yellow light like masks. She was unaware that she was seeing our eyes. They could have belonged to anyone in the world. But as she stared she found the answer to the question of her birds and laughed with pleasure and relief.

Her voice woke Mercedes who assumed the sound was the remnant of a dream until she heard footsteps, a crisp rustling, then the door of the girl's room closing. It worried her enough to get out of bed. She went down the hall and saw a sliver of light beneath the door, opened it.

The girl, who had taken a handful of typing paper from Roberto's desk, was sitting at the dressing table, constructing birds. Mercedes did not know what to make of it. She was a little disturbed by what had grown into an obsession and crossed the room, putting her hands gently on her shoulders.

"They're very nice," Mercedes said. "But don't you think you should go to sleep? You can work on them in the morning."

The girl smiled at her in the mirror, continued folding. When she finished the one she was working on she took up another piece of paper.

Since there was nothing she could do, Mercedes went back to bed, thought about waking Roberto, then decided to let him sleep. She told him in the morning and he said it was probably a good sign. It indicated that her mind was active.

"It's child's play," Mercedes said.

"I suppose you're right. But it might lead to other things."

Mercedes was busy in the kitchen getting a head start on the elaborate meal she always prepared on Sundays while the girl quickly ate breakfast and returned to her room. The discovery she had made the previous night was that the birds lacked eyes to see where they were going. She had made twelve new ones before getting back into bed and thinking of all the eyes she'd ever seen. She saw round eyes, elliptical eyes, blue eyes and yellow ones, regarding each judiciously, then discarding them one by one until she was satisfied with the shape to use.

The birds were neatly lined up on Ana María's dressing table. After rummaging through her cosmetics, the girl found a plastic makeup kit with eyeliner and several lipstick brushes which she used to decorate the wings with drawings of herself. Then she held each bird up to the light and slowly, carefully began to replicate the eyes that had appeared in memory, staring out of a golden mask. She recalled neither the figure's name nor the degree of his royalty. To her, they were simply Egypt's eyes. With the fine tip of the brush she drew the graceful upper lid and then the lower, outlining each with blue eye shadow, just as they had looked the night before. In the center she drew circles, leaving the irises white.

Once she finished, she put them all in a wicker basket and went out to the balcony, passing Mercedes who was engrossed in reducing a wine sauce. The girl looked up at the sky, searching for a route. Facing south, she picked up a bird and tossed it over the railing, releasing the others quickly and smiling as they climbed just as she knew they would.

Two people who happened to be walking in the neighborhood saw tiny shapes appear over the roof of the building adjacent to the Villa Deamicis and dismissed them as some species of migratory birds. Pedestrians on Calle Florida watched two fall from the sky, assuming they were a clever promotion stunt launched from an upper floor of one of the expensive stores. But when they retrieved them from the sidewalk they found no advertisements, only strange pictures on the wings, and eyes that made them feel uneasy.

Two flew through open windows of cars on the Riachuelo, causing a minor accident. Another impaled itself on the sharp hood ornament of a bus, distracting the driver so much that he pulled over and removed it, giving it to a little boy seated with his mother near the door. A dying man gazed out of his hospital window and believed he had seen the Paraclete. An hour later he went to his death happier than he had ever been in life. One flew over two parks before it reached a soccer field where it surprised the home team's goalie so much he let the opposition score to the disgust of his teammates and the contempt of the fans. Two more, flying in tandem like planes in formation, passed the window of the dingy apartment where Ernesto Siciliano lay with his hands behind his head. At first, he thought they were only finches, but then he looked more closely and their leering eyes made him scream. Minutes later one came to rest on the balcony of the Ruedas' apartment. When Carlos picked it up, it seemed to glow in the morning light. Another began to fall over Caminito Street, then rose again; borne south on a surge of wind it rode all the way to the top of a tree on the Sternbergs' *estancia*. The macaws, parrots and songbirds nesting in the branches, immobile as ripening fruit, flew from their perches in a flurry of squawks and beating wings, circling the newcomer like a moving rainbow. The commotion caught the attention of Sasha who had been standing on the veranda. She gazed, openmouthed, at the unblinking eyes.

The last headed straight for the port, passing over a crane unloading a German freighter whose crew was too busy with cargo nets to notice how it suddenly rose out of the salt-scented air, vanishing upward to the jet stream which carried it toward the pampas. It soared out of sight over tracts of sun-seared land, over ranches and endless fields of wheat, beginning its descent two days later above the plot of deep green grass that hid our bones, skirting dusty towns as it followed the road cutting through the fields, coming closer and closer to the treetops until it finally spiraled down, circled the blossoming acacia tree, the only thing that grew in the otherwise barren ground surrounding the Ponces' house.

The bird landed ten feet from where Tomás and Manfredo were playing with their soccer ball. Tomás picked it up by one wing, as if it were a real dead bird. The brothers inspected its markings, studied its piercing eyes, both enchanted by their unexpected windfall. Tomás gripped its body between his fingers and tossed it into the air. To their delight, it soared to the top of the acacia, circled the branches twice and came to rest at their feet, obedient as a boomerang. Manfredo had the same success. They passed half an hour taking turns until it was irremediably weakened when it landed on its beak.

Beatriz did not think one way or another about the dilapidated paper bird the boys said had fallen from the sky. Windblown trash tossed from passing cars regularly littered the ground. It was one of the difficulties of living where they did, so close to the road. She told them it was time to get cleaned up for dinner and returned to mending a sock stretched over a lightbulb.

Eduardo listened avidly when he came home half an hour later. He wanted to know exactly what time the bird appeared, exactly where it landed. He told them to show him the spot. Beatriz was putting dinner on the table and protested that everything would get cold, but Eduardo was already shooing the boys out the door. They showed him the place. He asked which direction it had come from but they hadn't been looking, they said. Besides, they were hungry. He asked if there was anything else they might have forgotten. When they said no, he relented and let them go inside while he stared at the sky, then calculated the distance of the spot from the road, pondering it all until Beatriz finally came out on the porch and said his dinner would be ruined if he didn't come in that instant.

After dinner he played chess with the boys, letting them collaborate as he always did. He was pleased with their progress. Tomás had a fine analytical bent. On the other hand, Manfredo, who was less gifted at calculation, was intuitive and always suggested moves that surprised Eduardo with their originality and verve. He often told Beatriz it was a pity they did not have the other's gift, saying that such a combination would help them make their way in the world. Beatriz was less interested in their minds than their hearts, which had seemed generous from the very beginning. She rarely made this observation out of deference to the pact she and Eduardo agreed to years ago, that it would be better not to mention the entry of the boys into their lives, contenting herself with saying they were a blessing and letting it go at that.

Eduardo said nothing more to Tomás and Manfredo about the paper bird, aware that he had frightened them with his questions. He let them win the third game, then sent them to bed with the promise that he would be more fierce tomorrow night. He would take their rooks in the first five moves.

While Beatriz returned to her mending, Eduardo took the bird over to a chair in the corner where the light was good and examined the wings. The drawing was forceful if crude, depicting a figure in a field, so tiny he could not make out the face, or tell whether it was a man or a woman. Interested as he was in the representation, it was the eyes that held his attention. Large and empty, they reminded him of a photograph he had once seen of a hex sign. He held the bird up to the light to study its eyes, moving it one way and then the other so that he could see the right eye and then the left, which was slightly larger and more elegantly drawn. The glare of the lamp bulb emphasized the black outline and made the empty pupil glow until he had a sudden image of the Sphinx looking unblinkingly across the desert. The pupil seemed to expand, showing the pampas where he lived. His house materialized, then the road. A car approached and stopped in front of the house. Four *abuelas* wearing white scarves got out. The one who looked especially aggrieved strode to the door and broke it down against his protests. The others followed her inside where they stood guard while she searched all the rooms until she found the one where the boys were sleeping. "Here they are!" she shouted triumphantly. The others followed her inside, emerging moments later with Tomás and Manfredo still in their pajamas and sleepily rubbing their eyes. He shouted at the women, cursed them. When that didn't work, he begged them not to take his sons. "Blood is blood," they said contemptuously as they walked through the room, which shook from their footsteps. He tried to follow, but some force kept him inside, making it impossible to cross the threshold. He could only watch and grieve as they piled into the car and disappeared in a cloud of bright pink dust.

The pupil was a circle of white again, enclosed by a thick black ring, empty now, immaculate, the images that had appeared there as on a screen now transferred to his mind. He glanced around warily. Beatriz was removing a sock she had finished mending from the lightbulb, slipping on another. He slowly turned his eyes back to the bird. Suddenly, he tore off one wing.

"What's the matter?" Beatriz asked.

"Shut up," he told her as he continued pulling it apart, shredding wings, body, beak, tearing them into smaller and smaller pieces.

Words like Fire

The girl waited with only the dimmest notion of how long it had been since she launched the birds. She had almost no sense of time. The past was a vagueness where things briefly appeared only to vanish without a trace. The present was not so much a matter of hours as the long stretch of morning, afternoon, night, the slow glide of the sun across the sky.

The first week of her vigil passed, then the second. She grew tired of looking at the empty sky, craning her neck, mistaking seagulls for one of her creations. In her dreams, paper birds sailed over the city, descending into neighborhoods where they glided through open windows into houses and demurely perched on tables or clung like parrots to damask curtains. She saw a drunken sailor in a bar laboriously try to reproduce the shape he had seen while working on the deck of a German freighter, folding and refolding a paper napkin. There was a man in the pampas who held one up to the light, fearful of its eyes. One sailed into an ombu tree where it clung desperately to the leaves as the rain came down, softening its beak, its head and neck, smearing the drawings on its wings until they were purple blurs.

She did not know what to do with the disappointment that lay like a cold stone beside her heart, and she was about to give up at the beginning of the third week when she remembered the gull in the door flying above the stained-glass town. And then she understood her mistake. She had not made enough. Remembering the endless stretches of the pampas, the city streets she had wandered through between tall buildings, the sounds she heard at night that came from far away, she realized that there was too much space for a dozen birds to cover, too many fields and districts and streets.

In the morning she made more birds in Chloe's apartment and flew them from the balcony. She repeated the process the next day and the day after that. As they passed over the roads and avenues that had once been taken by the green Ford Falcons, their stark eyes reflected skyscrapers, machine shops, police stations, abandoned torture centers and the River Plate.

We followed their flight even more eagerly than she did, privileged by our condition to see things beyond her understanding. What we knew most clearly was that the liberation of the stories had begun. Cecelia's book and other voices had already loosened Argentina's memory. Things that the generals and politicians, the foot soldiers and petty bureaucrats, thought would never, ever come to light were starting to emerge. As the paper birds fluttered into the hands of old men playing dominoes at outdoor cafés, landed on the soft blankets of infants being pushed in strollers and flew beyond the city to the pampas, the whiteness was being filled. Over the course of months, clues, facts and accusations piled up on the desks of lawyers, doctors, policemen, supplied by disaffected patriots like Alberto Marqovitch as well as housewives, laborers, secretaries, and watchmakers who came forward with scraps of paper, recollections, eye-witness accounts, memories suddenly freed of fear. And among the helpers, though she never knew it, was the girl.

Before the episode with the paper birds, she had confined herself to gnomic utterances followed by periods of silence that sometimes lasted for many days. The Cristianis feared she was regressing as Raúl Espinoza warned might happen. But the successful flight, attended by her hope that one of her creatures might reach a person who knew her name, was like a breech in a dam. She talked incessantly, eager to let the words flow out and see what shapes of meaning they might take.

She told tiny, shrunken stories with neither beginnings nor endings, offering word pictures of places and things devoid of context. One morning as she was having breakfast with the Cristianis, a morning when Roberto was scheduled to assist in surgery and was going over in his mind what he had done dozens of times, rehearsing his part as was always his custom, she put down her knife and fork so suddenly they clattered on her plate. Roberto was finishing his second cup of tea, thinking about where to place the clamps. He looked at her, startled out of his reverie. She was staring out the window, seemingly absorbed by the view of rooftops. Mercedes noticed, too, and they exchanged a glance, both worried but unsure what to do. The girl looked back at him, her eyes widening with surprise.

"There was a student," she said. "She had the tickets in her purse. They were going to an inn in the mountains. She had thought for days about the lake there and how they would make love at night and walk hand in hand along the shore every morning. It was the first time they were going away to a place where she didn't have to be afraid, where she wouldn't have to worry that someone who knew her would see them going into a hotel. Her heart was full and she had been thinking of all the things she wanted to tell him. She was happier than she had ever been. That morning she had studied herself in the mirror, trying to imagine what their child would look like, how their features would mingle in the child's. She was humming their favorite song when the men dragged her off the sidewalk."

Her eyes fluttered. She glanced at her plate, slowly reached for her fork.

Stunned by the clarity of her speech, Roberto recovered enough to ask, "Who is she, *cara*?"

"Is she a friend?" Mercedes asked. "Family? Do you know her name?"

"There were names before the darkness ate them."

"Try to remember," Mercedes said. "Was she blond? Brunette?"

"Only the darkness saw her. All we had were words."

"Who is we?" Mercedes asked. "Who was with you?"

The girl appeared confused. Roberto glanced at Mercedes, shook his head.

"It's gone. Can't you see?"

As the week wore on, she told Chloe about a metal tree with people in it, a man who followed birds in the darkest hours of the night, a guitar whose strings played words.

One day, while she and Gabriela were walking, she stopped suddenly and said, "There was a man." She remembered how he sat close to the door which sometimes opened. She saw his thin face glowing in the sliver of yellow light, his eyes slitted against the unaccustomed glare. He was waiting for her, turning to face her, an expectant, hopeful expression softening the morose curve of his mouth. "He was a singer," she said, her voice still tentative but her tone firmer, determined.

"What did he sing?" Gabriela asked. "Can you remember?"

His voice rose up in the girl's mind. The dark had always thickened with his songs. She heard the tap of his foot, the soft, complex rhythm.

"*Milongas,*" she said suddenly. "And songs of knives. His voice was like metal in his throat, deep and almost strong. He sang for money and he sang for free. In bars, he sang old songs of the pampas, gauchos' songs, but for his friends and then for us he sang new songs of freedom he made himself. He said he took the words out of the smoke that made it hard to breathe. One night he was singing about the dry hearts of soldiers when they came and took him away in the middle of a word. They did things to him, broke his voice. When they finished, they brought him to where we were, and then he sang in the darkness with his broken voice, keeping time with his foot, his words like flames that reached the rafters where bats hung, staring down. The fire made little pyres of freedom in their eyes. Even when he couldn't sing, when the metal hardened in his throat, we heard his melodies."

Gabriela could still see the place after the girl fell silent. The fire glittering in rows of eyes seemed to light an enormous room where shadowy figures moved to the rhythm of the singer's song. It was all there, in the girl's face whose whiteness was like a screen.

The girl met her eyes with an expression of hope which she clung to, desperately fighting off the darkness, refusing to look away. But it was too late. The gravity of her expression slackened. The pallor thickened, became muddied. She blinked as her face went blank. Gabriela watched the fire dance out of her eyes.

On several occasions she stopped people in the foyer when they returned from work, speaking with an earnestness that made some feel she had become a pest and almost wish for the days when she was mute.

Once she walked uninvited into Guillermo Calvino's apartment, and while the old man objected vigorously, he listened anyway as she talked about the need to name the spirits, the soft, singsong quality of her voice breaking through the crusted shell of his solitude. She insisted in her garbled way that her name was not the only one that had been lost.

Her need to talk affected everyone in a different way. The Cristianis were always patient. So were Chloe and Orestes. Eva listened until she had no more to say. Others who had refused to care for her became increasingly uneasy. It was not so much the attention she demanded when they were leaving or returning from the building as the way she looked. For months she had greeted everyone with a blank face and abstract stare. Now her eyes were bright and liquid, unbearably intense, though they refused to reveal what was hidden in their depths. It made no difference that everyone knew this was unpremeditated. Her gaze reminded them of a peculiarity associated with the insane; the normal eyes that mask a disordered mind.

But there was still plenty of sympathy, and none was greater than Gabriela Santini's. From the day she appeared, the girl had touched the deepest chords of her being, releasing emotions that were more complex and subtle than those she felt for her most gifted students. By introducing her to the feeling of motherhood, the girl had done what none of Gabriela's students could: softened the hard edges of the way she dealt with them in the classroom. She was more patient with the plodding ones, more praiseful of the best. The change was so pronounced that they talked about it after class, and finally agreed with Olivia Arnoldi that there was only one interpretation. Their teacher must be in love.

Gabriela would not have put it that way, though she would have admitted to the charge of infatuation. She was much taken by the girl's vulnerability, and acted protectively whenever they were together, the way she would have done if the girl were lame. So it was only natural that with the advent of speech, whose beginning she had witnessed and for which she felt a certain responsibility, that Gabriela became her ally and interpreter.

We weren't surprised. After all, her training allowed Gabriela to bring to bear a kind of attention that was unavailable to the others. Whereas the Cristianis' expertise lay in the body's exquisitely ordered functions, Chloe's in the interaction of the stars, Orestes' in the way things looked, Gabriela's devotion to literature made her uniquely responsive to everything the girl now said. She listened with the same attention she brought to reading texts that resisted interpretation and demanded puzzling over, approaching them from different angles to release their hidden meanings. Because she knew how signs and symbols carried the meaning of a book, she was especially attentive to recurrent images, phrases and motifs she noticed migrating from one story to another. There was a repetition of the color yellow, lanterns, the words "spirits" and "pampas" and "names" that Gabriela believed would lead her somewhere if she were patient. She looked for patterns in everything the girl said, tried to discern sequence, the *progression d'effet*.

We did what we could to help her see, tried to increase the glow of lantern light, guide her eyes to the pampas she knew like the back of her hand since she had been raised there. We encouraged her to use her abilities to ferret out connections so she could map a semblance of the world from the girl's enthusiastic but broken speech. But no matter how hard we tried, Gabriela could not find the key. Her ability to tease the deepest meanings from her texts, take her students on brilliant excursions through the most difficult passages, proved useless in deciphering what she heard. It was the first time in her life that her intellect proved insufficient, and it was as bitter to her as the taste of day-old maté tea.

One Saturday the Cristianis invited Gabriela to join them for a picnic in a nearby park. Everything looked normal. Families. Children playing. Ice cream vendors. Photographers with large cameras mounted on tripods. It was hard to believe that not long ago things were different. Gabriela thought of Hirsch, then put the thought away, storing it with all the others she could do nothing about, a lifetime's mistakes that surfaced from time to time to remind her that she was far from perfect. There was a rumor he had been seen in Paraguay. She hoped it was true. But if it was, did that excuse her silence? She would give anything to know. There was a life behind things, unseen, powerful. She recalled having said something to that effect not long ago. Two planes at once, something like that.

The girl babbled nonstop during lunch. Gabriela half-listened, giving her full attention only when she started in on the spirits.

"She's been talking about them a lot," Mercedes said.

Whenever Gabriela asked about them, the girl looked at her with a troubled expression and went on to something else. She decided to try again.

"Who are they?"

"Their names," said the girl.

"Where do they live?"

"In the place where light made bones."

"And where is that, *cara*?" Mercedes asked.

Gabriela had heard her talk of light and bones a dozen times. The conjunction always interested her, and she would interrupt, ask her to explain more fully only to see her turn away and then resume with another fragment of the story. She gave no indication that anything had changed, though Gabriela thought she seemed more pensive.

"Where did the bones come from?" Gabriela asked. "Maybe you could tell us that."

"Where no lights were," the girl said slowly. "Dark. Dark. The smell of hay and oil. Old things. Birds with funny faces, little noses, teeth, flew in the high window. They stayed when the dark was gray, upside down, hanging asleep in the ceiling, dark wings on rafters. The ones who went into the light heard their cries. They flew at night, made noises, 'Screech screech screech.' Then it was always dark and dark. The ones who went into the light talked then. One talked to me. Then another. Then cries. Dark and the skinny light and other voices and then more lights. The place moved. It bumped and made me fall and someone picked me up. A long time. And dark. And then lights like eyes, moving up and down, and the voices. I saw the faces, not what I thought. Different. The light moved too much and then it was dark again and then wet grass. Dress wet and cold on my legs. Cold and dark and then the faces in the lantern saying, 'No no no,' until the drums and the man who wanted to do it and then the other one saying saying saying laughing laughing laughing. He made the bones and then he made a light with stars. The bones made grass."

The room was very quiet. Sunlight poured through the windows, glinted on surfaces. The light caressed her, made her warm. She pushed the double doors open and stepped out on the balcony, looking over the iron railing at people strolling by on the street, then straight ahead where buildings framed an oblong sky. A seagull circled a cupola, rose suddenly and sailed away, becoming smaller and smaller but leaving a trail upon the air that drew her eyes to the horizon. There were a few clouds in the distance, beyond the receding shapes of the city's roofs. White and billowy, they floated slowly eastward above a place she could not see but which she knew was there. It seemed to be calling to her. Watching the clouds slowly changing shape, she began to recall a story, not its words or who had told it, only a bright flash of color against the sky, something that had taken form out of language and was part of who she used to be. It was somewhere beneath the clouds, she was sure of it. She stood with her hands on the railing, waiting for it to appear in her mind. For a moment it seemed as if it were going to happen, she was going to see it. But the clouds kept moving, passing over the buildings toward the sea without telling her what she needed.

There was something she had to do. Turning away from the railing, she went inside and left the apartment without bothering to close the door. At the end of the hall she descended the stairs soundlessly on bare feet to the foyer, where she stopped in front of the pier glass. She was wearing the white dress Gabriela had washed for her, its still faint stains offset by bright opalescent buttons. She remembered how she had looked the day she arrived. Now her hair was clean and combed, her face without a smudge. With a last lingering glance she turned away from the pier glass and went to the door. When she opened it, Guillermo Calvino thought he heard a click. He looked up from the paper he was reading with a magnifying glass, then decided it was only another random sound.

Uncertain which direction to take when she reached the sidewalk, she looked hesitantly up and down the street. A stop sign half a block away winked and she went toward it, crossing the intersection against the light. A cabdriver slammed on his brakes. She continued across the street, impervious to his blaring horn, a screed she passed through unaware, her desire rendering the sound substanceless as air.

The color of the pavements, the snowflake design of metal gratings surrounding *palo borrocho* trees, fluted water fountains, a solitary man bent over a cup of coffee in a sidewalk café, two women pushing strollers, a horse-drawn cart piled high with woven baskets, all verged on familiarity, their shapes and colors calling to images buried in her mind. She recognized something in the calls and wolf whistles of a group of laborers, the lovers embracing in a recessed doorway, the woman watching her over the man's shoulder as they kissed. Even the pulsing of traffic lights she did not obey seemed imbued with a former brightness. But just as she was about to reach out and claim the images as her own, at the moment it seemed she could fit people and objects into memory, they slipped away into strangeness once again.

As she walked on, pedestrians made way for the girl, turning to watch her as she passed, then looking at their companions and even at strangers to see how they were reacting to this oddity making her way barefooted through the old city of refinement and self-conscious style.

A boy swore to his older brother that she left no shadow.

An old woman victimized by superstition believed she was a spirit come back to haunt the streets, and to protect herself made a hex sign she had learned seventy years ago, amazed that she remembered how to do it.

Unaware of her effect, the girl walked on dreamily until she reached a square surrounded by trees and wooden benches. Cooing pigeons filled the air with sound. When she stopped beside the fountain people regarded her, puzzled that she was barefooted but quickly assigning her to the assorted crazies, drunks and wanderers they were used to seeing. They returned to their papers and magazines or sightless staring until a loud fluttering of wings caught their attention. A dozen pigeons were flying around her, their wings brushing against her face and upraised arms. No one had ever seen anything like it and they stared, a few with their mouths agape. The pigeons scattered like confetti across the square, waddled away from seeds and crusts of bread to join the flight, surrounding her with a gray-white blur, a moving vortex that guided her from the square to a nearby subway entrance where she passed from the onlook-

ers' astonished sight and descended the stairs to a tile-lined
corridor and went through a stile, ignoring the guard who
shouted but did not pursue her. Like everyone else in the
station, he was a little frightened by what he saw.

She stood patiently on the platform as a train emerged
from the tunnel and creaked to a halt. The car doors opened
with a pneumatic hiss, disgorging people with briefcases and
shopping bags and harried faces who jostled past her with
backward glances before they were absorbed by the crowd.
As soon as there was room to move she entered a car and
took a seat beside a woman in a stylish suit who raised her
eyebrows in disbelief, staring at the three downy un-
derfeathers caught in the girl's hair as she quickly edged
closer to the window. The remaining seats filled, portions of
the aisle. Hands grasped for straps, supporting poles. A
minute later the train departed into the tubed underworld of
movement and rushing sound and trapped air reeking of
diesel fumes. Even before the rumble of its wheels smoothed
out with speed, everyone close enough to see her was staring, doing what they could to make sense of her until their
stops arrived. Then they left with a final glance, intent upon
the story they would tell at work or home, spreading her
fame through high-rises and bars and suburban houses pro-
tected by walls of bougainvillea.

She sat motionless in her seat beside the door, eyes
fixed on the window across from her, noting people
bunched at stations, blackness flecked with bare lights
shooting by like stars, workmen in hard hats fitted with
halogen lanterns, the neatly lettered names on station signs.
Everything passed like images in a dream. It was all unim-
portant, textured trivia, background to something she was
looking for as the train stopped and sped, disgorged passengers, took on more who inherited the wonder she had cre-

ated from the departing crowd. She never turned her head, never looked up. When bodies obscured the window, she stared at belts and purses until the train finally stopped and a conductor came through, announcing that they had reached the end of the line. She followed the crowd into sunlight and headed down a narrow street, intent upon a half-remembered direction, her eyes fixed straight ahead, on a spot between old soot-stained buildings a block away.

At the flea market she walked up and down the aisles, passing booths and tables strewn with dishes, clothes, lamps, horse halters, mirrors, myriad objects waiting to pass from one life into another. She stopped only when she saw the birds.

Caged alone and in pairs, they perched on finger-thick bars, singing melodies she recognized from another time, two- and three-note songs belonging to an unremembered story. She wandered slowly along the lines of cages, stopping at each to look and listen. She could see the barred faces of people on the other side of the cages, men and women whose eyes met hers and flickered with the recognition of a common interest before they realized how odd she was and quickly turned away to engage a vendor in talk of pedigrees and prices, their words part of the ambient sound of metal clicking against metal, a called name, the voice of a fortune-teller at a nearby table expounding on a woman's fate.

"These lines that cross mean a journey. I see a large house in the country. There will be much happiness and sorrow."

The fortune-teller's voice faded as the girl went on to the end of the aisle where a vendor wearing a black beret was carefully placing a parakeet in a box for an old couple who were making clucking noises at the bird.

Suddenly, everything was clear. As the vendor watched the old man counting out bills from his wallet and reached into his pocket to make change, she stepped around to the other side of the cages, her movement startling the birds who responded with cockeyed stares, their heads bent to one side as if they were looking around a corner. She went along the row, quickly unlatching hasps and opening doors. In her wake the birds jumped from perch to sill, from sill into the air, answering the vendor's angry shout with songs she knew were pitched to tones they had never sung. As they rose, following a path she seemed to remember from long ago, the vendor shouted and looked around frenziedly, demanding to know who had done this and calling for the police. Surrounded by curious onlookers, she waited until the last bird disappeared over the rooftops before heading back in the direction she had come, stepping in exactly the same places she had on her way to the market, left foot over the invisible imprint of the right, right over left in what looked like a child's game but was as natural to her as the River Plate emptying into the thirsty sea.

The Cristianis were in the living room when she returned, windblown from her journey, but otherwise unaffected. Mercedes jumped up and went to her.

"We were so worried."

The girl looked at her absently, then went to her room and closed the door.

"I never thought she'd wander off," Mercedes said. "She was fine until now."

"We don't know that," Roberto corrected her. "We don't know anything, when you think about it."

Testimony of Jacob Levy

I used to go to that flea market, looking for odds and ends. Sometimes a decent guitar turned up, a harmonica or pitch pipe. I bought my metronome there from a music teacher who'd fallen on hard times. But I liked it for the people more than the goods. All kinds, all ages, rich, poor and in-between showed up. I think the place appealed to everyone because they never knew what they'd find, like a treasure hunt.

Afterward I'd go a few blocks in the opposite direction the girl took to a little park. When you make your living in smoky bars you take every chance to be outside. There was a fountain and benches and the softest grass you've ever felt. I'd lie on my back, looking up at the branches. Little slivers of sunlight came through the leaves. The sound of water in the fountain lulled me. So did the cool grass and the people talking low on the benches. It was intimate, peaceful, even after the *Proceso* started. I think we all went there to lose ourselves in the greenery and shade. I'd daydream about voice lessons, opera houses, imagine myself taking bows with Pavarotti. Everything was possible in that park.

I never thought I'd disappear because of my songs. Maybe if I'd made a spectacle of myself in front of the Casa Rosada, or sung on the radio, but my voice never strayed outside the cafés, was never heard in the middle of the night on street corners. I was more surprised than anyone in the Café de la Parroquia when four men came in and arrested me, men with faces no different than those in the café or the park, citizens of the port, all no doubt linked to networks of families and friends. We spoke the same language, shared the same referents when we traveled through the city. I could no more have isolated them in the crowd than you could have pointed me out and shaken your head knowing that I, rather than someone next to me, had stepped across a line, violated some belief. As they came through the tables, knocking over glasses and bottles, I could see the hatred in their eyes, even though all of them were smiling.

Nothing happened for a while after they locked me up in a basement room. A young man brought me food, said insulting things, but he left me in peace to eat. I thought maybe they'd just keep me awhile and let me go with a warning. I knew such things happened. It was an odd time. Even though I was frightened, I started feeling bored. I can't account for the strangeness other than to say that the source of the fear was outside the room while inside everything was quiet, peaceful. The fear was like a nagging but minor pain you get used to. Sometimes hours passed without my being aware of it.

Since there was nothing to do I slept a lot, long stretches of dreamless sleep from which I woke tired and with a clotted mind. Sometimes I'd sing to pass the time. Not the songs I'd composed about the regime. Folk songs, mostly, though sometimes I'd sing religious ones, especially those that my father loved and which he'd taught me when I was still a child. I'd remember his voice in the synagogue, the amazing things he could do which I'd never quite been able to master. At that time I had no idea why they left me alone so long. Now I see how their minds worked. They were waiting for me to sing, you understand. They wanted my voice to be strong and supple.

One morning two men took me to an office. There was a desk, half a dozen chairs. A tree outside bending slightly in the wind. A tall thin man wearing a colonel's uniform was filing his nails by the window, looking at it. After he finished he put the file in a drawer, regarded me in a friendly way. "So you're the singer?" he asked. I said yes, I was. "Your father was a cantor?" I nodded, wondering how he'd found out but not really worried because he was being so pleasant. He looked at me for a minute as if he were sizing me up. Then he signaled to one of the men who'd brought me. He opened the door and some more soldiers came in. "It's not much of an audience," the colonel said, "but it's the best we can do. Sing something."

I didn't feel like it, but it would have been stupid not to

so I asked what he wanted to hear. "What do you think?" he said to the others. "I'd like one you sing in the cafés." I sang one that wasn't very offensive, keeping time with my fingers on my leg. "You're good," he said when I finished. "Have you studied?" I told him that everything I knew I'd learned from my father, adding that I'd been too poor for a professional teacher. "That's too bad," he said as he glanced at the men behind me. "You have a nice voice. Listen," he added as he walked behind the desk. "What would you think about a free lesson? It won't cost you a thing."

They gave it with a piece of metal. I couldn't swallow for days. Not even water. I was afraid to speak, afraid of what I'd hear. I must have been silent for nearly a month. Then, not long before they took me to the warehouse, I tried an easy scale that sounded like metal grinding on metal. That's how it's going to be, I thought. And then, terrible as it was, I felt relieved. I was certain they wouldn't have ruined my voice if they planned to kill me. But when I was transferred to the warehouse, the smell of fetid oil, the semi-darkness, the fact that other people were there made it clear that we were all part of a different story than I'd imagined. I knew it when the girl arrived. I saw her clearly for a moment as they opened the door and pushed her inside. She was crying, and one of the women tried to comfort her but she was inconsolable. Suddenly I knew she was the piece in the story that was missing, proof of their intentions.

I sang with my broken voice while we waited, sang as long as I could. It helped ease the fear and seemed to make the others feel better, gave them the illusion that things might not be heading where they were.

So when I saw where the girl was going after she came out of the subway station I was happy. The flea market was like a visit home. As the birds winged their way to trees and rooftops I thought of how my voice once soared. I'll tell you this. If they hadn't taken me here, I'd have gone back to the cafés and sung in exactly the right voice for the times. No more sweet tremolo I was famous for. No high notes sustained longer than any singer in Buenos Aires. Metallic sounds would have risen from my throat like tongues of flame. If I'd returned, everyone who heard me would have taken up a gun.

Book

Four

THIRTEEN

The Ezekiel Squad

wo weeks after the girl's journey to the flea market Roberto

spent the morning in the operating room performing flaw-

lessly, conscious only of the movement of his scalpel

beneath the heavy whiteness of the six-bulb lamp. For

the length of the operation he reduced himself to his

functions, thought with his hands. But when it was over and he went into the locker room, discarding his soiled gown and gloves, he was acutely aware of his place in the world again.

After lunch with several colleagues he drove twenty minutes across the city to the Argentine Forensic Anthropology Unit. He had been excited when he first heard that a search was underway to recover the remains of the Disappeared and hopefully identify who they were. It was part of the effort by Alfonsín's government to make an accounting, tally the dead. Now he was going to be part of it. Even before he and Mercedes visited the grandmothers' office, Roberto had considered the implications of the unit's work. When he saw where his thinking was taking him he had backed away, frightened by images of bones. But the collage of missing children had broken his will to resist. He had thought of all the faces missing from the pictures, an array of men and women whose absence was somehow increased by the smiling children. He spent days wondering whether he was up to whatever role he might play. There were long discussions with Mercedes who said he should follow his heart. He knew little about forensics. If there was a place for him it would entail menial work, not that he minded. The only question was whether he could endure the process. When he called the team leader, Juan Gregorio Reyes had said of course they could use more help. He and his co-leader, an English anthropologist named Macalester, had more work than they could handle. Then he asked Reyes when he could start and there had been a pause on the line. "I don't mean to offend you," Reyes said delicately. "But doctors think they can take anything. Exhumations aren't like operations. We have the remains of a young man we've asked his mother to identify. Maybe you should come tomorrow and take a look. Then you can decide."

Roberto saw a white pickup truck with the unit's name on the door as he pulled into the parking lot. Picturing what he had come to see, he also remembered what the girl had said about the bones. The array in his mind suddenly became luminous, a necropolis without stones or earth.

When he told the secretary who he was she said, "The mother just arrived. It's the first room on the left."

He saw the door at the end of a long corridor, drew a deep breath, headed for it. The leather heels of his loafers made a loud clicking. Appalled by the sound, he slowed down, carefully letting his heels touch the surface more gently. It was the standard echo in halls in public places, generic, featureless. As he walked he had a precise memory of the professor in medical school who taught courses in forensic pathology. An émigré from Sweden, he was six feet six, with broad shoulders narrowing to a waist not much larger than a girl's. And he had loved his work, loved exploring the dead, finding hidden clues to whatever swept them away. A spelunker of body caverns. He would have been at home in this hall, Roberto thought. He stood a moment with his hand on the knob, interrogating himself one last time, as if he still had a choice. The feeling was no different than the one that had come upon him the first time he entered a classroom to dissect a cadaver.

Reyes and Macalester, both wearing lab coats, stood at the head of an aluminum table spread with a white sheet that formed a pristine backdrop for the bones. The mother, a tall, thick-set woman in her forties, was staring rigidly at her son's remains while Macalester watched, arms crossed, an unlit pipe clenched between his teeth, sorrow like a banner across his eyes. He was short and beefy, with a round,

ruddy face. A pale salt and pepper mustache made him look
both puzzled and jovial, though it could have simply been
the way the light from the fluorescent bulbs fell across his
face. He was well known, even more than the medical
school professor. Roberto had heard of him the way one
does the famous in their field, long before there was any
need for his services in Argentina. He had come to promi-
nence after exhuming Celtic bones from a peat bog. So far
as Roberto could tell, his fame was transparent. It was visible neither in his eyes as pride nor in the way he held himself. He seemed content, satisfied to simply be Macalester,
reader of bones and teeth.

Reyes, his protégé, was taller, very thin, younger than
he had sounded on the phone. He looked at Roberto as he
closed the door.

"Dr. Cristiani," he said. "This is Señora Helena Alberti."

Without looking up from the bones, the woman in-
clined her head slightly in acknowledgment. Roberto had
expected to find her weeping, but Helena's was a dry-eyed
sorrow. He was the one on the verge of tears as he glanced
again at the table.

Her son had been tall, probably slender. Beside his feet
were a discolored shirt, a belt with a small silver buckle
bearing his initials, J.A., and a wristwatch with one strap
missing, the crystal on its face smashed. Staring at the skeleton, Roberto felt a strange sense of intimacy. The emotion
was different from what happened when patients exposed
their bodies for examination in his office, or were immobi-
lized by anesthetic beneath operating room lights. Now he
understood what Reyes had meant. Flesh rode bones like a
pale velvet coverlet. This was essence, the final secret.
Looking at the skeleton was like reading a diary someone

had left open on a table. It felt like a terrible invasion of privacy, especially since Helena Alberti was there.

"Where did you find him?" she asked softly.

"A cemetery in the suburbs," Reyes said.

"Under an old grave," Macalester added. "It's not the first time."

"I knew he was gone a long time ago," Helena said. She stepped forward and picked up the watch, turning it over in her hands. "The time he died?"

"Perhaps," Macalester said in heavily accented Spanish. "That isn't something we're likely to know."

"I understand," she said as she put the watch back on the sheet. "It was a graduation present from his grandfather."

Roberto could see an inscription on the back of the watch; fortunately, the words were too small to read. His throat constricted. The bones blurred, swam into focus again. Like Helena, he harbored no more illusions that his child was still alive. For a long time he had nurtured his loss as an oyster does a pearl, until it was the best part of him. His pearl of grief had been the only one in the city, in all of Argentina, the only one in the world. After the girl came it lost its sheen, became a great aching void. And then it lost its uniqueness the day he saw the collage and had become aware that he was exactly like thousands of others deprived of the story that could fill the space hollowed out below their hearts by the generals. Because not knowing was a form of torture. No one could grieve properly, wring their hearts out when the last pages were missing. It was as if time had stopped for all of them and they were suspended in some terrible limbo of unknowing. What they needed, what they had to have, was knowledge. That was why he was standing there, beside Helena Alberti.

He watched her pick up the belt and run her fingers over the initials on the buckle. Then she carefully smoothed out the shirt, gazing at it with what seemed like an air of detachment, but which was really not that at all. He knew she was engaged in a silent act of repossession, as if touching her son's things, looking at them, would bring him closer. Darkened by its time in the ground, the shirt that had belonged to the boy who inhabited the bones was a relic as sacred to her as any a believer might gaze on in a glass case kept in a church. He was immensely relieved when she finally looked at Reyes.

"May I have his things? Do you need them?"

"Of course," Reyes said.

He removed a plastic bag from a drawer and handed it to her. After placing the watch, belt and shirt inside, she carefully sealed the bag and tried to put it in her purse, but it was too large and she clutched it awkwardly.

"Thank you," she said, letting her eyes stray once again over the bones. "At least now I know where he is."

Reyes said that in a few days she could arrange for the remains to be sent wherever she wanted. There were some papers to sign, if she was up to it.

"I'll show you out," he said.

She shook her head.

"I know the way."

When she closed the door Macalester stuck a match to his pipe and blew out a great billow of smoke. Roberto was wondering when she would let go, if it was happening now, in the corridor, or if she would wait until she got home.

"I'm amazed by her strength," he said.

"It's not unusual," Reyes replied. "People are relieved to know. Then it catches up, and they have to go through the grief all over again."

"The generals' gift," Macalester added dryly.

They all looked at each other, knowing there was nothing more to say.

Reyes sat down on a stool, crossed his legs.

"Do you still feel like getting involved?"

Roberto felt like going home. He wanted to draw the blinds and have a stiff drink.

"Yes," he said. "More than ever."

"Well," Reyes told him, "there's a site we need to start working on this afternoon. We use archaeological techniques. Applied to forensics cases, the methods allow us to recover much of the evidence. There are the bones, of course, teeth and hair. Bullet fragments help the ballistics people identify firearms."

"The bones are the primary evidence," Macalester said. "The ones who did the killing always stole the identity cards, but the clothes are almost always there. The bones are witnesses, the only ones we have in most cases. They all have stories to tell, but they're slow to speak. Finding out who they belonged to involves a long process. We measure the tibia, the femur, other bones and teeth, determine whether they belonged to a male or female. Then we compare them with medical records, dental records. If we're lucky, a name emerges."

Reyes said, "We'll fill you in on the rest at the site. We just received an anonymous tip. Someone photocopied the records of a suburban cemetery. It lists half a dozen N.N.'s. That's shorthand for no name."

Sorry as we were for Helena Alberti, we were also cheered by Macalester's tutorial. Hovering there in the room, aware of the brightness, the white walls, the depth of knowledge shared by the Englishman and Reyes, their words came to us like the promise of deliverance, like a match struck in darkness, for centered though they were on the loamy earth of the city, who was to say that their search might not expand? If the girl's memory did not return, then some other clue might emerge that would lead them to where we were, some unknown benefactor might point the way, indicate the place where a shovel's blade might pry up the rich dark earth, let in the light of day.

Roberto's hands began to sweat while Reyes backed the truck out of the parking lot. He could not recall it happening before. He tried to ignore the greasy sensation, but by the time they reached the cemetery his palms were as wet as if he had just scrubbed for an operation. He dried them on his thighs self-consciously, hoping that Reyes and Macalester wouldn't notice. It was a trivial thing, and he was slightly embarrassed that it mattered.

The mist that hung over the city in the morning had burned off and the sun was out, pleasantly warm. Roberto saw a line of roofs, power lines, let himself get used to the surroundings. The grass was half-burned, with splotches of green here and there among the stones. A young couple with two little girls in tow were kneeling beside a grave near the parking lot. The woman arranged flowers while her husband held the children's hands.

"Over there," Macalester said, gesturing with his pipe.

On the far side of the graveyard, in a plot of weeds backed by a wire fence, six men and women in work clothes were pounding stakes into the ground. The soft tapping carried a meaning far out of proportion to the sound.

"It's a slow process," said Reyes. "Once the grid is laid out we start with a test hole at what we hope is the foot of the grave. When the foot bones appear, we measure the exact depth so we'll know how far down it's safe to dig with shovels. Then we do some calculations, orient the grave to the area and the body. Let's go over and you can see how it's done."

After Reyes introduced him to the other team members, Roberto stood by the fence, watching them tie lengths of brown twine to the stakes, dividing the plot into neat squares. He admired the care they took stretching tape measures along the lengths of string, then recording the numbers in a notebook which replicated the grid they had made, each with its own coordinates. He wanted to immerse himself in the details, the science of squares, all of the coordinates, dimensions, contours, wanted to look on the process with the same detachment he had developed in relation to the human body. But as they worked he understood that this was only superficially a scientific enterprise. The truth was that they were exposing the flesh of the country crosshatched with accusations, each grid framing a testimony he clearly imagined, mirror images of the bones in the morgue, skulls with bullet holes, broken legs and arms. The vision was so real he had to turn away and look over the roofs of distant houses as he forced himself not to think of Ana María.

He was grateful when Reyes handed him a shovel and told him to start in a corner, take only a small amount of dirt and place it on a screen which the assistants would sift for clues. As soon as he began to dig he remembered the shattered watch, the buckle. He was immensely happy that all he found were a few stones and roots. It was Reyes who unearthed the left foot. Roberto watched until he reached the skull, turning away too late, its grinning jaw already reburied in his mind.

So it was that Roberto became a member of the Ezekiel squad, named by Macalester in ironic deference to the Scriptures. As the weeks passed, Roberto's once pale skin, almost sickly white from spending all his time indoors, turned brown under the sun. The smooth handles of shovels and picks raised blisters on his palms and fingers that slowly healed to calluses thick as any workman's. The muscles in his arms ached before they hardened. His back grew stiff, then supple. At night he studied books recommended by Reyes, often staying up well past his usual bedtime and retiring only after his eyes began to blur.

During the second week they went to a vacant lot in one of the city's poorer districts, a place once used as a soccer field by neighborhood boys who dreamed of fame and glory. The boys stood together at one end of the field, watching the squad pounding stakes into the ground, subdividing the bare earth into grids, returning the next day after school in time to see Reyes and Macalester exhume what remained of Mario Zefferelli, a philosophy student who had made the mistake of thinking he was free to speak his convictions one night when he was half-drunk at a tango bar. His bones were transported to the unit headquarters where they eventually supplied evidence against three old friends of Ernesto Siciliano. The men denied they had ever been to the district when they were brought before the judge who went home after the hearing, shaken to the core by the injuries Reyes had described.

A few days later they discovered Ricardo Galimberti in the backyard of a dilapidated house near La Boca where he had been buried after being tortured in the basement of the Naval Mechanics School. One rainy afternoon in a field where flowers were grown for city florists, they found the remains of a young woman who turned out to be Graciela García. Alicia Gillespie was found in a policeman's garden, Fernando Hernández in a car wrecking yard, under the fender of a defunct Renault. Week after week the bones bore witness, their stories separate chapters in a tale whose final shape still remained obscure. Relatives endured the silence, marched in the Plaza de Mayo, vowed never to forget. Some returned to the places where son or daughter, husband or wife, had last been seen, leaving flowers and other remembrances on a park bench, at a street corner, in the lobby of a theater. The man who had inscribed his son's image on the sidewalk, which the girl had passed on her way to release the birds, returned every Monday at noon with a box of colored chalk, carefully freshening the portrait of his son and the motto beneath it that the footsteps of pedestrians had scraped away. He worked diligently, passionately, as if drawing the image might collapse time, recall the past, so that he could pull his boy away from the grasping arms of the policemen who had jumped out of the car, its back doors left open to receive his son and close upon him like a vise.

These scenes and a hundred others unfolded before our greedy eyes as if we were in a movie house with a giant curving screen large enough to encompass every district of the city, watching people going through rituals invented to keep memory alive. We admired their strength, acknowledged their determination, but that was not enough to quench the bitterness of confinement in the white. Anger was as much our element as earth and grass, so it was only natural that our attention lingered on those who refused the well-worn shibboleths about life going on and all its attendant claptrap, which included trying to forget and even pretending the war had never happened. That was why we stayed so close to Roberto who ignored nostrums and platitudes, why we hovered over the marchers every Thursday afternoon, doing what we could to stretch their memories. It was why we visited the man patiently renewing the image of his son, and why we betook ourselves in ghostly silence every night to the Children's Theater where we perched in the rafters and waited apprehensively for the people who came to hear what Carlos had to say. We watched them coming down the aisles with the hope we would see a member of our families who might speak a name, telling enough of a broken story to enliven his imagination and release our bones from where they were interred.

Carlos had retreated into himself after the *Proceso* ended. Exhausted by the work he'd done, he grew skeptical of his abilities, saw his failure to find his daughter as a sign that perhaps his gift had departed as suddenly as it had come. Yet as the months wore on Carlos came to realize that he was no longer a private man, had not been since that night long ago when he had a vision of Enrico García's father in his prison cell and foretold his freedom. His gift had placed him outside the old world he had so happily lived in. Until Cecilia published *The Wall* he kept to himself. Afterward he took up his work again, this time in the theater where he had first discovered his powers and spoke of them so disbelievingly to Martín Benn.

Some nights only forty or fifty people showed up. On others, every seat in the house was filled with a mixture of newcomers and those who had once journeyed to his garden, restless, haunted people looking for stories that might at least confer the blessing of consolation. Whether the theater was half-empty or packed to the rafters, no supplicant ever waited more eagerly than we did for Carlos to appear from the wings and take his place on a wooden chair at the front of the stage. That was when we descended from the rafters quietly as spiders rappelling down a glistening filament, floating like motes of dust over the seats to the front of the theater where we appropriated the air before him,

gazing longingly into those cobalt eyes as we whispered our
names and those of the neighborhoods we had lived in.
There were nights when spectators craned their necks, convinced that words had come from the deep blue air, nights
when Carlos bestirred himself, attentive to a faint admoni-
tion. He still missed the aura of yellow light cast by paper
lanterns over the flagstones in his garden, missed the scent
of cyclamen and roses, trees that bent to the wind, the ritual
attentions of Cecilia and Teresa which, even on the worst
nights, when all he saw was devastation, had shielded him a
little from the things he had to say. But he did not dwell on
these absences. He accepted them, exchanging the warmth
of the garden he had abandoned because of the memories it
held of Teresa, for the bare boards of the stage where he
always sat immobile as an effigy before finally signaling to
the stagehand that the time had come. As the houselights
dimmed a single spotlight slanted down, its light surrounding him like an aura. Then he began to say what it was he
saw, responding in a voice wearier than it once had been
because only rarely now could he describe a journey, encourage a father to wait by the river, a mother to listen for a
knock at the door. Most often Carlos tilled the past just as
the Ezekiel squad tilled the earth, discovering places thick
with bones and dresses, shirts and plastic berets that once
held lovely hair in place, his stories and the unit's work
coalescing from time to time, proving Macalester prophetic
in the matter of tales that bones could tell.

In the course of Carlos' visitations to places only he
could see, basement cells in provincial police stations, neglected fields, rooms shuttered by venetian blinds in whose
soft light unspeakable things had occurred, he traversed the
length and breadth of Argentina, his memory cross-hatched
with roads and highways, alleys and narrow paths snaking

through tall grass. He had followed them so often in his imagination that he began to think of Argentina not as a dagger whose scabbard clung to the flank of a continent, but as a network of routes so numerous he was no longer sure which went east, which west and north and south. For a long time it seemed as if he were at the center of a hub whose spokes spread like ganglia pointing in the direction of the latest sorrow that was his gift to find. But one night he was struck by a singular revelation that shook him to his core.

Dolores Masson had gone to see him once again after learning that a promising lead about her grandsons had turned out to be false. He asked her name as he always did, listened as she repeated the story he remembered from her visits to his garden on Calle Córdoba. He saw a battered truck raising dust from a narrow rutted road near the mountain town of San Carlos de Bariloche, but even though he lost it then, the brake lights vanishing in a cloud, he made a discovery that would have stilled his voice even if he had been able to follow the Ponces' flight. For that road was no different than all the others his imagination had traveled down. The scattered routes he had traced from homes and schools and factories to where the abducted were taken was really only a single road leading into the whiteness where Teresa disappeared, a road cut through the heart of Argentina that now guttered out into nothingness.

That night we were perched in the rafters, content to watch and listen. But when the lines on the map of his mind converged, wrapping round each other until they were tight as braided steel, we descended until we swung back and forth just above the stage where we could get a good look at his eyes. What we wanted to see there was the ribbon of blacktop stretching through the pampas and branching off into the fields anchored by the ombu trees. But Carlos could not see that far, not that night. The revelation had exhausted the resources of his imagination, dried them up as desert air does shallow pools of water. A moment later he cut the evening short with a curt apology, then left confused and uncertain about what to make of the vision that had come upon him.

We hung there as the supplicants filed out into the night. Carlos left and the doors were closed and locked. In the darkness we saw the road all the way to its end, looking down the next morning upon the fields when the Carranza brothers, owners of an *estancia* called La Paloma, near Santa Rosalita, left their stables on an inspection tour of their property. It was a ritual with Luis and Alonso to drive an old horse-drawn carriage on these outings, which they went on once a month, even though their foreman or one of the gauchos they employed could have done it for them. They owned a new Land Rover and Honda dirt bikes that would have cut the time by several hours, but surveying their livestock, wheat fields and grasslands from the carriage their grandfather had imported from Spain at the turn of the century made them feel close to the land that had been in their family for over a hundred years. Gazing on the green-brown fields, letting their eyes roam across the horizon beneath the morning's overarching sky, was both an act of homage to their family and a way to swell their pride.

They had been riding for an hour behind the matched chestnut Percherons when they approached an ombu grove and Luis pointed with his whip toward a flock of sheep moving lazily in a circle from left to right. The animals' instinct was to bunch, and the configuration was peculiar enough for them to stop and watch. A buck strayed inside the circle and walked slowly, its head lowered, toward the trees. Then it froze. The Carranzas were close enough to see its soft brown eyes dilate with fear before it suddenly ambled back to graze.

If Luis and Alonso had not driven so slowly on the way out they might have gotten down from the carriage and inspected the site more closely. But they had miles to cover, and since the sheep appeared healthy despite their odd behavior, the brothers drove off toward the dirt road that intersected a paved one half a mile away, neither interested enough to look back where a flock of birds wheeled over the grove as if to perch on the branches, only to fly off in confusion and finally settle in the field well away from the trees.

The Carranzas did not know that the grove had a special place in the minds of gauchos. Unlike their grandfather or father who had maintained close relations with their men, Luis and Alonso had grown up surrounded by wealth and privilege, strictly limiting their contact with the gauchos and never crossing the line into intimacy. Because of this distance they remained ignorant of a discovery made by a man named Domingo who had worked on La Paloma for forty years.

Months earlier, as he was riding back to the bunkhouse after a day of mending fences, Domingo had stopped to rest his horse in the grove. He went under the trees to take a nap in the shade, and was about to settle down when he saw a strange and fearful thing, the outline of a woman impressed on the carpet of dead and decaying leaves. Domingo stared long enough to be certain it was not a trick of the light or his less than perfect eyes. The shape remained when the wind changed the pattern of the shadows. It was clear, unambiguous, precise. He took one last look and fled, riding so hard that his horse was lathered and wild-eyed by the time he dismounted and handed the reins to the stable boy, quickly instructing him to curry and comb the animal, which he had always enjoyed doing himself.

What Domingo saw quickly became a legend in the bunkhouse at La Paloma as well as those of nearby ranches. Though he had a reputation for veracity, he had been afraid to reveal the location of the figure, contenting himself with saying that he had seen what he had seen and keeping his own council because it seemed foolhardy to do otherwise. The story he told passed from ranch to ranch, added to by every mouth it passed through, especially those of men who were as superstitious as Domingo. By the time it reached an *estancia* a hundred miles to the west, the shape had become a spirit who wandered far and wide on nights when the moon was full. People heard her calling in the fields, begging someone to take her home.

For months the story was the exclusive property of gauchos who embellished it with every telling, but soon it migrated from the ranches to the towns. Children heard their parents tell it late at night, listening through closed bedroom doors, and they in turn brought it to school yards where they scared each other with lurid details more macabre than any their parents or the gauchos thought to add. By the time Tomás and Manfredo heard it at recess one hot afternoon, the spirit was capable of withering a limb if you were within the sound of her voice. The sight of her could blind an eye, make you deaf. She could, at will, bring the dead to life. Like other children, the Ponce boys sometimes dreamed of her chasing them down and taking them back to where she lived. In their braver moments, they speculated about where she might be found.

Living on the outskirts of Santa Rosalita had been hard on them. They chafed at the isolation, begged Eduardo and Beatriz to find a house in town. They resentfully watched the occasional car coming along the road, and then wished they were in it, going anywhere, so long as it was away from Santa Rosalita. Only gradually did they accept their lot and develop an interest in the gauchos they sometimes saw riding in the distance. These men became romantic figures to the boys who thought of being like them when they were grown. Their capes, wide-brimmed hats and thick knee-length boots had a fine appeal that turned into a kind of fascination. They began to appreciate adventures denied the boys in town. Manfredo discovered old trails and caught and pinned butterflies to pasteboard squares. Tomás became a budding entomologist, fascinated by ugly insects he kept in a dozen jars on the shelf above his bed. On Saturdays they went on expeditions, supplied with sack lunches Beatriz made for them, with the warning that they had to return well before dinnertime.

One windless spring day they left soon after breakfast, armed with Manfredo's butterfly net and Tomás' rucksack filled with bottles. Tomás wanted to follow their usual route, angling northwest from the house, but Manfredo was tired of the same old thing and persuaded his brother to go in the opposite direction, which led them, hours later, to our grove.

We heard them coming long before they reached us. Except for Domingo and the Carranzas, they were the only people who had approached the site after our killers drove away and the girl rose from the leaves imprinted with her shape. The soft padding of their feet, the rhythmical measure of the living, was sweet as music to us. We listened for the faintest inflection, the subtle lulls and crescendos of their movement, as if our bones were arrayed in the plushest seats of an opera house.

So it was that they came to where we were. When they

stopped at the edge of the grove we urged them forward, pleaded with them to explore the soft green shade further into the grove where they would have been struck by the way the light came through the canopy of leaves, bright as fire. A shape on the ground would have caught their eyes. They would have been drawn to it, would have approached and then stopped suddenly, gasping with surprise and fear because there on the ground, surrounded by leaves, was the shape of the girl that had entered Domingo's imagination. They, too, would have gaped at the outline of her head and disheveled hair, the way her arms were thrown out on either side, the line made by the hem of her dress ending just below her knees. A deep thrill of fear would have risen up from the very core of their beings as they backed away, remembering the stories, afraid she might be somewhere near, ready to pluck out an eye, shrink an arm or leg. They would have carried the story home and then to school where the other boys and girls would have taken it with them and offered it to their parents. Within hours scores of people would have ventured out to the spot.

But that was not the way it happened. Just as they were about to enter Tomás stopped short.

"What's wrong?" Manfredo said.

"Look," Tomás answered as he pointed to the grass. He stooped and retrieved an earring, holding the small oval shape up to his eyes where it glittered in the sun.

"It's gold," he said excitedly. "Maybe there's another."

There was, of course, five feet underground, its brightness interred with Alessandra Ricci who had put the earrings on the morning of her abduction because they pleased her lover, Marco. Never in all the time that had passed since we were trapped in lantern light had we coveted the power of speech more than at that moment. Our efforts in the

Children's Theater to plant our names in Carlos' mind seemed like a game compared with the opportunity that was so tantalizingly close. Alessandra's name should have leaped like a bird to the earring Tomás was burnishing on his shirt. It should have announced to everyone who cared to know that we were there, opened the final chapter of our stories. All that was necessary was air passing over vocal cords, the softest enunciation of those syllables. But yearn as we did for sound, coaxing what passed for our voices into a chorus chanting, Alessandra, Alessandra, the weight of the earth kept us mute, the sound of a bird's wing creaking in its socket a thousand times louder than any we could utter. So we could only watch despairingly as the boys eagerly combed the grass before heading home, delighted with their treasure.

Beatriz immediately assumed that the earring belonged to a rancher's wife who had lost it while out for a ride. For safekeeping, she put it in the basket with her sewing things.

"I'm sure it belongs to one of the women," she told Eduardo when he came home.

Without crediting her interpretation, Eduardo questioned the boys sharply. When they finished telling him everything, he asked each of them if there was anything they might have forgotten. They looked at each other, then at him, shaking their heads. He thought about what they said during dinner, considered Beatriz's idea. There was an hour or two of daylight left, plenty of time to drive out and take a look.

When they reached the grove Eduardo carefully examined the ground. Except for the strange color of the grass, nothing seemed unusual. He gazed beyond the space to the dirt road where he had parked his truck, turning the earring over in his fingers as he made some calculations in his head, measured distance, considered time. He did not like the feeling of the place. In its isolation it seemed to avail itself of augury, bad luck, his old familiars. The site was a minute's walk from the dirt road, isolated, unlikely ever to be visited. There was only one reasonable explanation for the earring being there. Stories of *matanzas* he had heard in the old days came back to him, and by the time he herded the boys into the truck he had decided there was only one possible conclusion to be drawn: his sons had stumbled across a killing field.

Back at the house he locked the earring in a strongbox, brusquely telling Beatriz to mind her own business when she asked what he was doing. Then he apologized, saying he was sorry he had shouted. Her eyes looked bruised as they always did when she was hurt, but he was not in the mood to coax her out of it. He had his own problems to deal with, starting with the boys.

"I want you to promise me something," he told them. "I want you to promise you won't say anything about this, not even to your best friends."

There was a seriousness in his voice they knew too well. Crestfallen, they agreed and were only a little mollified when he said he would take them to a soccer game the following weekend and to lunch in the café where the players ate. Then he sent them to bed, looking in after they were settled and telling them he hoped they would sleep well.

In the living room Beatriz looked at him. She was perplexed and still irritated.

"What was that all about?"

Eduardo sat down beside her, avoiding her gaze. He had hoped she would catch on, but one look at her made it clear she hadn't.

"Maybe somebody did lose it, but there's another explanation."

Beatriz had no idea where he was going.

"Bodies are out there," he said quietly. "People are buried there."

"Who?" she asked.

"Do I have to tell you?"

Beatriz had approved of the war, never questioned the need to repress the traitors. Her ideas had always been married to Eduardo's, but when it came to discussing the methods of repression she turned a deaf ear to her husband, telling him emphatically that she had no interest in learning about what was done. She had lived in a cocoon of self-imposed ignorance throughout the war, and now Eduardo's announcement struck her like a fist. She stared at him ashen-faced, appalled by what she'd heard.

"That's right. Not three miles away. If anyone finds out there'll be an investigation. The authorities will ask questions. They'll come to the house, go to the neighbors. You have no idea where it'll end. I need to think about this."

And think he did, long into the night, hours after Beatriz fell into a troubled sleep. There was undoubtedly more than one body since the death squads favored groups, massacres being more efficient than single executions. He felt the old panic surfacing. Then he tried to calm himself. There was no reason to worry. The bones weren't going anywhere. If word of them did not get out they would remain lost, unknown. He could easily live on their margin because he felt no guilt. His part in the *Proceso* had demanded nothing in the way of overt violence, left him with unbloodied hands. He recalled his work with a sense of pride and then regret as he saw how quickly it had disappeared once the regime disintegrated. Memory served up images of all the

places they had lived since then, always running to save the
boys from the grandmother he knew was looking for them,
some old crone he imagined in a shapeless dress, working
toothless gums. No matter where he went he could not leave
the war behind, never get far enough away. It followed him
like a wind, was as tenacious as disease. He saw himself and
Beatriz and the boys as refugees. They weren't in rags, they
always had enough to eat, but they had learned to carry
their lives on their backs, whittling away their possessions
so that everything could fit into the truck he had bought
after having to sell the old but still elegant Alfa Romeo that
had been his pride and joy. Miserable as these recollections
made him feel, there was no sense of panic rising from his
heart following the initial fear. This new state of affairs gave
rise to no intimations of danger that had always been the
case before and was the signal to pack and run. Nothing
connected him to the grave. He bore no responsibility for
what had happened. His panic had been generic, a gut reaction, nothing more. He did not have to pull up stakes again,
be driven away by the undiscovered dead. The only tie was
the earring whose circle bound nothing to nothing. Tomás
and Manfredo were sensitive, obedient boys. One of the
pleasures of fatherhood was molding their minds, teaching
them the virtues of prudence and responsibility. But this
situation was different he thought as he turned on his side
and looked at his sleeping wife. He had taught them principles, insisted on good behavior, obedience to their elders.
Their backsliding was never serious, never occasioned more
than a mild rebuke. Now he questioned the nature and
depth of his instruction, the roles the boys played in his life.
He was more than a little horrified to discover the truth that
we had patiently, joyfully watched making its way to the
front of his consciousness. His sons had become antagonists,

the possibility of their youthful indiscretion the source of danger and undoing. In the morning he would have a long talk with them, make it clear that the subject of the earring was beyond debate, their silence a vow they dare not break. Then he would have Beatriz talk to them, too. That would be enough to keep the bones interred.

FOURTEEN

The Good Wife

You know as well as we do that a shift in perception sometimes has to occur before certain objects take on their true significance, come out from behind the mask our ignorance has imposed and show themselves for what they are. Such was the case with Beatriz Ponce and Alessandra's earring.

Before Eduardo's visit to the fields, Beatriz was certain she knew the earring's history. She had a precise image of a wealthy woman, Alonso Carranza's wife, riding in the pampas on a blooded mare when the jewelry had come loose from the lobe of her ear because of something as simple as having neglected to slip the catch firmly into place. In a life that had become increasingly uncertain since the advent of the boys, Beatriz liked giving order to chance events. It made her feel more in control of her destiny. The story of the earring was easy to invent since she had actually seen the woman riding with friends on half a dozen occasions, and had come across her in town where Beatriz admired her clothing and jewelry. The picture in her mind had been precise enough to make her feel jealous of Silvia Carranza, and then think longingly of the time when she was so much better off than she was now. To her credit, this envy did not dampen her inherent sense of honesty, which made it impossible for her to keep the earring, or sell it and give the money to the boys, which was what they thought might happen.

But everything changed the moment Eduardo told her about the site. Silvia Carranza and her rich friends vanished, leaving an image of green grass circling the earring whose old-fashioned oval shape and lustrous glow reminded her of things she would rather not confront but found impossible to avoid. She imagined the popping sounds of gunfire. Her mind's eye filled with toppling bodies. In an instant the reality she had refused to acknowledge came to life. She would never forget the suddenness of it, nor the sickness that came upon her as she lay in bed later, pretending to be asleep because she was afraid to speak.

The most important thing was to protect herself. Beatriz was glad when Eduardo locked the earring in the strongbox. She approved the sternness of his lecture to the boys. But within a day her determination to forget she'd ever seen the earring turned into nagging curiosity. The more she tried to ignore it, the more it played on her mind. She resisted the temptation for a week. Then one morning she rushed into the bedroom for the key and unlocked the strongbox.

The whorls of Eduardo's fingerprints were visible when she held it to the light. She polished it with the cloth she used on her remaining jewelry. Her thoughts strayed to the stores and bars where she had handed over most of her bracelets and necklaces and rings to men who bought them for wives or girlfriends. She imagined women wearing her things, and then she tried to imagine who had worn the earring in her hand.

Every day for the next two weeks Beatriz removed the strongbox from the kitchen drawer. Sometimes she unlocked it only minutes after Eduardo and the boys left for work and school. Often, though, she waited until lunch or late in the afternoon. On weekends her obsession was dictated by the comings and goings in the house.

The routine was always the same. First she went into the bedroom and got the key from the top dresser drawer. Then she returned to the kitchen, took out the box and unlocked it, slipping the curved arm of the padlock through the D ring so she would be sure not to misplace it. She had wrapped the earring in a square of tissue paper that she unfolded as carefully as a diamond dealer preparing to display his wares. Holding it in the flat of her hand, she let the light from the kitchen window bring out the deep yellow of the gold. Then she put it on the table where it glowed against the white oilcloth, studying it with the same intensity of purpose an anthropologist brings to a shard of pottery, someone who sees far more than a faded object, letting it build in his imagination, filtering its shape and markings through his knowledge until it becomes part of an amphora, acquires a history replete with date and place.

Working backward from the false origin of Silvia Carranza, Beatriz first imagined the way it had looked to Tomás, a small circle of gold lying in a bed of grass, half-obscured with dust. From that point she slipped further into the past. A faceless woman appeared, neither young nor old, standing in the pampas. It was the moment that the anthropologist would have seen the shard become part of an amphora, but whereas his discovery would have been occasion for celebration, Beatriz Ponce burst into tears.

Shuddering, she tried to decide the age of its owner. For some reason she concluded it must have belonged to a young woman who might have looked like Camila Estragón, the daughter of the couple who lived half a mile down the road. She wanted to freeze her imagination at that point, concede the resemblance to Camila, isolate her the way a cameo's profile is set against a pure white background. That way she would not have to see the family. It was the same thing she had done in the past whenever she started thinking about the boys' relatives. She had succeeded in confining their family to the faceless cadre of enemies of the state, but her effort to shut out the woman's people failed. Despite everything she did to stop herself, she imagined a mother and then a mother's grief, sympathetically entering it with the crushing knowledge of how it would feel to lose her sons.

After that Beatriz tried hard to stay away from the strongbox. She cooked elaborate meals that required hours of preparation, cleaned the house until it gleamed, took long walks on the road. When none of these distractions worked, she acquiesced and placed the box on the table but did not go into the bedroom for the key, thinking she might be able to satisfy her need by simply staring at the gunmetal gray shape the way an alcoholic does an unopened bottle as he imagines the scent and taste of the liquor. But her determination to go no further always failed, and she would retrieve the key which she put on the table before walking into the living room where she looked miserably at the box for upward of an hour at a time. Eventually she opened it, removed the earring, felt anew the grief of the unknown mother.

Beatriz understood exactly why Eduardo had demanded that the boys say nothing about their discovery. She respected his wishes and valued them, sometimes even more than she did her own. She was a good wife and she loved Eduardo as much as she had when they were married twenty years ago. She grieved more for him than for herself or the boys whenever circumstances drove them away from one place in search of another that might be safer. But the story that began to fill the whiteness behind the profile of the daughter, the grief of the faceless mother, the sense of loss she continued to feel with every passing day, soon began to override Beatriz's natural affections and to erode her respect for what Eduardo wanted. She imagined the mother sitting alone in a room, looking at a photograph, imagined her helplessness when she tried to conceive of what had happened to her daughter, where in all the vastness of Argentina she might be. Against her will, she began to consider the nature of her fidelity to Eduardo.

We felt no sympathy for Beatriz's dilemma. She was part of the *Proceso*, after all. We would have made her see even more if we had the power, made her think not only of Alessandra's mother but of all the mothers of all the Disappeared. We would have shown her things from which she would never have recovered. But our pleasure and our hope remained a matter of observation. We listened greedily to the dialectic in her mind, approved of the way her conscience bit into her heart, applauded the day she suddenly rose from her chair in the kitchen, groaning because she had reached a point where she could no longer stand the pain.

The next Tuesday morning, an hour after Eduardo and the boys had left, Beatriz sat in the kitchen, her heart filled with recriminations and self-loathing as great as she would feel if she had just returned home after leaving the bed of another man. Her conscience was stronger than her sense of loyalty. It filled her up, displacing Eduardo as water does the emptiness of a glass. And so she dried her eyes, carefully wrapped the earring in its tissue and placed it in a zippered compartment in her purse. At the door she hesitated, standing with her hand on the knob and hoping that something would change, that she could find a reason not to go outside. When she took her first step toward town she was overcome with a feeling of betrayal.

Beatriz wanted to walk the two miles like a blinkered horse, but she could no more keep her eyes on the road than she could will her heart to stop. The grove was partly visible in the distance, a dark smudge on the horizon, slightly round on top. She wondered how long ago the *matanza* had happened, how many people had lost their lives and whether Eduardo and her boys had stood on the spot where they were buried. It would have been at night. She had seen headlights from time to time when she stayed up late, and the lights of the cars or trucks that had taken them there would have looked exactly the same. She imagined the beginning of a scenario, heard doors opening, voices, and then, fearing illness, she shut her mind down, willed it closed.

It was a relief to reach the first buildings that cut off the view. She stared at the storefronts, grateful that the place where Eduardo worked was on the far side of town, well beyond where she was going. She stopped at the grocery and made herself look at the vegetables neatly piled in pyramids and the cases of melons glowing in the midday sun. She passed the pharmacy, the veterinarian hospital, a bar. When she reached the police station, a squat, one-story white building with a patrol car parked outside, she let it swim past on the edge of her vision as she quickened her step and kept up the pace until she reached the corner half a block away where she sat down heavily on a shaded bench and watched people strolling by. Aware as she was of her distress, she also felt disengaged, as if she were hovering above the street looking down at her body, regarding herself as someone else would, as Eduardo would. She wondered what he would feel if he learned what she was doing. Until she had conjured the mother of the woman whose earring was in her purse, she had never believed very strongly in the ability to enter into another's emotions.

Now she did.

Now she was an expert. She knew exactly how the betrayal would cut like a knife, how his mind would reel with disbelief. What she imagined was horrible, but the mother's grief was worse. The anguish of this woman she had never seen was already pulling her up from the bench and propelling her in a slow, halting walk back down the street.

It was cool inside the police station. The main room was bright, neat, orderly in a military way. A sergeant named Constantino asked if he could help and she said no, she wanted to see the chief.

"It is an emergency?"

"Yes."

She watched Constantino enter the door in the back and come out a minute later, followed by Fernando de la Hoya who was a little more overweight than she remembered. He had gray hair and a neat mustache and brown eyes that seemed kind and gentle.

"I have to speak to you," she said haltingly.

"Yes?"

"Privately, if you don't mind."

She managed to hold back her tears until he closed the door and offered her a seat opposite his desk.

"What can I do for you?" Fernando asked quietly.

In response she opened her purse, removed the square of tissue. With shaking hands she unfolded the paper and put the earring on his desk. It looked very small, tiny, its size wildly out of proportion to what it signified.

"I want you to see this but I can't let you have it for long. Please understand. Tell me I can keep it. Otherwise, I'll have to leave."

Fernando de la Hoya looked at her, then nodded, acquiescing against his principles and good investigative procedures because he did not like the idea of adding to her pain. He picked it up.

"You found it?"

"In a manner of speaking."

"We usually don't deal with lost property."

"It wasn't lost."

"You know who it belongs to?"

"In a manner of speaking."

"Why don't you just give it to her?"

Beatriz's breath caught. Looking down at her lap, she stared at her intertwined fingers. Her wedding band glowed like a beacon of accusation.

"That's impossible," she said, her words heavy on her tongue, leaden, more bitter than she thought they could be.

"Why?"

"Because she's dead. It came from the pampas."

She raised her eyes. Fernando de la Hoya was looking at her, obviously waiting for her to go on. She could not. She thought of Eduardo's trusting expression, the way he always confided in her even when he was angry. The demands of the unknown mother had reached as far into her soul as she could permit and she could only return the officer's gaze, look at him with unblinking eyes.

"From the pampas," she said slowly. "From the pampas," she said as if repeating a catechism.

And then she saw it happen. She had never actually spoken to Fernando de la Hoya, had only seen him a few times, yet in that instant she felt she knew him intimately. He had become transparent to her, the working of his mind as familiar as her husband's. He had been smiling quizzically, but with the repetition of the word his face settled into a startled, then a fixed expression. Not a muscle moved. It was his eyes that gave him away.

"Yes," she said. "The ombu grove."

Fernando watched her get up shakily and leave, moving as if she had aged ten years during their interview. She passed Constantino without looking at him and went through the entrance, leaving the door ajar so Fernando could see her standing on the sidewalk, her purse clutched under one arm as she stared across the street. He was worried about her and was ready to go out and ask if she would like a cup of tea when she took a step with what appeared to be enormous effort and passed out of sight. As Constantino glanced back at his boss, his eyebrows raised in curiosity, Fernando de la Hoya quickly got up and closed the office door so his assistant would not come in and ask questions he was not prepared to answer.

Fernando had expected some petty complaint, at the

most a story about being abused by her husband, a strange, off-putting man with a sour expression who always seemed to be hiding something. He wished that had been the case, wished it had been anything but what it was. Before she arrived he had been enjoying the day. He was in the middle of a report to the regional director and had found a perfect way to request additional funds. Now he could not even remember what he had planned to say. The earring which he picked up and held to the light so he could see the jeweler's mark proclaiming it twenty-four-carat gold cut him off from the present and sent him reeling into the past, collapsing time and all the efforts he had made to forget, its tiny circle framing his sister's distraught face as he opened the front door of his house and let sorrow in with his nephew's name.

Víctor had been his favorite among Consuela's three boys, more like a son than a nephew. When he was a boy, he had been in love with the idea that his uncle was a policeman and had told Fernando dozens of times that he wanted to be just like him. Fernando had been happy when Víctor grew up and went off to Buenos Aires to study medicine. A doctor in the family would be wonderful. He had received a letter from Víctor only a few days before Consuela appeared on his doorstep, just as he and his wife were getting ready for bed. Ever since then he had been trying to forget the horrible sound of her voice when she told him that Víctor had disappeared.

A thin crust, like a scab, had formed over the remembered sound in the years since then, muting it enough so that sometimes it seemed far away. But he heard it again now, remembered the look in Consuela's eyes, the way she had stuttered and sobbed as she begged him to do something, anything, to bring Víctor back. He remembered the way her eyes had gone dull after he told her there was nothing a provincial policeman could do. He remembered his helplessness, his rage, the little daily battles to go on with his life. He stared at the top of his desk, at the half-filled page, the sentence that had been interrupted by the plain-looking woman in a worn print dress. There was nothing he could do for Víctor, never had been. Cursing, Fernando swiveled in his chair and picked up the phone.

Roberto went along the hall toward Juan Reyes' office, thinking of all the times he had gone down that pristine tunnel before driving to a site whose every detail mocked the purity of its shining walls. He had begged off for three days running, and wished he had called again today. What he had seen recently, harrowing things all his years of practice had not prepared him for, left him exhausted long before he returned to the Villa Deamicis where he spent the evenings drinking too much and looking for an excuse to quit.

He was on the verge now. He did not want to be here, approaching the door. What he wanted was to turn around, return to the hospital and call Reyes, say that he had reached his limit, that the exhumations had tattooed his mind with images that came back like a plague in the middle of the night, and stayed long after he woke up sweating, his heart beating wildly. He could deal with the hypocrisy of quitting. The slow sloughing off of his commitment would leave him raw but intact. The problem was that he had developed enough skills to be useful to people like Helena Alberti. He was trapped in his burgeoning expertise, a prisoner of bones and measurements.

Reyes had his feet up on the desk, the cleats of his work boots studded with dried clay.

"You look like shit," he said as Roberto sat down.

"Thank you," Roberto answered crisply. "It always helps to hear something cheerful." He glanced at Reyes' boots, the papers piled high on his desk. "Where to today?"

"The same as last week."

Roberto groaned inwardly. It was one of the worst sites he had seen.

Reyes studied him over the top of his glasses.

"You don't have to."

Roberto made an impatient gesture as Reyes skimmed a sheet of paper from the pile and handed it to him.

"This came yesterday. Macalester went down to investigate."

Roberto scanned the report stating that a policeman in Santa Rosalita had evidence of a possible site. An artifact had been presented as proof.

"What do they mean, 'artifact'? It sounds like a treasure hunt."

"An earring. I called the source in Santa Rosalita, a provincial magistrate. Someone found it on the pampas." Reyes swung his feet off the desk. "I can't get away if this turns out to be something, but Macalester could use you. You could go with the second crew."

Roberto saw a teardrop shape, distinct, unusual, glittering against his daughter's ear. He saw her face break into a smile as she stood in front of her dressing table, heard her saying thank you.

"Did he say what it looked like?"

"Just that it was gold."

"How long?"

Reyes shrugged. "A week? It's hard to tell. Could you get away from the hospital?"

"I'll take some vacation time."

Roberto would have probably agreed to participate even if there hadn't been an earring. Despite the nightmares, the fear of what he would have to see every afternoon, the emotional exhaustion, the team needed him. Reyes had appealed to his conscience as well as his vanity, but his decision rested on the earring. It's important to know this because it marked the beginning of a new phase in the Cristianis' lives and in the life of the girl as well.

Roberto's memory had cast up an image of a birthday present to Ana María clear as a photograph, chilling as a piece of tagged evidence lying on a courtroom table. It had taken an enormous act of will to deny the certainty he felt at that moment that it belonged to his daughter, but it had been absolutely necessary. Otherwise, the ground would have opened up then and there, swallowed him whole. Roberto forced himself to consider possibilities and was encouraged by the infinite numbers he conceived. Though the odds against it belonging to Ana María were huge, the doubt did not go away. It was like a hairline fracture in a bone, ready to cause untold damage at some unforeseeable moment. We sympathized with him of course, but not enough to affect the excitement running through us. Forces were convening on people separated by hundreds of miles. Who among you would not have rejoiced as we did when it became apparent that the hunt was on?

Roberto did not mention the earring when he told Mercedes about his conversation with Reyes. He said only that there was evidence of a possible site in the pampas. Later in the week, after Macalester confirmed it, Roberto said he had to go and she did not object. Grim as the occasion was, she agreed that it would be good to get away for a while. Besides, her aunt lived a day's drive from Santa Rosalita, on the coast. They could visit Flora when he finished. In the meantime, she and the girl would come out in the car. A change of scene might help her, too.

Half an hour before dawn on the following Monday, the unit's Ford Broncos headed out of the city along streets that were deserted except for the occasional delivery truck and garbage vans pouring diesel smoke into the violet air. Sitting in the back of the first truck between two of Reyes' graduate students, Roberto stared absently at the thin ribbon of sky that looked tentative and weak against the roofs and cupolas and spires. He was beginning to hate the city. What he had loved about it, the frenetic, crowded avenues, the store windows presenting glitter and amusement, the vast kinetic energy of the place where he had been born and raised had become mendacious, sinister. Nothing was as it seemed.

Before long the suburbs thinned out. The driver switched off the headlights when the sun came up, and they rode into the brightening day, stopping at a roadside inn for lunch and then continuing through the monotony of the pampas, which was broken occasionally by stands of trees, ranches, dusty towns.

The sun swept across the sky. Night came on. The headlights of approaching cars revealed five faces, stark and unarticulated in the glare.

During the day they had talked to kill time and boredom, but since dusk they had ridden in silence, caught up in thoughts of what lay ahead, the preliminary effort with shovels, picks and spades, then the work that could only be done on bended knees with paintbrushes whose soft bristles would sweep away the last layer of dirt, with toothpicks they would use to pry into fractures, and finally with their breath blown through pursed lips brought close to bones. They were reading from the same script, preparing for a task none of them had ever gotten used to but which they performed because no one else had the skills to make lost bones speak, give up their secrets. They all saw the things that would accumulate in neatly labeled piles, clothes, shoes, keychains, good luck charms, but only Roberto saw the earring, thankful that it was still only a circle of gold that did not necessarily bear any resemblance to the teardrop shape of those he had given Ana María. He thought of crowded streets, the flashes of color half-hidden between neck and hair, the thousand shapes he had never noticed but took comfort in because they numbered the odds against the one that had been found.

The Hotel Olimpo was nondescript but serviceable. Macalester greeted them in the lobby and insisted on buying a round of drinks in the bar where a sleepy young man in his twenties seemed put upon by the latecomers. Roberto's legs felt rubbery. He said a glass of wine would finish him. They agreed to meet at six for breakfast. He went upstairs, looking at the room numbers on the doors until he found his own. After putting away his things, he ran water in the sink and bathed his face. Dark half-moons bloomed under his eyes. He pulled down one eyelid, inspected it balefully. Then he got out of his clothes and slipped on his robe against the chill.

He stood by the window that opened onto the main street, dully noting the signs. *Almacén, Tienda el Cielo, Farmacia.* A truck with a defective muffler roared by. His eyes followed it down the street, then swept left toward the site Reyes had circled in red on the map. It glowed in his mind like the truck's single taillight, refusing to vanish into the night. He felt profoundly lonely, isolated from everything he knew. It would have been better if they had driven all night and arrived at dawn, just in time for a bite to eat before going to the fields. That way he could have had company and talked about a thousand things that might have spun his mind away from the idea, the possibility, captured in the red circle. Because being alone was dangerous. There were no barriers to deflect an idea, no voices to draw out the one thrumming in his head, no faces to blur his daughter's face hovering in front of him, inches from his eyes. He tried to concentrate on the signs dimly illuminated by the streetlight. Suddenly he wished they were the brilliant greens and blues and yellows of the city's neons, a cacophony of color that might distract him. But nothing worked. He could conjure neither the faces of the Ezekiel squad nor the broad sweep of the pampas nor the lights flashing off and on along Calle Florida. Only the red circle.

He was shivering. He pulled the lapels tight as he looked toward the darkness. The idea slipped out from where it had been hiding, like the moon from behind a cloud. It fit perfectly over the red circle in his mind.

Oh God, he whispered. Don't let her be there.

The girl sat in her slip at Ana María's dressing table while Mercedes combed her hair. She had been agitated all morning, wandering restlessly around the apartment and asking Mercedes every fifteen minutes when they were leaving. She had only grudgingly submitted to Mercedes' comb.

"You'll like Flora," Mercedes said, looking at her in the mirror. "She's my favorite aunt. They have horses. We can go riding."

The girl smiled vaguely as her eyes followed Mercedes' hand whose rings reflected the light with every stroke. She seemed calmer, less agitated, and Mercedes was grateful. She had enough to worry about with Roberto whose work with the unit had worn him down. There wasn't much left of him when he came home. She hoped they found the bones right away because she wanted to see him walking on the beach, and later stoking a fire at night in Flora's spacious living room. Most of all she wanted him to come back from where the work had taken him.

The girl broke her thought with a sudden movement of her head as she looked toward the window.

"Did you hear?" she asked.

"What?"

She cocked her head, listened.

"Bells."

Mercedes hadn't heard a thing. She glanced at her watch. It was twenty minutes before the carillon in the church down the street would sound.

"You're imagining," she said lightly. "Now hold still. You have a snag."

"They were like bells, the noise she made in the dark. The morning they took her she had on a long-sleeved dress and they couldn't see her bracelets. She had rings and a pearl necklace that they stole but not the bracelets and the earrings. I always knew where she was, like a bird that sings while it's hiding. I heard them in the grass and in the yellow light, but it was different then. The sound was cold as ice. The lawyer talked about the sound because it reminded him of his wife. He was writing when they came, sitting at his desk. His boys were playing on the floor. He said it was only to help an old woman with her bills, but they said he was writing things against them and that was why they'd come. He told his wife to run. She took the boys and they ran away and his heart broke when he saw them go. He said their names over and over. I think . . ."

Mercedes stared at her. The brightness in the girl's face was already replaced by the familiar mask.

"What do you think, *cara*?"

The girl stared at Mercedes, her brow furrowed, sunk back into wherever she lived her days.

Mercedes watched her in the mirror, amazed by the animation that came into her face, bright as a handful of coins, whenever she delivered herself of a story. Odd as they were, they seemed to pave the way out of the interiority she lived in, like the round stones in the garden leading to the gate. She waited, not wanting to break the spell, hoping that more stories would be put down. But the luster was gone from her eyes. Mercedes had stopped combing the moment the girl cocked her head. She lowered her hand, rings gleaming in the vanity's bulbs, and began again, wondering if the soothing action of being groomed might have triggered the story.

"Let me finish. You're still tangled."

The girl did not want any more. Twisting away, she went over to the bed and sat down.

"I'll get your dress," Mercedes said. She removed a green cotton print, slipped it off the hanger and put it down beside her. "This is perfect for travel. It won't wrinkle or show dirt."

The girl crossed her arms, regarded her petulantly.

"You don't like it?"

She shook her head.

"Which, then?"

"The white."

"That's not a good idea," Mercedes said patiently. "It's linen. We'll be driving all day. You'd be a mess before we got there." She touched the green dress. "Just try it on. You'll look pretty."

Glaring at Mercedes, she shouted, "White white white!" She put her hands to her hair on both sides of her head, pressing her temples. Then she ran her fingers through her hair, fanning it out in disheveled wings so that she seemed to be facing into a high wind. Without looking at Mercedes, she skimmed the green dress from the bed-spread and tossed it across the room. Mercedes shrugged and nodded. There was something manic about her, a kind of desperation as she went to the wardrobe and removed the dress. Pulling it over her head, she smoothed the skirt, then fastened the buttons. The stains were still faintly visible. She seemed calmer as she looked at Mercedes. The anger was gone from her eyes, replaced by a slightly dazed concentration.

"Riding," she said in a pinched, almost frantic voice. "When are we riding?"

Mercedes felt out of her depth. It had happened before, on more than one occasion, but never like this. All the progress the girl had made seemed to be unraveling.

"Everything's packed," she said evenly.

Mercedes carried the luggage to the elevator. Neither spoke on the way down. Their silence was broken by Guillermo Calvino's blaring television as soon as the door opened. The voice of the soccer announcer filled the foyer. Telling her to wait until she came for the other suitcase, Mercedes picked up the heavy one and went out to the car.

The girl watched the door close and stared a moment at the seagull before approaching the pier glass. Above the shouting crowd she heard the jingle of bracelets, the fragment of a song. She looked at herself in the mirror, ran her fingers through her hair. Something was happening to her. There was a pressure deep inside her chest. She stepped closer, touched her reflection, as if trying to make contact with herself through the glass.

Mercedes appeared behind her.

"Come," she said, and taking the girl by the arm, guided her through the door.

The girl was restless as they drove through the city. The shapes of buildings, lamp poles, cars, vacant lots reflected off her eyes, leaving no impression save for the faint residue of frustration. Why should it have been otherwise? What had drawn her interest long ago as she emerged from the alley, the infinite weave of stone and glass and metal into what then were strange and frightening shapes, was now a veil separating her from what she wanted to feast on, the open endlessly rolling fields that had begun unfolding within her mind the moment Mercedes had announced where they were going.

Mercedes had no idea that images were struggling up from the girl's memory, curling like smoke into forms as suggestive as those of puppets in a Balinese shadow theater that cavort between flame and sheet to the rhythm of bells and drums. Nor did the oddness of the girl's expression strike Mercedes as extraordinary. As far as she could tell, it was only an intensification of what she'd seen before, a composite confusion changeable as air.

Shifting her eyes back to the road, Mercedes said, "You can see the ocean from Flora's living room. At night you can hear the waves. I always sleep like a baby when we're there."

She had tried to pitch her voice to cheerfulness, but as the words came out she heard the strain, a half-harsh tone that gave away the worry nestled in her mind. She had been upset since the girl had told her stories which had stayed in her consciousness like fragments of colored glass that made no pattern she could understand. As soon as traffic permitted she increased her speed. She wanted to tell Roberto about the morning's outpouring because it had frightened her and seemed pointed toward the place Raúl had warned of, the irreversible plunge away from sense and any vestige of sanity she might have reached.

The girl acknowledged Mercedes' comments about the sea with neither nod nor glance, content, it seemed, to watch the last of the city trail out of sight like the caboose of a too-long train. The odd building still appeared here and there on the verge of a road or at the end of a littered field, as if Buenos Aires were struggling to retain its claim upon the land. But eventually they too were gone and the pampas rose up around them, brown as the palm of some great hand. The girl followed the flatness with her eyes as the steady thrumming of the tires gave way to other sounds. She heard once again the way our voices echoed in the warehouse, the softly reassuring sound of speech whose only purpose had been to assert our existence. Then the sounds and shadows merged. She bunched a handful of her skirt tightly in her fist and looked at Mercedes with urgent eyes.

"Arturo was running shirtless on a Palermo street and they caught him in the middle of his stride and after that he was always cold because he had only shorts and running shoes. After we were together in the place with the tiny eyes, the one with the bracelets and earrings let him have her shawl and he cried before he told his story. Everyone was cold. Kikki made jokes about being naked, but she always warmed me with her arms, and when that was not enough she gave me her body and her legs, wrapped me up in flesh. When her time came to talk she said she took men to a room in La Boca. One was a policeman who liked to visit every week and that was her undoing. One night she answered his knock wearing a negligee he'd given her, but couldn't let him in because she was already doing what she had to do to pay her rent. The next week, to make it up, she bought wine and candles and she was waiting when he came with all the others. They took her for revenge, a favor to their friend. I could see their faces in her words, tiny as little dolls. Then they grew and became familiar and I cried because they looked like the ones who came to the place where the mother was, where she saw the girl in the corridor lined with blue chairs she was trying to grab, knocking them down while they dragged her away."

Testimony of Kikki Alvarado, a.k.a., "La Gioconda"

ull up a chair, have a drink, snort a line, whatever makes you happy. All I care about is whether you're listening. It's Kikki this time, a.k.a. La Gioconda. The cops always put it on their reports when they hauled me in.

La Gioconda, the Mona Lisa. What's a hooker doing

with a name like that? You want to know, I'll tell you. It's a laugh.

I got it from an art professor who turned up one night at Yolanda's when I was still working in the house, before I decided to go into business for myself. Suit, tie, the works. Distinguished. Not bad-looking, either, even if he did have a scrawny neck and one of those little Hitler mustaches like a bug on his lip. He was carrying a gym bag and a portfolio. I told him to leave them at the office, but he said no deal unless he could bring them up to the room. I figured he was just jumpy being in a whorehouse and said okay, I don't want you worrying about being ripped off.

Soon as I closed the door he unzipped the bag. His eyes looked kind of weird. I didn't know what was happening except I didn't like it. You want bondage or some sick shit like that, I said, you got the wrong girl. Line up for Ana down the hall, she's the specialist.

Well, he looked like I'd hit him in the gut. He said all he wanted was to make me beautiful. That's when he pulled out this black dress, like old ladies wear. He'd pay double if I put it on. For that kind of money I'd have run around the block stark naked. It was nice, crepe de chine, something like that. Comb out your hair, he said. I combed it out. He looked at me with these jelly eyes for a minute before he took a reproduction of the *Mona Lisa* out of the portfolio and tacked it over the bed. See how she's sitting? he asked. I'm not blind, I said. What happened is that I had to sit like that for ten minutes before he could do it.

He visited once a month for about a year. Same routine every time. I didn't pay much attention to the picture at first, but then I started looking at it while he was staring at me. It gave me something to do. She didn't seem like such a big deal. In fact, she reminded me of a nun. Then she started getting under my skin. I liked her face and her smile and wondered why she looked that way and why I felt like I did, sort of calm and relaxed. I finally figured out it was because she looked the way I sometimes still felt inside, like everything I'd done was a bad dream and hadn't really happened. There weren't any pimps or madams in her eyes, no rough trade or hard times. She reminded me of goodness.

Anyway, one night he told me he wasn't coming back. It was a letdown because I liked him. I'd gotten used to wearing the dress and the way it made me feel. And I liked looking at her. By that time everybody was calling me La Gioconda, like I was one of those one-name movie stars. It set me apart, you know? Gave me status. So I asked if I could have the picture. You really want it? he said. Why do you think I'm asking? I told him. When he wanted to know why, I said it was because she made me feel good and reminded me of better things. Well, he got tears in his eyes. I think what I'd said made him happier than anything I'd ever done. First thing I did when I got my own place was put that picture on the wall.

The cop the girl told Mercedes about, Geraldo was his name, said it made him nervous. Every time he visited I had to take it off the wall and put it face down in a drawer. Other than that he was okay until he started getting possessive. He wasn't the first client who wanted me all to himself. When I told him to straighten up he said he wasn't just an ordinary cop. He had power, influence. So what? I said. I had to make a living. I had rent to pay, food to buy, expenses. What he paid wouldn't cover more than a day's rent. He didn't care. He started talking about the other guys, what he'd do to them. I was worried the night he showed up when he wasn't supposed to. That's why I promised something special for the following week, something he wouldn't forget. There were candles on the table, champagne, but as soon as I opened the door and saw his friends I knew I was in trouble. I had no idea they'd take me away, couldn't believe it when they locked me up and said they'd found out I was a Communist. You don't have to be a genius to figure out that Geraldo told them that to get even. I tried to reason with the guards. They wouldn't listen. I was there. That was enough to make me guilty. I'd been removed from the world in less than an hour. I knew what was going on in the city. Everybody did. Aside from being sorry for the Disappeared, I never gave politics a second thought, didn't have a political bone in my body. It didn't take long to change that, maybe a month. Not that it did me any good.

Before I go on, let's get something straight. I'm not proud of the way I lived. If it hadn't been for my uncle maybe I wouldn't have ended up on the street. I might have finished school, made something of myself, maybe been a professor, like Gabriela, or a doctor. That's not how things worked out. You have a table, you've got to put food on it. You want a roof over your head, something to drink, you have to buy it. I was a whore but I was still a human being. I had feelings like everybody else. But they didn't believe it. They did it to all the women, but it was different with me. They thought I liked it. They tortured me a little, enough to be satisfied I didn't know anything, then they did it every way you can imagine and some you can't.

After a few weeks I didn't care what happened. It wasn't the pain. It was what they'd done to who I thought I was. They stole my pride like they were scooping seeds out of a melon. By the time they sent me to the warehouse I just wanted to die, go to sleep, not wake up.

It wasn't pitch dark. During the day enough light came through the boards so you could just make out the silhouettes of faces, like seeing somebody on the street at twilight.

I felt sorry for the others but I didn't feel like talking. I just wanted to curl up inside myself until it was over. They wouldn't let me. One after the other said I had to be strong, insisted there must be something I wanted to live for. What? I said. I haven't exactly had a pretty life. There must be someone, they said. There wasn't anybody, I answered, no family, no friends.

I'd just started to go over to the corner to be alone when the girl arrived. It was daylight, the door was still open, I could see her plainly. She was in her teens, pretty, had the face of an angel. All of a sudden, a strange thing happened. She wasn't smiling, but she reminded me of what La Gioconda had meant to me. It was who she was. Maybe there was something in me that had been waiting to get out all along, I don't know. Maybe it was something about her. You know how she affected Mercedes and Gabriela and Chloe. They all wanted to mother her. And so did I. I took her under my wing like an old hen does a chick, warmed her with my body, wiped away her tears. We'd sit together when Jacob sang, slept beside each other. And we sat side by side when they put us in the truck.

I was afraid we might be separated when we got here and I was ready to fight to hold on to her, scratch their eyes out. But they kept us together, bunched up, as we went through the field. She was holding on tight when that bastard lit the lantern and a minute later I saw Alberto Marqovitch coming toward us, smiling in a way I understood. Nobody hated it more than me when he took her away. It seemed like a hole had been gouged out of the world because I believed what he said he was going to do. Then I really didn't care what happened. It was too much. I didn't even scream when the first bullet hit. I was glad. My only regret was that it took two more to finish me off.

So now we're all holding our breath, in a manner of

speaking, waiting, hoping the unit can find out where we are. But I have to tell you something. I'm not as excited as the others are because I've seen enough to know that things have gone beyond us now. God knows, I want a proper burial, my name on a stone, no matter how small it is. But it doesn't mean as much after thinking about all that happened. It's more than a battle between the generals and the ones who were against them. It's about something in the human heart that denies the goodness of La Gioconda's smile. Our bones testify to that. Will it make a difference if they're found? Has it ever? Can anyone prove her smile is stronger than what they did to us?

Book
Five

Full Fathom Five

O nce Mercedes had settled the girl in her room, drawn the

curtains, and turned out the light, she went back down the

hall and told Roberto about the stories, describing as well as

she could the tone of the girl's voice, her expressions, which

had subtly changed from narrative to narrative, the way

each ended as if clipped off in mid-sentence, suggestive of a loose connection, a short-circuit, or perhaps merely a sudden lack of words or the will to speak them.

"They make sense, in a way," she concluded. "In another, they're no more than the sounds of madness. I'm afraid for her. For us."

So was Roberto. For all he knew each person the girl described was a creation of her shrouded mind, no more substantial than the paper birds she'd tattooed and sailed with the seeming innocence of a child releasing a balloon over the River Plate. But for Mercedes' sake rather than the truth's he said, "She could be coming out of it, finding her way back."

Mercedes looked hard at him, eyes glistening.

"Don't patronize me, Roberto."

She looked tired, half-distraught. After asking how she planned to pass the time while he worked, and hearing that she intended to explore the town with the girl, he convinced her to go to bed, saying that he would come in shortly but that there were things he needed to prepare for the morning.

With the door to the bedroom closed, Roberto collapsed into the dusty smell of an armchair, turned off the light beside it and looked out the window at the street where the light from signs and lampposts paled the immediate edge of night. Glad as he was for Mercedes' presence, buoyed by the comfort she offered against the strangeness of the town and his purpose for being there, it would have been better if she had waited. He should have called when the work was finished, the bones and trinkets removed, cataloged, put away. He was afraid that, dreaming or awake, she too might stumble across the same fear that had come to him last night when he saw the shape of the earrings they had bought for Ana María. For a moment he remained on the cusp of what he perceived as a terrible paradox: every shovelful of dirt he'd carefully scattered on the screens, every length of twine he'd stretched and tied to wooden stakes, every indrawn breath he'd taken as bones and belts were raised to sunlight, had been done in the belief that knowledge, certainty, the end of the story was what everyone like himself wanted to fill up the void of ignorance. Now, confronted with the slightest chance that tomorrow or the next day or the next he might come upon the last detail of his daughter's story, Roberto questioned himself, doubted the truth of all he had believed, saw the look on Helena Alberti's face not as relief but as the prelude to sorrow that would never heal.

But it was too late. Run or stay, the earring was planted in his imagination. It had a life of its own along with the strange affliction of the girl that wove through his thoughts like a golden thread. He considered her wound for the thousandth time, remembering the smoothness of the scar, the tiny indentation in the skull. Raúl's diagnosis was meaningless in the face of the mystery which deepened each day until now he was caught up in something beyond his control, as if he were oarless in a boat at the mercy of a current whose direction was unknown. But that wasn't true. It was merely a subtle lie of the mind. He did understand. All along the way his puzzlement had verged on something he had refused to credit. His disdain had veiled his fear of what lay on the other side. It shone like the headlight of an approaching train coming from the darkness he had believed to be the end. It glowed with certainty that was accompanied by a roar as it passed through his consciousness and in its wake left him with a single thought. If he told Mercedes, she'd think him mad.

That night we became the acolytes of his dreams, casting images into his mind. We showed him display cases

filled with earrings shining beneath the glass. Images of Ana
María. The girl standing against a darkened sky. We
brought bones and the secrets bones can tell not to torment
him but to goad him on. And when we finished with Roberto we visited all the others in the Ezekiel squad, helped
them dream of what they'd see, muttered names they never
heard.

Everybody was wearing jeans, old sweaters, scarred work
boots. They were drinking coffee in the lobby, talking in
hushed tones, looking nervous the way they always did before they converged on a new site. Macalester tipped his
cup, drained it, said, "Let's go," as he put it down on the
reception desk.

"We probably won't be back until dinnertime," Roberto told Mercedes.

He was turning away when the girl touched his arm.
He looked at her over his shoulder, saw her frowning.

"Take me," she said.

Roberto glanced at Mercedes who gently disengaged
the girl's hand.

"Roberto has to work," she said evenly. "We'll go for a
walk, find a nice place for lunch."

The girl pulled away. Macalester was standing in the
doorway. She looked at him as if she were about to speak,
then changed her mind. Taking a step toward Roberto, she
said, "Take me," her voice plaintive this time, edged with
urgency.

"I can't," he told her, gesturing toward the others filing
out the door past Macalester. "We have to leave now. I'll be
back before you know it."

She looked at him without saying anything, as if she
were searching for the right words to persuade him.

"Maybe you should go," Roberto said to Mercedes.

The girl shook her head. She stood with her fingers splayed out on the reception desk, making a sound low in her throat, somewhere between a hum and a groan, as she watched him pass through the door. Before it closed she was running, pushing it open. Everyone in the unit was already in the trucks. People were standing on the sidewalk, gawking as she ran to Roberto. She was crying now, desperate.

"Take me," she pleaded. "Take me. Take me. Take me."

As Roberto looked at her in consternation Mercedes came outside.

"What do you think it is?" he asked her before he looked worriedly back at the girl.

Mercedes shook her head. The girl glanced at her, then Roberto, her eyes red and desolate.

"Please," she said. "I need to see."

Roberto put his arm around her and spoke quietly to Mercedes.

"Why don't you follow us and let her see where we'll be."

"All right," Mercedes said.

The girl wiped her eyes with the back of her hand.

"Spirits," she said quietly. "In the little corners of the night they talk."

Her words seemed to come from the light he'd imagined the night before. With an inward shudder Roberto turned and climbed into the Bronco beside Verónica Flores.

"She seems confused," Verónica offered.

"No," Roberto said as he watched the girl and Mercedes going toward their car. "She knows exactly what she wants."

In addition to the people gathered on the sidewalk, a dozen cars and trucks were lined up behind the Broncos, spectators, drivers and passengers having gotten wind of something strange as soon as the unit's trucks had appeared two days earlier. The bartender had told his cousin, his cousin told his wife, the story circulating as quickly as the one about the spirit in the fields and affecting them as deeply. Horrified but fascinated, they had congregated like sports fans waiting for the doors of a stadium to open, crediting and discounting rumors which sent their heads buzzing and filled their hearts. Their motives made no difference. We wanted eyes other than the unit's, the more the better. If we could, we'd have brought in a dozen buses, enough to transport everyone in Santa Rosalita to where we lay.

Macalester's truck pulled away from the curb, followed by the remaining Broncos and the townspeople's cars, the procession moving solemnly as a cortege along the main street while shopkeepers and customers emerged from the stores to watch, returning the somber stares of Roberto and the others. Even the followers in their cars looked grim now that they were moving toward the site. Half a minute later the sun glared on the rear window of Mercedes' car, the last in line, and the procession disappeared in that square of yellow light like a match going out. They drove through fields past outlying houses that looked soft as pastel drawings in the morning's freshness, their windows circles of reflected sun hiding the faces behind them, veiling Beatriz Ponce's miserable eyes as she watched and imagined the mother's sorrow and felt the pain that would blight Eduardo's heart if he ever learned of her betrayal. Of course no one in the procession knew she was responsible for the news that had brought them there. For all of their anxiety, the countryside looked boringly normal, innocent of guile and deceit. They could have been on a Sunday outing, and everything they saw for the first few miles reinforced the notion. They passed a boy walking a nondescript dog on a leash, then a family in good clothes who must have been on the way to mass in Santa Rosalita. The green-gold pampas stretching to the horizon, encompassing as the sea, seemed to belie the purpose of their presence.

But that was before Macalester ordered his driver to make a hard left onto the narrow dirt track leading to the ombu grove half a mile ahead. The ruts jarred their bones, rattled their teeth, jostled them out of the false complacency of the paved highway they wanted to sustain because none of them were ever ready to see a killing field, especially one like ours which wore a bucolic mask, inviting them into its shade and coolness.

The sound of fifteen motors merged in a grating hum as the cars and trucks pulled off the track and parking brakes ratcheted on and the dust hung in the air, bronzing sky and trees. For a minute or two everyone stayed inside, aware of the quiet which was deep without being peaceful, charged as clouds with energy that could explode into lightning, pouring rain. Finally, a door opened, then another and another. The clatter of picks, hoes, shovels broke the silence with the sound of metal striking metal, wooden handles banging together, the soft voices of Macalester and the Ezekiel squad.

Without a signal of any kind, with neither nods nor words, the spectators arrayed themselves in a semicircle forty or fifty feet away from where the team set to work, acknowledging an unspoken protocol that turned the grove into an open-air theater staging some ancient rite. The edgy excitement they had felt as they lined up in front of the hotel was replaced by respectful silence, their eagerness by apprehension because what had been abstract and dramatic in town was frightening and unseemly in the quiet field.

The girl and Mercedes sat in the middle of the circle,

arms clutching their knees, the girl rapt, uneasy, her eyes following every move. She was perplexed by what she saw, her consciousness, awareness, whatever it was she might be said to possess, focused on the look of things the way one's mind does when searching for a word memory refuses to surrender. She watched Roberto shoulder three shovels, others picks, hoes and canvas bags they carried to the edge of the green sward and put down neatly as a nurse arranges the scalpels, probes and needles the surgeon will use to examine the unfeeling flesh of his patient. Roberto's face was set. She could see the muscles working in his jaw and her pity went out to him because she understood instantly what he had kept secret from Mercedes and hoped he would not find.

Once the tools were laid out Macalester flipped open a notebook and walked around the site, poking at the edges with his boot. A minute later he signaled to the others and the girl watched them begin cutting the grass with machetes, then getting down on their knees and clipping it shorter with shears, being careful to avoid uprooting anything. As the grass was removed the sun climbed higher and the onlookers watched silently, fascinated and appalled as an oblong of rich dark earth was exposed to light.

No one said a word. The members of the unit spoke only when necessary, conscious of being watched, isolated by their work that was binding everyone together as they dug into the country's sorrow and its shame. Late in the morning a few spectators left, replaced by others who drifted in, drawn by rumors to this place they should have shrunk from but whose meaning claimed their hearts. The pharmacist and his wife appeared. A gaucho who had been riding back to La Paloma came over to investigate. After questioning one of the men, he tied his horse to a low-hang-

ing branch and joined the crowd. Five boys who had promised their parents they would stay away were breathless after the long ride, dumping their bikes unceremoniously in a
heap and running toward the place they had heard about
only to stop when they saw how somber everyone was.

At noon they broke for lunch. The spectators had
brought food and bottled water. The girl ate some fruit,
nothing more.

An hour later the team resumed its work. The girl
edged closer to the oblong of bare soil. She was drawn to it,
as if she had entered a magnetic zone, felt her body being
pulled toward the center. She sat cross-legged and watched
them drive wooden stakes into the ground which they connected with white tape. She listened to the hollow sound of
more stakes being pounded into the earth, watched them
making quadrangles with twine, neat little brown squares
that hovered like spiderwebs in the heat haze. She watched
them bring out tape measures and write in their notebooks.
She watched Macalester signal to Roberto and two others.
When they began digging something came loose in her
heart, a wave of sympathy that flooded through her and was
shared by everyone who heard the scrape, watched the
earth being carefully unveiled. Macalester hovered over the
site, directing the work like a conductor does an orchestra.
He signaled with his hand for them to pause and take up the
smaller instruments, trowels, dustpans, brushes, the music
so faint now that only the diggers heard. By five o'clock the
ground was prepared and the unit packed up their tools.

The girl stood on rubbery legs. One after the other we
spoke to her, imploring her to remember, our voices joined
in a recitatif that swirled round her deafened ears while we
pleaded for her to bring the force of her sojourn in the
world to bear on our intestate bones. She walked away arm

in arm with Mercedes as if she were striding through the inchoate rubble of a dream.

That night, townspeople huddled together over dining room tables or leaned on café bars, wondering if they were strong enough to deal with the horror of what they would see if they had the courage to return to the site. The Ezekiel squad discussed the next day's work. Later, as the moon rose over the pampas, Eduardo Ponce drove down the dirt track and parked where the grass had been crushed by the tires of cars and trucks. He had come hoping that some sign, some yet unknown detail might ease the sense of jeopardy that had been building all day and was manifested in the rapid beat of a vein in his left temple, a ticking of the blood regular as a metronome. With one last glance at the trees, he switched off the headlights and the motor. He reached for the kerosene lantern on the floor and got out, pressing the door gently until it clicked. Even then the sound seemed loud as a gunshot.

We heard the soft scratching of a match as Eduardo lit the lantern and a moment later we felt the faint warmth of its fire. We heard him coming through the grass, heard the droplets of dew slide from the blades and cling to his shoes, little chimelike sounds measuring his progress. We heard him breathing, taking air in short, troubled gasps, as if he could not get enough. The soil vibrated with each step and slowly sifted into air pockets left when Ernesto Siciliano and the others had stamped it flat. Then the sound and vibrations stopped and all we heard was his breathing as he swung the lantern slowly in an arc, following the tracery of the twine. The faint warmth of the light was companioned by soft curses uttered more out of despair than anger, the words of a man who had seen his fate and knew that he could not change it. Eduardo turned the dial at the base of the lantern and the yellow glow gave way to moonlight. He stood with his hands plunged in the pockets of his jacket, looking at the faint silver squares, the neat geometry laid out during the day while he was working, tormented by his knowledge of what was happening in the grove, perplexed by the sudden descent of the team on the sleepy town. There must have been other clues, he thought, things he and the boys missed, or that someone found earlier. He cursed the informant, the police, the members of the team. He had watched them gathering in front of the hotel that morning, had felt his heart jump and skip a beat when the girl came out the door. All day long Eduardo told himself that it was a trick of his eyes, a fragment of memory broken loose. But in his heart of hearts he knew who she was and the hours had passed slowly as days.

Only when he began to shiver did he turn away and return to his truck. As he drove off, the headlights revealed the loneliest road he had ever seen.

Eduardo's sense of loneliness had nothing to do with us. None of our names would have been meaningful, nor would the sight of our bones have stirred a thrill of guilt. The accusing earth did not speak to him, but the image of the girl did, and the moonlight that clothed her form. Soft as it had seemed to lie upon the spreading branches of the ombu trees, it had the force of acid, burning away the last vestiges of hope and sending him on his way with an ache in his heart he could not quell.

He did not want to be with Beatriz. When she asked where he had been he said only that he had gone for a ride and wanted to be alone. Without another word, he went out to the porch and dragged a chair to the edge, where the moonlight was. The whole of his life since the night the

boys had been delivered played itself out before his eyes, a
multitude of separate threads. He knew where they converged, but he turned his eyes away. He had a little time left
before he had to look, and wanted to think about things as
they had been, before he saw the girl, the white trucks, the
grids. He saw the shelves of the store, the implements
stacked in corners, the order he made in the storeroom. The
work that had seemed to debase him was a sanctuary now,
a source of pride and pleasure. He gave himself up to precise pictures of cans, wrenches, rolls of wire. He was not
ready to look at the future. He thought about the boys, let
them fill his heart. He loved them in a way that was indistinguishable from the emotion that would have come if they
had been his own flesh and blood. But his fatherhood had
always been encumbered with the constant threat of loss, no
different than it would have been if the boys had suffered
some dire affliction of the blood untreatable by medicine.
He had known it from that first night, and he had done his
best to keep it at bay. But it returned now, growing
stronger as the moon sailed overhead, driven by the black
unseen wind of space. He would stay put until the moon
was captured by the branches of the acacia tree. He
watched it slip behind an outstretched branch whose leaves
made the pattern of a bird, watched it glide behind the full
leafy crown, its silver face broken by the dark branches
streaming down like water. Then he let himself see where
he was going.

Hours later, in the cool night air, Eduardo guided the
truck onto the road. He drove all that day, stopping only
when necessary for food and drink before heading south
again. He drove into the heat and the silence that was his
own making, for he did not have the heart to speak. He
drove all the next day and the one after that as he headed

into the remoter regions of Patagonia, leaving behind him only a trail of sun-brightened dust to mark the direction of his flight.

Sorry as we were for the grandsons of Dolores Masson masking their troubled thoughts with silence and brooding looks, even for Beatriz, whose guilt was greater than her despair, we rejoiced in Eduardo's suffering and took pride that the story slowly springing to life from Alessandra's earring had brought him to this pass, that the glimpse of our girl had blighted hope. Determined as he was to put all the space in the country between himself and the prospect of our risen bones, we consoled ourselves with the knowledge that his flight was double-edged. Like the uroboros feeding on its own tail, Eduardo would never escape himself, not even after he reached a remote village in the south. For even though he would welcome the sight of the squat buildings backlit by the sun, their outlines low to the ground as is appropriate to an outpost, his relief would happily be short-lived. He would rent a tiny house with a view of the slate-gray sea, find work on a trawler, implore his benefactor for help again. But Eduardo would have lost all hope of safety. He would remember the face of the girl while he worked, dream of her at night. And at the end of the day, when the boat headed toward shore stinking of its catch, he would see the little town growing closer but without relief or promise of relief, for Eduardo Ponce would know that it was only one more way station on an endless road.

But that was in the future. Much as we wanted to dwell on it, savor his frustration and despair, there was something far more important that lay in the foreground of our vision: the promise of reprieve. No eyes ever watched more diligently than ours the next morning as the team and then the spectators returned just after Eduardo's footprints had dried in the sun. Macalester and Roberto walked over them. The feet of the others obliterated the grass that had held the outline of his shoes, breaking the spines of the blades that would dry to powder and blow off in the slightest wind.

The protocol of the first day had been ad hoc, uncertain. Now the spectators led by Mercedes and the girl spread their blankets and folding chairs in a line parallel to the grids. Once again the team laid out their tools. And then they began to dig, loosening the earth with shovels and hoes and pouring it carefully into bright red pails that Reyes' students emptied onto screens. The chuffing sound of the shovels was joined by the rhythm of the sifters who gently rocked the screens back and forth, back and forth, their eyes avid for the smallest sign, a button, perhaps a pin. Except for the occasional cry of a bird, and once the distant rumble of a jet miles high, the only sounds were the call of the shovels, the response of the screens until the hole was three feet deep. At a sign from Macalester the diggers went to work with trowels and small brushes, their tempo slowing, pianissimo now, soft as muted flutes.

The girl was intent on the process, her eyes half-closed against the sun. She had insisted on wearing her white dress against Mercedes' objections and she glowed among the spectators, bright as a lighthouse. Her mind was empty, a tabula rasa. Neither stories nor images violated its purity, as if she had prepared herself for some unknown knowledge to be written across it in the tiny letters of an unsteady hand. Though she did not understand the goal, she knew there was purpose in every movement, every glint of sun on the rising blades of trowels and the brushes' metal handles. To the others the tedium made the work seem like some arcane ritual of polishing the soil, as if the Ezekiel squad were engaged in a mad enterprise, a collection of lunatics let out of an asylum to entertain the locals, men and women disporting among twigs and roots and clods.

But their boredom fled the instant Macalester stood up, arching his back against the strain of digging on bended knees. The sifters stopped their work. Suddenly the site was plunged into silence as Macalester pointed to the ground, called for a spade and bent, alone this time, surrounded by members of the team. He scraped the earth with the side of the spade, brushed the earth with his hand, scraped again. The spectators rose and went up to the tape separating them from the team, the girl leading, followed by Mercedes. Macalester scooped again, brushed. The film between us and him was paper thin, as if we were looking upward through a frosted window. Suddenly, there was a point of light, the sharp end of the spade, a wider wedge of blue.

Half an hour later, with infinite tenderness, Macalester used the soft bristles of a shaving brush to clear away the last layer of earth from the earring that lay against Alessandra's skull. Murmurs rose from the crowd. Some looked away, but not Roberto and not the girl. As soon as he saw the faint glow of gold Roberto began to weep, and he did not stop when Macalester exposed it to the sun even though he saw no resemblance to Ana María's earring. He wept with relief and he wept from sorrow for Alessandra and the rest of us still straining toward the light. Slowly his eyes rose to Mercedes and the girl standing together in a close embrace, the girl's face moving through horror to something he could not name but thought was almost beatific. All he knew was that a brightness came upon her eyes which seemed to fill with recognition before she buried her face against Mercedes' shoulder.

By the next afternoon they had recovered all of us. Then the sorting began, the search for clues. Our still-mute bones were marked with pieces of tape and numbered. Matted, bloodstained clothes were laid out in rows through which Roberto strayed like a derelict, staring at the array of shirts, dresses, shoes, jewelry, his hope bolstered by the fact that the earring had not been his daughter's but his mind still filled with apprehension. He was afraid to look, more afraid to turn away in the event that a bone might call out to his blood, crying, "Father, this is where they took me. Now you know."

But no high-pitched, still-girlish voice rose from the bones and rubble to pierce Roberto's heart. The only sound in that corner of the plot came from Verónica Flores. With her dark hair pinned up and covered with a scarf, she knelt over a pile of clothes and other objects quietly describing them to Sofia Benveniste as she placed them in a basket labeled 119.

"Skirt of some fine material, silk or rayon. A shawl, loosely woven. Adidas athletic shoes, men's. Woman's shoe with stiletto heel, no mate. Three silver bracelets with tribal markings."

Her voice droned on, quiet, businesslike, edged with pain each time she removed something from the pile, identified it, placed it in the basket. Neither woman looked at the other and Roberto refused to look at their faces, keeping his eyes on the twisted mass, knowing that no matter how impregnated with blood and dirt he would recognize anything that had belonged to Ana María.

"Small leather purse, clasp closed, strap broken."

Roberto watched Verónica open it, peer inside, remove a stained envelope.

"What appears to be a letter," Verónica said.

Folding back the flap she removed a single sheet of blue paper she slowly unfolded.

"It's addressed to someone named Marco."

She read silently for a moment before she replaced it in the envelope and quickly retrieved the next object.

"Wing-tip shoe," Verónica said in a hoarse voice, whispering the words now, brushing away the tears with the back of her hand. "I need a break," she told Sofia and wandered off toward the grove where she stood looking into the shade.

When Verónica finished cataloging the evidence an hour later nothing that could reasonably have belonged to Ana María had turned up. Roberto stared at the plastic baskets. He knew what was in each of them and could have recited their contents perfectly, but it seemed that he had to look one last time to reassure himself before admitting that nothing belonged to his daughter. Then, exhausted, he gazed toward Mercedes and slowly shook his head. She was searching his eyes, making certain that it was fact, not hope, she had seen. That was when Roberto understood how stupid he had been. She had the same fear, all along. He went to her, aware of the paradox of his relief in remaining ignorant but not caring. As he stepped over the tape, Mercedes left the girl's side, whispered, "I know, I know."

The girl watched them walk away, keeping her eyes on them when they stopped beside one of the trucks and embraced. She could see Roberto's face over Mercedes' shoulder. Then her eyes swept back and came to rest upon our bones.

Understand, that's all we were to the spectators, a neat array of femurs, tibias, skulls, metacarpals attended by what remained of the things we'd worn. But not to her. The excitement that had gripped her mind since Mercedes announced their visit to the pampas, and had hardened into rapt attention over the last two days, was like an invisible thread binding her to something beyond the bones. A force had been working on her from the moment Alessandra's earring had gleamed in the sun. She had felt it growing stronger throughout the night, beckoning to her like a voice she knew from long ago. We heard it, too, and urged her on as she rose and headed back along the dirt track to the road where she stopped and scanned the fields, as if seeing them for the first time. She raised her eyes to the sky which darkened as she looked, its blueness fading to dusk and night. She heard the creak of hinges as the truck's door swung open, terse commands, Kikki's whispered entreaty for her to be strong, the grip of her hand on her arm.

And then she began to walk, entering into the overlaid darkness that filmed the day, obscured our bones and the faces of the crowd. The sound of birds and the clipped voices of the Ezekiel squad gave way to the rustling of feet in the grass, the dryness to moisture weighing down the dust. She moved toward the grove on a path of words that rose up to greet her, shelter her in an embrace of sound only she could hear, her eyes widening as she heard them breaking out of the past, chiming clear as bells.

Teresa feels the grass against her bare legs. It is wet from dew and soon the hem of her dress is soaked and the coolness feels pleasant. As she walks she thinks there may be a house out there in the dark where they will be greeted by men who look the way some did in an early story I told. Because of this she is less frightened. She whispers to the girl next to her that everything is going to be fine, that they are on the way out of the terror that has been their lives. Teresa thinks about her mother, wonders if even at this very moment she too is being led somewhere. She thinks about me, and wants to be here with all of us in the garden. The darkness is filled with images of her life before the men came to our house, and it is so dark that she returns to the idea that perhaps she has dreamed all of this, that this is part of the dream just before she wakes up. It is so dark that even the flashlights are no longer visible.

As she entered the grove her nostrils flared at the musty scent of leaves. It was cool, dark, but the shape in the matted leaves glowed like the phosphorous that sometimes rims a crashing wave. The shape rose up to receive her, gently pulling her down, wrapping itself around her as she lay back among the leaves. Then it was pitch black. Alberto's voice was lost in our shouts and cries. The owl, perched on a limb above her head, flew off, entering the moon like an arrow and passing through to the other side.

It is pure darkness, blackness, but Teresa doesn't care. She believes she is in one of her father's stories, that this is being made up. The dark contains all colors. Sound, and no sound. The dark gives birth to lanterns, to klieg lights, to a thousand suns.

Light filled the darkness, pressed down upon the leaves, made the great limbs groan. And when it was most intense, when the light and the voice were one, she rose from the shape into the shade of the newborn day, bearing with her the sound of her father's voice as she returned to the place of grids and quadrants, bones and beads. The girl looked at Roberto and Mercedes as she emerged from the grove, her eyes gleaming bright as double suns.

"This is where I came from. Where I left my name," she said slowly, evenly, her voice resonant with assurance they had never heard. "I am Teresa and these," she added, gesturing toward our bones, "these are my friends."

It was as if her name had been exhumed with what remained of us. Roberto's eyes rose to Teresa's scar. From the moment he first saw it and diagnosed its source, he had fought against its meaning even more strongly than he had the story Carlos told that brought her to his home. He had resisted every intimation that she was taking him beyond his depth, coaxing him out into the deep unknown with a voice that always seemed to know more than she could say. Now the current pulled him out and further out until the old

familiar shore was lost. He watched Mercedes take her
hand, embrace her. Teresa. Her name sounded again and
again in his mind. He remembered Carlos looking at him
with that uncanny expression in his eyes, validating the reality of all that remained unseen. Roberto glanced at the
bones, tools, piles of clothes and trinkets neatly arranged on
the ground.

"Come," he said, driven by a sudden urgency that
bound him to Carlos in fatherhood.

When they reached the car he turned and looked back.
His friends were working diligently. The squad was more
aptly named than they would ever know.

In the hotel lobby Roberto asked the desk clerk if he could
use the phone for a long-distance call.

"You'll pay?" the clerk said warily.

"Of course."

The man nodded. Roberto picked up the receiver and a
few minutes later reached information in Buenos Aires.

"Please," he said. "The number of Carlos Rueda."

He jotted it down hurriedly on a pad, depressed the
cradle with his thumb, released it, glancing at Mercedes and
Teresa before he dialed.

The phone rang eight times. Then he heard a click and
Carlos saying, "*¡Holá!*"

"Señor Rueda, this is Dr. Cristiani. My wife and I
came to you once, long ago. You probably don't remember."

"I remember telling you a girl was coming."

"Señor, I have something to tell you."

As soon as he was certain Carlos understood, Roberto
handed the receiver to Teresa. Half a dozen people were
passing through the lobby, impervious to the extraordinary
thing that was happening before their eyes. If he told them,

they would not believe it. He was still amazed he did. When they went by he crossed to where Mercedes was waiting and slid his arm around her waist. There they stood a moment, long enough to see the brightness in Teresa's eyes, her lips break into a smile. Then they turned away, toward the stairs. Roberto knew exactly how her voice would sound on the phone, and he also knew what it was doing to Carlos, how it entered all the way into his bones.

Epilogue

N eed we say the obvious, that Carlos and Cecilia were wise enough not to question Teresa's return too closely? Given what you know about the conditions of their lives, how could it have been otherwise? Schooled in legends of the doomed and saved, they saw her return, *of necessity*, in the

same light that flickered across Carlos' stories. The moment
he heard her voice the whiteness into which she disappeared
exploded like a supernova, showering her with shards of
broken light. He called to Cecilia, handed her the phone,
and while she stood there crying, starting sentences over
and over, as if it were impossible to find words to express
what was in her heart, Carlos understood that they had all
been reunited in a garden of their own devising which required no explanations but simply was.

By the time they arrived at the Villa Deamicis two days
later to take her home, Carlos knew her place in the family
was destined to be as bright and ghostly as a hologram.
Light and shadow, flesh and spirit, she had ridden his half-
told story back into the world bearing with her, like strands
of kelp clinging to a diver who breaks the surface of the sea,
lineaments of the darkness he had visited night after night.
Unlike himself, Teresa was no mere visitor to that place, no
Dante led by Virgil, but part of it, an intimate of blood and
cries that hung like phosphorescent kites in darkened air.
The authority expressed in her eyes and in her voice that
seems to echo Jacob's metallic songs was of another order
than his could ever be.

Though what Teresa learned shines in their family life
like Venus on a windswept night, her outward life appears
unexceptional. When she approaches a subway entrance no
flights of birds swirl her underground. Her hair is no longer
a wild, unruly tangle. Neatly trimmed and combed, it cas-
cades over her shoulders in a graceful fall. The only resemblance to the girl who appeared at the Villa Deamicis is the
pallor of her skin, the white dresses she always wears and
eyes that gleam with an elegiac light, the look of someone
intent upon a notion.

Nor is there anything to distinguish her on Thursdays

when she arrives at the Plaza de Mayo to join those who
search and hope to find. Only when everyone has gathered
in the middle of the square does her difference become apparent. Before the march begins Teresa studies all the signs
emblazoned with names and pictures, concentrating her attention on frozen eyes and arrested smiles as she runs her
fingers across the letters and the faces. Once she has
touched them all, she offers small white cards with the address of her new home and directions for those who wish to
visit. After that she joins Roberto and Mercedes, ties a scarf
over her head, slips her arms through theirs and walks for
an hour into the shadow of the Casa Rosada and out into
the midday sun.

The Cristianis still grapple with an experience they will
never understand, but which lights their way with a certain
glow. Teresa's sojourn in their lives has joined them to everyone who seeks the rags and tatters of vanished stories.
Four afternoons a week Roberto and now Mercedes pile up
bones with the Ezekiel squad, but every Thursday, rain or
shine, they carry signs, Roberto's bearing the inscription,
"Never Forget," Mercedes' "Never Again." Marching arm
in arm with Teresa, the three of them chant the marchers'
demands that never seem to leave the plaza, not even in the
stillness of midnight's air long after everyone has gone.

As for the other residents of the Villa Deamicis, Chloe
continues making her charts, Orestes has begun working in
bright acrylics, Guillermo watches television happily because his team has not disgraced itself badly in recent
games. They all think of Teresa, but Gabriela has enshrined
her in her heart. The girl's mystery, the courage she displayed has altered Gabriela's life, soothing her with a balm
of love, strengthening her resolve. She has begun to make
amends for her moment of weakness by giving fiery lectures

during which she insists that what has been knitted together under President Menem may unravel in the future. That, she says, is the way things have always been in Argentina.

Pacing back and forth, she tells her class that history is rarely what it seems. "What's missing sometimes tells you more than all the statues in all the squares," she says. "Think about the way our city looks."

She goes on in that throaty voice of hers, asserting that Buenos Aires is a forest of monuments unfurling its history like a banner against the sky. She reminds them of the Liberator sitting astride a stallion in the Plaza San Martín, the obelisk in the Plaza de la República intended to look like the axis of the world, the helmeted women in flowing robes who lead the eye to a warrior's chariot above the facade of the Palacio Nacional de Congreso, the pedestaled busts of the ancient great gazing impassively over the heads of museum patrons.

"War heroes, saints, martyrs, civic leaders, artists, visionaries," she says, "they're all remembered in stone or bronze. And this is not unique to Argentina. The impulse is universal. It is impossible to consider civilization without its monuments. Even the surface of the moon bears the boot-prints of astronauts."

Pausing, she looks at them, letting her words sink in. "Well, then," she asks quietly. "What of the Disappeared? Surely there's a place that honors them. Down some avenue or cobbled street, in the shade of a suburban park, a form must have risen from the mind of a sculptor. So you go to take a look, traverse the city, pass along teeming streets lined with office buildings, car dealerships, tango bars until you find yourselves alone in a quiet residential neighborhood, gazing at the blank face of a stucco wall. An interior voice offers you the reassurance that perhaps there's some problem with zoning laws, or that those chosen to execute the project are still at work, the challenge of representing an absence so far having baffled the minds that would conceive an image of it."

She goes over to the window and looks out at the quad before turning around. Her eyes are filled with anger now, and so is her voice.

"It would be comforting to think so," she says, "comforting but stupidly naive, a willful turning away from the facts. Because there is no bronze shape, not one stone in the humblest plaza. For just as Argentina chooses to raise images of its triumphs, it also chooses to ignore its disgrace. The art that would render the fate of the Disappeared is not even that of the air brush which requires an image to do its work."

Are Gabriela's words our epitaph? Are we doomed to official silence, empty air?

Not at all. For though it is true that no shape dedicated to us rises against the noontime sky or takes the glow of evening's floodlights, we are remembered by those who march in the plaza and especially by the girl who dreamed of bones.

It happens this way, week after week throughout the year. Late on Thursday afternoons Teresa goes back to the house Carlos and Cecilia bought after the birth of their son. There is a garden in back that she and Cecilia have decorated with potted plants, birds of paradise, cyclamen and roses. At twilight mother and daughter hang lanterns in the trees, then go inside to wait. Well before dark grim-faced people appear, loss etched in their eyes deep as the lines in steel engravings. Carlos plays his guitar while Teresa watches from the window until the lanterns glow like tiny suns. Then he strums a final chord and they go out together, walking side by side to a chair standing alone in the middle of the lawn. There Carlos makes a courtly gesture with his hand, a slow, sweeping movement of relinquishment before taking his place beside Cecilia and their son.

Teresa's eyes glide from face to face registering expressions, gauging hopes and fears. When she has made contact with everyone, she sits down and puts her hands delicately on the arms, but before she engages the sorrows in her father's garden she walks again through the dew-wet grass and sees again our faces in the lantern light. And then she names our spirits.

"Jaime Goyisoto," she says, pronouncing each syllable as carefully as if she were offering a benediction. "The one who was lost because of his son. Alessandra Ricci who wore her lover's gift beyond the end. Jacob Levy, singer of the metal songs. Kikki Alvarado who warmed me with her body when I was cold."

She goes on like that until she has acknowledged all of us. But that is not the end, for even as Teresa asks for stories and begins to tell what she has been vouchsafed to see, our names continue to be heard, filling the precincts of this garden with sounds more durable than the bronze that will never hold them.

ABOUT THE AUTHOR

Lawrence Thornton is the author of *Under the Gypsy Moon.* His first novel, *Imagining Argentina,* won the Ernest Hemingway Foundation Award, the Shirley Collier Award from UCLA, the PEN American Center West Award for Best Novel of 1987 and a nomination for the PEN/Faulkner Award, and was chosen as one of the Notable Books of 1987 by *The New York Times Book Review.* Thornton, who has lived in France, Spain, and England, is a native of California, where he lives with his wife.